TERRA NULLIUS

TERRA NULLIUS

CLAIRE G. COLEMAN

Small Beer Press
Easthampton, MA

Winner of the black&write! State Library of Queensland Fellowship 2016
Lyrics on page vii: 'Solid Rock', written by S. Howard (Mushroom Music). Reproduced with permission.

Small Beer Press
150 Pleasant Street #306
Easthampton, MA 01027
smallbeerpress.com
weightlessbooks.com
info@smallbeerpress.com

Distributed to the trade by Consortium.

Library of Congress Cataloging-in-Publication Data

Names: Coleman, Claire G., author.
Title: Terra Nullius : a novel / Claire G. Coleman.
Description: First edition. | Easthampton, MA : Small Beer Press, [2018]
Identifiers: LCCN 2018014330 (print) | LCCN 2018018069 (ebook) | ISBN 9781618731524 | ISBN 9781618731517 (alk. paper)
Classification: LCC PR9619.4.C64 (ebook) | LCC PR9619.4.C64 T47 2018 (print)
 | DDC 823/.92--dc23
LC record available at https://lccn.loc.gov/2018014330

First edition 1 2 3 4 5 6 7 8 9
Cover design by Grace West
Author photo courtesy Jen Dainer, Industrial Arc
Text design by Bookhouse, Sydney
Typeset in 12/17.16 pt Bembo by Bookhouse, Sydney
Printed on 50# Natures Natural 30% PCR recycled paper
by the Maple Press in York, PA.

For Lily

Always

'They were standing on the shore one day,
saw the white sails in the sun.
Wasn't long before they felt the sting,
white man, white law, white gun.'

– 'SOLID ROCK', SHANE HOWARD (GOANNA)

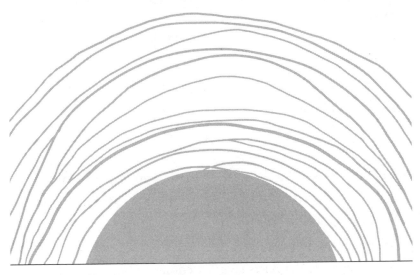

CHAPTER 1

When I saw the squalor they lived in, without any of the conveniences that make our lives better, dirty and seemingly incapable of being clean, I was horrified. When I discovered they had intelligence I was surprised. When I was told their souls had not been saved I resolved to do something about it.

– THE REVEREND MOTHER MARY SANTESLOSH

JACKY WAS RUNNING. There was no thought in his head, only an intense drive to run. There was no sense he was getting anywhere, no plan, no destination, no future. All he had was a sense of what was behind, what he was running from. Jacky was running. The heave of his breath, the hammering of his heart were the only sounds in his world. Through the film of tears and stinging, running sweat in his eyes there was nothing to see, only a grey, green, brown blur of woodland rushing past. Jacky was running. Other days he had felt joy at the speed, at the staccato rhythm of his feet, but not today. There was no space in his life for something as abstract – as useless – as joy. Only a sense of urgency remained. Jacky was running.

@

Sister Bagra paced the oppressively dark, comfortably stuffy halls of her mission in silent, solitary contemplation. She was dedicated to her duty, to bring faith to these people, if they could be called people; to bring religion, to bring education to these savages. An almost completely thankless task, a seemingly pointless, useless task. The recipients of her effort seemed totally incapable of appreciating what was being done for them, even going so far as resenting her help.

No matter how much she questioned the validity of the task at hand, it mattered not. She twisted, writhed, fought like a hooked eel, trying to throw off the pointy bit of steel in its mouth, inside her head where nobody else could see. She moaned, bitched and complained behind her nearly always expressionless visage, careful to ensure nobody else would ever know about it. She would persevere, she would fulfil her duty to the best of her ability.

They may be out in the middle of nowhere, there may be nobody to see them bar the ubiquitous Natives, but that was no reason to allow decorum to slide. The walls glowed faintly; an observer would guess rightly that in daylight they were a blinding pure white. The sort of white that hurts your eyes if you are foolish enough to stare at it for too long. There would not be a speck of dirt on the walls, no sand on the floor, no scuffs, nothing to demonstrate that the building was used. An army of hands kept her halls spotless.

Her robes, her habit was too thick, too stiff, too warm for this ridiculously hot place, yet to not be dressed in the full dress of her Order was unthinkable. She would never suffer a lowering of the standards of any of the women under her command, and she was always far harder on herself than she was on them. Far better to pray, again, and then again that the weather in this godforsaken place where she had found herself would get better, get cooler, or wetter. Her role, her duty was to suffer through discomfort if needs be; her job was to be disciplined, to teach discipline, to bring the Word to the ungodly, so suffer she must.

There was no escaping the certainty that she did not belong in this place, it was too hot and too dry and the food – the quickest way to earn her ire, the easiest way to unleash her famous temper was to mention the food. Certainly, there were local plants and animals that the savages seemed to relish, but surely she could not be expected to actually eat them. Attempts were being made to grow crops from home but they were hampered by the lack of rain and lack of farming expertise.

So many people kept arriving: troopers, shopkeepers and merchants, missionaries and thieves. What they needed was just one decent farmer.

Over half the colony were still totally reliant on rations delivered by ship from home, and what arrived was barely edible after the months of transit. Most of it was barely edible before it even left home, after what they had to do to make it survive the trip. Once it arrived at the colony it still had to be transported overland in the heat to the mission. The food, don't get her started about the food.

Stopping suddenly as if startled, she listened. She could hear the susurrus of voices – no intelligible words, just the faintest of tiny noises like the scurrying of the infernal mice that infested this unliveable hellhole no matter what measures they took to eliminate them. Wrapped in the comfort of her accustomed silence she followed the faint, bare trace of sound, finally tracking it down to the correct door.

Talking after lights out, and in that jabber as well – that nonsense the Natives use instead of language. Will the little monsters never learn?

She opened the door and slipped through it, the hems of her neat pressed habit cracking like a whip with the speed; she moved so fast she was almost invisible. Two children were kneeling beside their beds whispering prayers to whatever primitive god, or gods, they worshipped. Surely they were newcomers to the mission school if they knew no better.

They would soon know, that much was certain; both would be in solitary before dawn. Why wait, why not this instant?

She dragged the little animals by their too thick, too curly hair, chastising them in a constant hissing monotone, ignoring their screamed, unintelligible complaints. They had fallen before she had dragged them through the kitchen courtyard, past the new plantings she had been eyeing earlier that day in anticipation of their future fruit. The dead weight of the children was no hindrance to Bagra in her fury, they left two uneven runnels in the gravel and dust.

At the far side of the dusty red-brown courtyard, past the straggling green, yellow, brown weeds that needed pulling by the too-lazy Natives, was a neat line of three sheds. They were rough but strong, constructed of sheets of iron and local wood, barely the size of kennels. Two of them she opened, the bolts sliding with a snick like a drawing blade, and the windowless doors were yanked ajar. The screech of the doors opening was even louder than the wailing of the children as they were each in turn dumped unceremoniously in a box.

They kept wailing after the doors were locked, screaming more of their jabber. She suspected that they were new to the mission but surely someone had told them enough to fear the 'boob' as the

4

Natives called it. Some other little monster would have terrified them with the story.

Sister Bagra had never bothered to learn the noises the Natives made instead of speaking; she could not see the point of learning a language so close to extinction. She berated them in hers, totally unconcerned whether or not they could understand her. Kicking each door once for emphasis, the sheet metal emitting a yell like a cross between thunder overhead and a church bell, she stormed away.

In the dormitories the other children were silent in deep pretence of sleep. To hear Sister Bagra at all was rare, to hear her in a fury was something few forgot. Like an ill-mannered ghost she stamped and clattered her way back to her room to pray for the strength to survive these little beasts, this terrible place.

Several hours later, over an irritatingly bland breakfast – the best the nuns and their Native servants could pull together from the rations they had claimed, begged, cajoled or scavenged from the last ship and from the poorly grown crops of the local Settlers – Sister Bagra held court. 'We will continue to try and help these "people".' Her voice was firm, leaving no room for dispute. The word 'people' she said in such a manner, with such venom, as to leave no doubt she did not consider the Natives people at all. Pausing to think, to choose her words, she continued, 'We will do our best, whether or not they can be helped.'

One of the younger sisters was new to the mission – only days, a couple of weeks at most, off the latest ship. She was too new to know when to open her mouth and when to stay silent. 'Are we so sure they have souls to save?'

Sister Bagra stared blankly at the young woman, trying to recall anything about this nun: even her name would be a start, a handle to hang other information on. She recalled nothing; it was as if the girl had arrived unannounced to the table from the ether. Racking her brain for at least a name, she almost forgot she had been asked a question, rather, a question had been thrown into the air of the room and someone would have to answer it. She was that someone.

'They have language. It might be vulgar, it's horrible really, but they can communicate with each other. They have names. They have at least enough intelligence to learn a little; they must have souls.' A name swam into her vision, faint but she could read it: Mel, that was the foolish child's name.

Sister Bagra waved a slice of toasted bread – the poorly made primitive bread she tolerated, although she hated it – in a long bony hand for emphasis. 'What souls they have, we will save. Whatever it is they use for brains we will educate it –' she smiled the self-satisfied smile the other sisters most likely hated though they should be scared to say it, '– whether they like it or not.'

@

Jacky ate his meagre dinner crouched furtively in the dappled golden light under spreading branches. It was not a lot of food, certainly not the abundance talked about in the old stories the older Natives told each other. An old servant had heard about it from his father who had heard it from his grandfather: there was a time before the Settlers, when everybody had plenty of everything.

It was, however, something – a handful of small apples from the ground under a tree in a too-neat park, a couple of eggs stolen from the cages the Settlers keep their birds in.

Nobody prefers raw eggs over cooked. The texture is too much like mucus: not quite drinkable, not quite chewable. Jacky drank them down as if he was starving. He was not starving, not yet, although he had been hungry a long time. He knew too well what it was like to be hungry. He knew hunger well enough to eat anything he could get, whenever he got it. His frame, slight for his size, short for his apparent age, was all the evidence needed that he had been a long time underfed. Only his muscles were mature; he had the aura of wiry strength earned during a lifetime of hard work.

His muscles and his scars, his body made of barbed wire and leather, betrayed that his life had not been easy. A young man, not much more than a teen, he was scarred like an old soldier. He had a young face, if you could see past the habitual look of pain that belonged on the features of a much older man. Nevertheless, his back and limbs were straight. His agony had the aura of something more emotional than physical.

He could not risk a fire, he knew the Troopers were still out there, would always be out there, looking for him, and a fire in the bush would be as bad as shouting, as announcing where he was. He felt his face harden, his shoulders tighten at the thought of going back there. That last beating was more than even he could tolerate, even habituated to beatings as he was. It was surely not his fault that the dinner had burned; cook was drunk, cook was always drunk. He should have never left Jacky, whose job was mostly stacking wood on the woodpile, alone to look after it.

The decision where to go was almost impossible to make; all he knew for certain was he was not going back to that place. His decision to leave had been so sudden, so unexpected it had not really been a decision. It was more like a reaction, an inevitability. All he could think of to do next was not a decision either, any more than deciding to eat when hungry was a decision. He would do what many others would do if they had no idea what to do next: he would go home.

The choice had been so simple it should have been just as easy to start. He would already be on the move if only he knew where home was.

He had been so young when they had taken him, so far from his home, from his people. Nothing of that trip remained in his memory, though logically he must have come from somewhere. They had taken him to the farm from the school. Nothing remained of the time before they gave him a new religion, a new language, a broken degenerate version of the Settler tongue he could never learn to speak well enough.

For all their big talk they seemed to have no real intention to help him to speak their language as well as they. Near enough was good enough, whether the Settlers could understand him well or not. From the school he was sent to a house to be a servant, so long given orders, so long without freedom of action that he had almost forgotten who he was.

I am Jacky, he thought, I belong somewhere, I had a family once, I have a family who misses me. This litany played over and over in his head. I have a family, I have a family, I am Jacky.

What memories he had of family were nebulous at best, painted on clouds, on a sky bleeding red, breaking up at sunrise. He knew he must have a family – everybody has a family, he was not born at the school – if only he could remember them. Weeping, staying silent despite there being nobody to hear, he prayed they would remember him.

He did not know where he was going yet was certain that getting home was going to be many, many days, weeks, on foot. He was an escaped servant and had no money and no papers, no permission to travel, by foot was his only means of transport. Knowing he was still hunted he could not even dream of getting help, almost anyone he approached would send him back there.

Even his own people would think of nothing else, they would not hide him, not help him. They had their own problems.

The sun was setting; its comforting warmth, its amber light, fading. It was a wrench to lose the light, yet the darkness and cold held no fear for someone for whom bed had been dirt, in a cold, dark woodshed for years. Besides, those few times he could get away, escape, run out into the bush, were the only times he had felt safe. The cold and the dark were far less frightening than being beaten, far less discomforting than the cramped claustrophobic shed he lived in before his sudden escape.

His preparations for the night were devoted to not being found. Careful to leave no trail he wandered deeper into the bush, walking only on leaves, on rocks, barely able to see in the half-light. He knew the Settlers were at least unnerved, at most terrified, by this landscape that Jacky found increasingly familiar. Finding a dry enough hollow in the roots of a giant tree, a washout where it overhung a dry stream, he crawled in. Safer but not safe, he burrowed into damp, bug-infested litter and fell into a restless, fear-filled sleep.

@

A runner was sent out not long after dawn, when Jacky failed to bring in wood for the fire. Nobody had seen him the whole day before, nobody could even remember seeing him as the servants ate their scraps for dinner. The senior servants who had been there most their lives, who knew exactly how to survive, were taking no risks. They had a runner ready before a volunteer informed their master Jacky had taken off. Such swift action took some fire from the Settler's wrath.

Immediately, the runner was out of sight. The station was as if abandoned; the small cluster of buildings, made of tin sheeting and local wood, deathly silent. The Settler hid inside, took out his frustration and anger on a bottle. The servants, Natives all, were hiding, or finding some, any, work to do in hidden places, or outside as far from the buildings as possible. They knew it was too hot, the sort of heat that melts the new paint off your walls. They knew that in that sort of heat the Settler would stay inside.

Only the young were talking, not yet completely enslaved in their hearts, they spoke in hushed whispers of Jacky's audacity. Sure, he had run away before but always for only hours at a time, taking off into the bush he could still remember a little, though they could not. Never before had he still been gone in the morning. This time he had really run away; the youngsters had never even entertained that thought before.

They had learnt a new word 'absconded', and they knew it had something to do with freedom.

'Run away,' what could that mean, could they all do it? Where would they go? Where did Jacky go, where will Jacky go? Some of the younger servants had been brought to the station before they could remember, others had been born there, the children of servants, they had never known any life other than servitude.

The older men, when they heard the young ones talking were quick to shush them, before the master heard. They too would love to be free, though many had forgotten what freedom was, but their fear of being caught talking about it, their fear of even thinking about it, was greater than that desire. Many had been there too long and had almost forgotten what the word 'freedom' even meant. They did not wish the youngsters to get in trouble for thinking of the impossible. Jacky would be caught, he would be punished, that is what happens to everybody who runs. The youngsters would see the punishment and then they too would learn to fear.

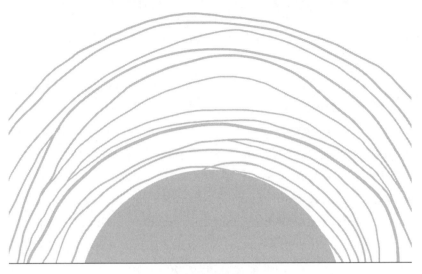

CHAPTER 2

They took me from my family when I was just a little thing, took me from my mother, from my father. They took me far away and made me work, I didn't even know where my family were, didn't even know I had a family poor thing. I never saw them again.

– BOBBY KEN

JACKY WOKE AS the first tentative tendrils of light worked their way through the trees, clawing through the branches, pushing softly through the leaves. It was not the light that had woken him, rather it was a relentless gnawing hunger. If the pain hadn't caught his attention, the grumbling of his stomach, almost a roar, nearly a scream, would have. Not that this was intolerable, it was even normal. There were few times in his memory that he had been given or even stolen enough to eat.

There was no time to mope, to fear, to eat or even to be hungry. He knew the Troopers would still be out there, still searching for him, and his only chance was to move as fast as he could. He knew he could go a day or two without food; hunger had been a normal punishment for minor mistakes, small rebellions. It would take a couple of days before hunger made him weak or foolish. So, for the moment at least, running was more important than eating.

Move was what he did, as fast as he could away from the settlements, away from the roads, through the bushland, through dripping trees and scratching, tangling, grabbing bushes. He tripped, almost fell, on clumping grasses, stumbled over unexpected, hidden rocks, slid back almost as much as he climbed on gravel-clad hillsides. There was no opportunity to think where he might be going; all that mattered was getting away from the house, away from the settlement and away from the Troopers.

The Settlers would be afraid of the bush, of the deep woodland, so different from their home. That would be the safest place for him in whatever tangled, green and brown, scratchy and dirty, trackless and untidy scrub he could find. North-east was the best direction, the settlement from which he had escaped was west. Native servants don't move around much, but when they arrived at the station, from other stations, they mostly came from the south and the west. He'd been told most of the settlements were to the south and west, in that part of the world at least. North and east were drier, the woods thicker, the Settler population thinner, north and east should be safer.

Unfortunately, soon they would have the help of a Native tracker, someone from his own people, or someone like his own people, someone from far away so they would not feel too much compassion, to help them find him. A good tracker, a skilled tracker, a clever tracker would not make his escape as easy; he really had to get moving fast, but not too fast.

He needed to be fast, yet careful; no amount of speed would be enough if he left signs of his passage even Settlers could follow. If he was careless enough there were trackers out there who would be able to track him even in the dark, he would never escape them. Chunks of red-brown ironstone, shapeless boulders like stuck-together pebbles, were scattered between the trees, most knee-height and a few as tall as his waist. He bounded from rock to rock as fast as he could. There were rumours of trackers who would not be fooled even by such a move, though he had to try something.

Rain, if it would come, would be a mixed blessing at best. The hammering of water on the ground would clear some of his track away, making it harder, even for a good tracker, to find him. On the other hand, if it rained it would not be as hot, and the Settlers would travel easier. When the rain cleared, as it always does, the wet ground would hold tracks even better than when it was dry. Jacky knew he lacked the experience to decide what was best, not that it really mattered in the middle of a drought. He could wish for rain but he was unlikely to get it.

It was good to be out in the bush again, even though it was not his own bush, the bush around his barely remembered home. He could not quite see, though he strained his mind's eye, the forest back home. Yet he knew these trees felt wrong, they were not his trees, that was all he had left of home, a half-lost feeling. Behind him now were the foreign-looking, alien-feeling houses of the Settlers, the strange trees they had planted to make it look more like wherever it was they had come from. That at least was a relief. For the moment it didn't even matter which direction home was in, at least he was away.

For fleeting moments while running he could almost forget his desperate peril. In those moments he ran for the joy of it, free in mind and body, his own man, running in his land. They did not last long, those moments; soon he was reminded that he was being hunted and the grim determination returned, the joy receded.

All day he ran while the sun kept him just warm enough, lit his path, forced hope into his heart. 'Where there is life, there is hope'; it felt that day like 'where there is light, there is hope'. The light that day was bright. He ran, as if hope was entirely fuelled by the sun.

All day he ran, flitting through trees on leaves and bark, clambering over boulders, leaping from boulder to boulder and from fallen tree to fallen tree. All day he ran, splashing along creeks to leave no tracks and no scent for dogs. All day he ran until the setting of the sun stole his sight leaving him helpless.

The sun rose and with it his hope, again. He spared a moment to bask in the sun, to bask in hope before starting again to run. He ran in fits, walking when running was too hard, when he was too tired, his muscles turning to pus. He walked when he could not run, because he also could not stop; if he stopped he might as well just give up, may as well surrender.

Another fitful, terrified, cold and damp night of sleep, buried under the driest bark and twigs he could find for what meagre warmth and cover they provided. Another day-and-a-half-running later and he got lucky. Before him, casting almost no shadow in the noon light, was a rock so large the Settlers had curved their road around it rather than attempt to destroy or remove it. It was an unusual shape, almost exactly the shape of a horse's head, jutting from the wet grass as if a giant animal was below the ground staring at the stars.

This was his first breakthrough. He remembered that rock, remembered staring at it in unaccustomed wonder as they took him in a great curve around it on the road. It was a rare moment of wonder, something unexpected, something almost magical on the road from the school to the settlement where he had been a slave for those terrifying years.

There was no way he could have known then that the horror of the school, the beatings often for no reason he could understand, the torture, the hunger, would be the best days he would remember. At the time he was excited, travelling when before he had spent his life in the school, seeing the world outside the fences for the first time in countless years. For a time everything around him was suffused with wonder, for he did not know, then, what sort of life he was being taken to.

He had stared in mute awe at that rock as the road curved around it, how could it have got there? What beautiful, terrible magic, what history led to a rock that looked like a horse, or a giant stone horse stuck in the mud, dead, it had to be, but staring at the stars? Maybe, being a horse of rock it was merely resting; one day it would rise, shaking off the entrapping soil, climbing from its pit, running off to . . . well, Jacky had no idea where.

As frightening as the thought was, he would have liked to have seen that.

Surely there could not be another such rock, if he had passed it on the way to the settlement from the school for Natives then he could follow the road. The road would take him to the school and there, maybe, he could learn more, something to show him his way home. It was not much of a chance and maybe, for someone less desperate, not even worth entertaining. For Jacky it was the greatest hope he had ever experienced.

Finally he didn't feel helpless, probably for the first time since he had been taken from his family, for the first time he could actually remember. It was not much of a landmark, not big enough to see among the trees if not for the road it rudely interrupted, but to him it loomed large, for him it was the centre of the universe, at least briefly. He could follow that road and make good time, not on the road of course, that would be suicidally reckless, but he could move through the bush in view of the road following it.

The forest, always a sanctuary from the terror, the constant labour of his day-to-day life, was, in his eyes that day, in the glowing afternoon light, beautiful beyond his imagining. He walked as fast as he could without running, delighting in this glimpse of what heaven must surely look like. The greyish trunks of the trees, festooned with hanging bark, reflected the light of the slanting afternoon sun. Waxy leaves, a shiny blue, green, grey, caught the light like glitter. There was almost too much light that time of day but feeling hopeful Jacky barely noticed. Even as the light drilled, painfully, into his eyes he didn't care, he was going home.

He started running, almost skipping through the bush, through the trees, glad of the times that he had practised cross-country running as a way to escape the almost constant, inevitable beatings. Settlers ran for fun, he had seen it but never understood why they did it. He was alive because he could run, maybe this ability would continue to keep him alive. There was no way to take the time to hide his trail, not at the speed he was moving, not when hope gave energy to his legs, drove him forward without volition.

He hoped that nobody would work out he was using the road as a guide, hoped they had already lost his track. He hoped for many things, knowing in the depths of his heart that to hope was foolish. He hoped because he knew that to lose all hope would lead to despair. To lose all hope would be to die.

There was little hope of escape, not with the hue and cry he knew was being raised behind him. Not that there was any more chance of fighting his way out if he was caught. There was even less chance of fighting his way to freedom than there was of him staying free by running.

All he had to defend himself was an old kitchen knife stolen from the kitchen, its handle of bone worn narrow from decades of handling and its once straight blade carved concave from many years of sharpening. It was more a liability than an asset, not much use as a weapon and almost certain to get him in more trouble if he was caught with it.

Not that he could get in much more trouble; absconding was a serious crime where he came from. Doomed, terrified, far from anything that he could call a home, alone, nothing on Earth could make him lay down the only weapon he had.

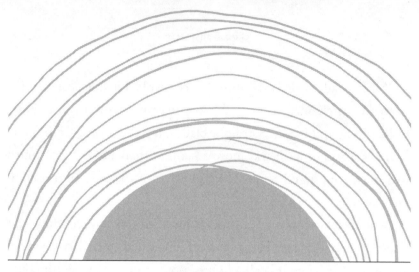

CHAPTER 3

When you landed in our home we knew you were like us and yet not like us. You eat, you sleep, you care about your children, you love one another, just as we sleep, eat, care for our children and love. Yet you brought your own ways, your own customs, your own religion, your own law, your own language. You brought your own crops and your own animals.

We saw little evidence of a desire on your part to try and understand our ways. We tried to understand you yet we could not. I don't know if you made any genuine attempt to understand us but if you tried you failed.

– JOHN FARMER, NATIVE ADVANCEMENT LEAGUE

THE HEAD OF the Department for the Protection of Natives was drowning, in a flood, in an avalanche of paperwork that had lately become more important than fulfilling the actual duties of his office. It had reached the point where the uninformed would believe from a glance at his office that paperwork was, in fact, all he actually had to do. That had to change, he just didn't know how to do it.

Few remembered his name, fewer used it, everybody had called him 'Devil' for so long, the infernal Natives and his staff alike, that he had simply accepted it. Even his wife, when she talked to him at all, used the epithet rather than the name his parents had given him. Oh well, he didn't need a name, not really, names are for people who need to identify themselves. Everybody knew who he was, everybody who mattered anyway.

He was average height, average paunchiness, his age although indeterminate was the indeterminate age you would expect from someone in his position. There was not a single physical characteristic that would make him stand out in any group of senior bureaucrats. His clothes were expensive, neat yet relatively plain. It appeared that he had been careful that morning to ensure that his clothes would demonstrate nothing about him other than his status in society.

His office, his desk, however, would give the alert observer at least a faint clue to the sort of man he was. The desk was well made though simple, of the dark local wood that was a trade commodity often sent home. Unadorned, it was polished until reflective, until almost a mirror, a dark rectangular pool in the daylight spilling through the window. There was nothing personal on the desk, just two trays full of papers, one on the left and one on the right, with a pad and a pen between them.

Anyone with a measuring tape would no doubt discover the pad was not just between the trays, it was positioned exactly in the middle between the trays. The only other furniture in the room was a single wooden filing cabinet, it stood alone – nothing around it, nothing on top of it.

The walls of the room, however, were covered in so much loose, barely pinned paper the room could have been a square clearing in a forest, a forest of trees with rectangular leaves. On the windswept coast near the colony there was a type of tree with flaky bark, bark like paper. It flakes off and hangs in sheets. Lacking imagination the Settlers in the area called the tree 'Paperbark'. The walls could have been made of logs of those trees, when a lazy carpenter had not even bothered to remove the loose bark. There were so many pieces of paper pinned to the walls that, surely, nobody could ever examine them all.

It did not help that there was absolutely no discernible pattern to the visual riot. Pictures of smiling Natives in Settler dress standing with depressed, traditionally dressed Natives were half pinned over scrawled notes, photos of trees, both native and from home, hand-drawn and printed maps, some maps a mixture of both. There were letters, some scribbled wildly and others handwritten neatly, every letter different, photos that made no sense without context, a child's drawings and pages from schoolbooks. Articles torn roughly, raggedly, from the local papers were side by side with wanted posters, with leaflets produced by his department. Much of what was on the wall was annotated in a small, crabbed, terribly untidy handwriting. If there was some sort of a pattern, method to the madness, surely only its creator could understand it.

All the work before him, all the work he had already completed that day was routine, although he did manage, as always, to take some small satisfaction in it.

'Dear Sir, I am writing to request an increase in the rations for our camp of Natives, they have been breeding like little animals and the children need feeding', one surprisingly neat, though poorly composed, letter read. 'I am willing to pay for the rations myself if you would give permission.' His manner might have been smug, was certainly filled with satisfaction when he wrote 'deny' in his almost illegible scrawl and dropped the letter in the tray for his secretary to handle.

To the casual observer it could have almost been an afterthought when he casually, almost sleepily wrote a note requesting the Troopers go to the camp in question. There they would find plenty of children to take away for education. It was not, however, an afterthought. He was not a cruel man, he believed, rather he was a plain man trying to do a difficult job well.

He smiled a faint smile, so faint there was almost nothing to see. There was nothing to like about the job except the satisfaction he received from helping the Natives to help themselves. Natives raising their own children to the primitive ways they lived before he came was unacceptable, they would have to be elevated. The school would help elevate the Natives.

There were many entreaties, great piles of letters that morning: 'Dear sir, I would like permission to see my child, taken from me . . .', deny; 'I have a good job and would like to apply for . . .', deny; '. . . my shoes are wearing through . . .', deny; '. . . good standing. We would like to marry', deny. Deny, deny, deny.

Despite his speed in filing the denials, there seemed to be no end to the pile before him. Maybe he should have handed this work over to another, an underling, but he felt this work was important. However, there was other work that was far more important that he seldom had time to do simply because he was handling all that boring, eternal paperwork.

Maybe, he thought, he needed a 'Deny' stamp to process this time-eating paperwork faster. It would certainly be more efficient and it was not the first time he had entertained that thought. As with every other time he rejected the thought: it is the personal touch that makes the job worth doing. A stamp just would not have the same effect for him or for the recipients. He mentally scrawled 'deny' on the thought.

No doubt everybody prefers to know a real person has made the effort to reply properly and personally, not least of all his secretary who, he knew, hated her job. Devil was certain she would hate it even more without that personal touch. He had been told many times it was important to be a people person, whatever that means.

On the pile, finally, and just in time to wrap a bandage around his bleeding sanity, was something a little different from the usual applications for privileges, petitions and appeals, complaints and whining. It was a card, small, hand painted, surely by Natives, the colour of the picture standing out brightly, like a gemstone, against the finger-stained and ink-scrawled pile. The picture had no appeal to him, it was poorly executed and not even the greatest artist in the world could turn the ugly forests here into something beautiful.

Oh how he hated the landscape, so different to the comfortable lush beauty back home. He would never admit it to anyone but the alien landscape in which he found himself both frightened and sickened him. He hated it almost as much as he hated the people . . . No, that was not right, he didn't hate them, mustn't hate them. He pitied them, they were merely children, he wanted to help them.

As much to hide the picture as to read the message, he turned the card over slowly – no need to rush – to reveal the other side. Yes, there was writing on the other side, in a neat hand, far more exciting than the ugly picture. 'Dear Sir . . .' it began, the handwriting somehow rendering the 'Sir' genuine, creating something special, a statement of real respect, not just a formality.

Dear Sir

I am writing to thank you for the essentially thankless task you have undertaken. The Natives, although possessed of the intelligence they needed to survive without us, and even more cunning than that, would be unable to survive the changes facing them. You and your department in forcing and assisting the assimilation of these 'people' are giving them the only chance they have to survive and one day be useful to society.

In Thanks
Doctor Des Asper

Devil allowed himself a still, silent moment of self-satisfaction. Finally somebody appreciated his hard work and believed in the great, certainly critical, task he had undertaken. Even the government, who paid his bills, reluctantly paid his salary, funded the work, seemed uncertain of the overall validity of the project. It was popular with the Settlers, at least those who didn't favour outright extermination of all the Natives, and no politician or bureaucrat had the courage to close his department, to cancel his project.

A tiny bead of moisture fell from his face onto the card he had forgotten he was holding. How he hated the heat of this place. He was prone, when insufficiently in control of his thoughts and emotions, to ranting about the state of the weather, to the point where whoever was listening would do anything to shut him up. Why his people settled the place was beyond him – there was nothing, from what he had seen, but desert. Once they had settled there, his arrival had become almost inevitable. As much as he hated the weather, they needed him, or someone like him, to manage, protect and elevate the Natives.

He had needed a promotion, they had needed a man, he had theories and ideas on how to perform the task before him. It was perfect. Or it would have been perfect if his office was not in the oven-hot, foul-smelling, fauna-infested dump where they had posted him.

In a silence broken only by his rapid, excited breathing, he rose from his chair, slowly, laboriously, with self-enforced calm and patience. Nobody could know how excited he was at such praise. Carefully searching the walls he selected a place and pinned the card, writing out, next to a child's drawing of a house and garden. There was not really any clear wall, this new addition obscured something less important.

One day everyone will understand, even appreciate, what he has been doing with his life. When they do, his walls, his entire office, will be a museum, a shrine. Just as carefully, walking backwards so he could keep his eyes on his walls, he returned to his chair.

@

Esperance had not slept well, again, the shouting and brawling had not ceased all night. Every time she tried to sleep she was woken by the clamour of voices and more than once the nauseating sound of fists pounding into flesh. Obviously someone, and she would find out who, had made it to a town and brought back some grog, either that or a smuggler, a trader had made it to their camp, had found them somehow.

The grog smugglers always find them, and somehow the drinkers always find a way to pay for a drink. Everyone was hungry, everyone was always hungry, yet somehow someone, everyone, always found a way to get grog.

There was little worse than the drunken fight over the last dregs of drink; grog seemed to destroy everyone's sense of proportion and their self-control, they fought for it, some would die for it. Stopped dead in her thoughts, she prayed it was drink that had brought the fighting and the fights were over the last of it. There are worse poisons than drink, and worse disasters than it running out. If it had run out at least the immediate problem was over.

Sighing she examined the shabby hovel she called home. She had seen other homes, real houses, from a distance, but she had never lived in one, never experienced four clean walls and a roof that did not leak. She had never even experienced a real floor, a clean floor, a hard floor, a floor not made of dirt. Everything was filthy, which is what happens when you live in dirt and can spare no water to wash anything, but at least nothing was broken. The single sheet of tin roofing held up with scraps of wood was at least still in place, giving the illusion of shelter if not the actuality of it.

If it ever rained there it would doubtlessly destroy the illusion the roof was waterproof. If it actually rained she would have to patch all the holes, although the repairs never lasted long. When it rained, and at night, her shelter was essential but in the day it was no better, worse actually, than the shade of a tree. Uninsulated, made of tin, you could bake bread inside by midday. Once the daylight hit the roof she would have to get out and find some shade.

Her meagre belongings were arranged carefully on an upturned wooden crate. She only owned what she could carry with her if they had to run, not that she had any way to get more stuff even if she wanted to. She knew where to find everything: the stub of candle she used on the rare times she needed light at night; a larger knife than the folding knife always in her pocket, scratched on the blade from constant sharpening on rocks; her tin cup; a carved wooden lizard as long as her forearm that was her only toy as a child and the only decoration in her adulthood.

She lay watching the first light peeking through the gaps in her walls, making motes of dust glow and dance. There was no chance of returning to sleep now and nothing else to do, certainly no reason to just lie there. She slid out from under the pile of dusty blankets that had kept her alive another night in the desert cold. The cold at night, out there where they lived, always surprises the unprepared after the scorching, dry heat of the day.

The eye-watering reek of a smouldering campfire wafted past as she clambered out of her shelter, stinging her tired eyes and surprising a weak cough from her lungs. The small fire pit, outside her hut, was cold, the ashes white. She rarely lit it when there was always a fire in the middle of camp. It was that pit in the middle of camp that was untended, smoking, stinking.

In the pre-dawn light the camp looked like a battle had passed through; bodies lay around the fire wherever and however they had fallen. The first light of day glinted off fallen bottles, dropped casually when empty, at least none seemed to have been broken. In the dirt they lived in, broken glass could bury itself, not to be found until it entered someone's foot, for shoes were hard to come by out here. Esperance was deeply relieved she would not be spending the day on hands and knees looking for shards of glass before they entered someone's body.

There was even less medical aid in camp than there were comfortable places to live.

Nobody in the camp lived in buildings; Esperance's hovel was not so much an example of the housing in the camp as it was something for people to aspire to. There were shacks of wood and canvas, always arrested in the act of slumping onto the ground, misshapen, bulging where the addition of sticks had been used in futile attempts to slow the collapse. There were sheets of tin like Esperance lived under, some of them only held up, held in place, by a single prop of bent wood. No walls, nothing to keep out the wind or give the dwellers privacy. There were humpies and lean-tos of bark and sticks, almost waterproofed by the addition of leafy branches. Everywhere under the trees were shacks made of sticks and discarded hessian sacks.

Here and there, in the half-light, she could see piles of blankets and belongings, some neat, some decidedly chaotic, where people, families, had failed to provide themselves with any sort of shelter at all. Those unfortunates who had no shelter and couldn't convince someone else to share their home – she had seen families of six under a single sheet of tin – had to resort to sleeping wherever they could. If they were lucky they had a scrap of canvas with which they could waterproof their bedroll; a canvas tarp as a ground cover was a luxury.

Fights over those scraps of canvas had kept her awake at night, many times. The issues most likely to cause long-term problems were also the issues most likely to cause fights, keeping Esperance awake at night. She was a great barometer of the camp's problems, what friends she had could tell how the camp was faring by the size and colour of the black rings under her eyes.

Esperance felt again the recurring guilt; she really should share her camp with someone, some homeless soul, someone with nowhere to sleep. Yet again she rejected the thought; she had tried sharing her scrap of shelter and the fights had nearly torn apart the camp. She liked people, that was not the problem, but she did not like people in her space, changing things, moving things. She realised every time she had someone else stay with her that either they would have to leave or she would, and she was not going to abandon her home. Curing someone else of homelessness by giving homelessness to herself would be a very stupid move.

It did not take her long to find her grandfather. He lay, asleep or unconscious, on the ground along with most, if not all, the other men and some of the older women. Fortunately, he was near the campfire. Esperance was grateful for the warmth that would have kept him alive and somebody had thrown a blanket over him where he lay. Somebody clearly had a spare blanket, a rare thing out there, or one had been sacrificed.

This was the strongest sign possible of the deep respect in which Grandfather was held. When she found out who had slept cold last night so Grandfather could be warm she would thank them profusely. She would also ensure their blanket was returned to them, which would not happen if she left it there.

He was an old and frail man, all wrinkled skin and spindly limbs; what muscle he had was strung around his fragile-looking bones like rope. Nevertheless, Esperance made no attempt to carry him to his shack. She was as sick and malnourished as everybody else she knew; they were a desperate and destitute mob. There had not been enough food since they had been driven into this part of the desert by the relentless advance of the Settlers long before she was born. She had to wake him, help him to his bed; she gripped his shoulder lightly and gave an almost imperceptible shake.

'Grandfather −' she shook him again '− wouldn't you rather be comfy in your bed, it might rain.' She shook his shoulder slightly harder, pulling on it as if to lift him by that barely flesh-covered joint. Grandfather merely mumbled − sounds but no intelligible words, a long moan and some heavy breaths. 'You shouldn't have drunk so much, you are going to feel like shit later.'

Releasing a toneless, formless litany of moans and grumbles he rose laboriously to his feet, helped by the loving hand of his granddaughter clamped firmly, respectfully, around his twiggy shoulder. His breath was light but laboured, as if fighting for every shallow inhalation he took.

Bundling the blanket under her left arm − it would be safer in Grandfather's shack until she found out whose it was − she held him up with her right. Several times they stumbled, tripping over detritus, human and otherwise, each near fall merely giving him something more to add to his constant, pained monologue, his speech rendered almost completely wordless by age, drink and the residue of sleep. It seemed an age, rather than only a few minutes, before Grandfather's ragged, misshapen shack loomed out of the rapidly rising mist.

'You are funny, Esperance,' Grandfather mumbled, the words unexpectedly intelligible, 'it's not going to rain, it never rains here, that is why we are here, why we came here.' It took Esperance a moment to think why he said that, to recall what he was responding to; his reaction had been slow enough to become disembodied, a non sequitur. As suddenly as the words had appeared they were buried once more under a mound of mumbles.

At least he had a proper shack, a roof with four walls, which was more than pretty much anybody else in the camp had. Waterproofed with oiled cloth and scraps of metal sheeting it was almost certainly the oldest, and most liveable, structure in the camp. Grandfather had been the first to set up camp on the banks of this dry riverbed, sheltered and hidden by the giant twisted hulks of red gum trees, leading a small group of lost souls.

For years, for decades, he had built, repaired and rebuilt his shack as others came to rest around him; repairing and rebuilding, helping others build, until old age and malnutrition began to take their toll. Every addition and repair to his shack was visible, the diverse collection of materials not quite blending together. They did not need to camouflage the building – it had little shape and colour to notice and already blended into its environment perfectly.

The camp stretched out along the riverbank – if you could call the edge of a ribbon of red sand a riverbank – and part of the way into the trees on each side. A few dwellings even sat precariously on the riverbed itself. If and when the rain came those living in the river would be homeless again.

Children had been born there, in the dirt under those trees, yet nobody really belonged. Everybody there had come from somewhere else, thrust together, unintentionally, by the Settlers who had merely pushed them away from their homes, expanding to cover more country. Others had arrived there running in terror, barely escaping the violence that had killed everybody they knew.

Over the years the camp had grown to over a hundred refugees, all malnourished, all dirty, destitute and homeless. Among them there was likely not one, not even a child, who did not relish a thought of returning home one day, returning to wherever they had come from. Every child knew they did not belong there, on that dry riverbank, although every child had been born right there in camp.

There were even some, like Esperance, whose parents had been born there, although she was the oldest of the second genera-tion born in the camp. Although they had been there for years, decades, everybody knew they might have to run one day – that the Settlers could come, the Settlers would come. Their lives were partly those of settled refugees, partly those of fugitives on the run and, like all fugitives, they were paranoid.

The sun was finally rising over the camp, casting that first warm light that filled the heart with hope while encasing the world in a soft glow, a light that blurs everything. Even the debris, the rubbish she knew to be scattered in almost every space between the humpies and shacks, was softened into insignificance and painted with a comfortable warm gold. The sun was higher already when she stepped back out through the patched hessian curtain that served her grandfather's shack as a door.

The marginally higher sun cast out a harsher light, thrusting fingers of shadow westward from every piece of fallen trash, every collapsed body too tired or still too drunk to stand. Stopping only once to pick up a dropped bottle, she made her way carefully through the mess to the riverbed, turned and walked upstream, or where upstream would be if there was water in the river. The last place to hold water every summer as the never plentiful water in the river dried up was a pool at the bend – now dried to nothing more than a slight darkening in the sand, shaded by overhanging trees, invisible to anyone who did not know where to look.

She could only hope there was water still; it had been a couple of years since it had rained. Nobody could guess how long the last of their water would remain. If it ran out they would need to go further in the search for water, or move camp completely.

Someone had been busy before the grog had arrived and there was a small hole in the right place as wide as the length of her forearm and deep enough that it would reach her knees if she stood in it. At the bottom was a film of water over the damp sand, if she stuck her finger into the water it would reach to the first joint. She knelt in the soft, damp sand at the edge. Desperate not to tumble over the edge into the hole, careful also not to disturb the sand in the bottom, to muddy the precious water, she lowered the bottle into the hole. She pushed it into the damp sand until the water flowed in, held it there until the bottle was full.

Drinking, she winced at the faint sweet taste of rough wine that the unclean bottle imparted on the water; it almost but didn't quite cover the fainter taste of mud and dirt. Later that day, when more had been there to collect their water it would get dirtier, until it was the colour of the milky tea she had been fortunate enough to taste once, until only the desperate would drink it. For now it was drinkable, even if there was no certainty it was safe.

The sun was completely risen, though still low on the horizon, its light cutting itself ragged through the bent, scraggly, dust-grey trees. It was early yet, but even these early shafts of light warned of the scorchingly hot day to come. Drinking down her grog-flavoured water she knelt to refill the bottle; she hadn't found a cork in the dark so a broken stick was utilised, if not to hold the water in, to at least stop it sloshing out while she carried it carefully back to camp.

Before the sun hit the waterhole it would need to be protected. Finding a broken branch with leaves still attached she covered the hole; it was not enough, the heat and the sun would still get in. A couple of leafy branches, from a tree across the river, were pulled down and broken off carefully to damage the precious trees as little as possible. The water should be protected by the green leaves almost as much as the sand had protected it before. If not, if it got too much hotter, the hole would have to be filled before midday once everybody had a chance to fill their bottles or to at least have a drink. Not everybody had bottles.

Stopping at the edge of camp she studied it carefully, as if this might be the last time she would see the place. It was almost a daily ritual, and with good reason; every morning might be the last time she saw that camp. Already there were rumblings from some; it was time to move, they said.

She agreed with them on one thing: the camp was no longer safe. The Settlers were getting closer and when they arrived it would no longer be safe for Esperance's people. People would die, others would be enslaved, their children taken. So far they had escaped notice, not been discovered; that would not be true forever. They were becoming lax in their secrecy – the presence of booze was proof of that. It was time to consider moving the camp, or if she couldn't convince anyone else to move, she and Grandfather should go at least. Unfortunately she did not like her chances of convincing him to leave.

There were people in the camp who had come there from other Native camps, and the stories they told were terrifying. Every story ended the same: people died, many of them, and those that survived were herded and collected and taken to fenced camps, to so-called missions. Once there they were used as cheap labour, or just allowed to die.

They called it protection, these Settlers, 'protecting the Natives', although it was hard to imagine what they were being protected from. The only danger they were in was from those doing the 'protecting'.

'Conservation', it was a word in the newspapers that turned up in camp from time to time. The only things Esperance had ever seen 'conserved' were already dead – fruit in jam or pickles. Maybe that was the plan – to pickle her and her people. In spite of herself, she laughed at that.

That was not what she wanted for her or for her grandfather.

The camp was not her home; she had no home, no sense of belonging to a place, she knew no life but that of a refugee. It was, however, as close to a home as she had ever known, would ever have. She did not want to leave it.

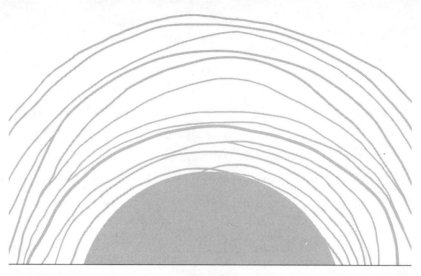

CHAPTER 4

Natives, you can't live with them, killing them all creates too much paperwork.

– CAPTAIN BLACK, COLONIAL TROOPERS

SERGEANT ROHAN HELD the letter in his hands as if it was a piece of stinking filth, as if it was one of the venomous animals that infested the forest around his office. Animals – venomous, Native, filthy – they even infested the cracks in the walls, crawled under the walls through the countless gaps.

The letter had started normal enough, with the standard greetings and enquiries about his health and the state of his station. Both were excellent, he would be proud to reply – he had continued to maintain law and order in this town, as he was required. There were no Native problems where he was, none that he couldn't handle anyway – no drinking problem, no fights, no crime – his was surely one of the most orderly settlements in the colony. Even the Settler boys, who never seemed to do anything other than drink, then fight when drunk, were sensible enough not to do so when he was in range. Not that they fought much; it interrupted the drinking. He could say in all honesty he did his job.

It was the second part of the letter, the part that traditionally dealt with the problem at hand, that was causing him some serious distress.

In mounting apprehension, in the certain knowledge that his upcoming leave, his chance to travel to the city, would need to be cancelled, he skimmed the letter again. 'Absconded . . .' his eyes read, 'on the run . . .' he wished his eyes did not see, 'headed your way . . .' was almost the worst part but the worst was, he knew, next.

'He must not make it to the deep desert; you must in your capacity as local representative of the department, as a local Protector of Natives, ensure he does not make it past you.'

He was deeply and thoroughly understaffed, his office consisting of basically, well, himself and whoever he could deputise among the local Settlers. This had long been enough to maintain order, especially when the entire town was terrified of his infrequent yet massive flights of temper. He had long been proud of his ability to terrify the town into maintaining order despite an almost complete lack of help.

Now, surely he alone would not be enough. His mind, known for thoroughness if not for speed or for dazzling flights of intellect, flicked rapidly through the files in his head. He needed help, needed a posse, needed a lynch mob if he was to be honest and he needed it fast, if the Native called 'Jacky' got past them they would be forced to pursue him into the desert or face serious reprimands. Only a madman would pursue a Native into the deep desert if they could avoid it. Rohan did not want to go into the deep desert.

It had been a long time since a Native had absconded from a settlement – well, a long time since one had made it far enough to be a concern. They were afraid, these Natives, and Rohan was part of the apparatus in place to keep them afraid. Efforts to integrate the Natives were working, they were doing their job, they were staying put. Yes, it had been a long time since he had been forced to chase a bloody Native.

He looked again at the name of the station from which the Native had run. Yep, he knew it all right, owned by one of the Governor's friends. He would have to be careful to succeed, this Native must be found.

From the outside his station appeared to be making a serious effort to disappear into the alien forest behind it. The Native timbers still had some of the bark on them; it peeled off and hung, never quite falling to the ground, making the building look like a filthy Native who needed a haircut. The roof of sheet-metal had long ago started to rust into the same colour as the red-brown dirt surrounding the building. In the harsh yellow sunlight the entire building stood slightly askew, built straight and true but so poorly it was beginning to fall over.

At least things were looking up, even if only slightly. Five years ago his police station was not even a building, all he had was a droopy canvas tent. It had cracked like a stockwhip in the wind, it had leaked at night, worst of all it was infernally hot in the sun – the dirty white fabric seemed to think heat precious, holding on to every fragment it got hold of. Every moment he had spent campaigning for a real building was worth it even though the place he received was only a building by the loosest definition.

Surely the authorities understood that you cannot keep order if everyone is laughing at you for trying to police from a tent.

Sergeant Rohan emerged walking briskly, his uniform clean and neat, contrasting profoundly with the building he had just left. He walked purposefully, shoulders back, throwing all his arrogance into his walk: someone might be watching. He was a representative of the Settler government, out here he was the only representative of the Settler government. It was important to keep up the appearance that everything was under control, all was well.

Mounting up he wished there were enough roads, and good enough roads, to allow him to have a car. No matter, if he had to ride, then ride he would although being from the city by nature it did not come easily to him. He did not wish to be seen to be rushing in an undue manner so he rode off calmly, cautiously in the direction of the centre of town, hoping some young men from the surrounding farms would be available.

Only half an hour later saw him riding back out of town towards what the letter told him was the last known location of the fugitive. There would be, of course, no need to go all the way there. He planned to pick up the trail well before that – last location and direction of travel of the Native was known – it should be easy enough. With luck they could catch the Native immediately, and he could be away on his delayed trip to the city.

Neither the sergeant nor the four young men with him had the slightest notion where Jacky was going. Nobody could have expected them to have a clue; the motivations of the Native were opaque, and often made no sense even if you asked them.

Surely the life they were given in the settlements was better than living pointless, aimless lives in the dirt like they always had. There was no purpose to their lives now and had surely been none before the Settlers had arrived to help them. They lacked ambition, lacked energy and drive, seemingly their only direction was towards alcohol, their only desires to drink, to breed and, unfortunately, to escape. Those first two desires had little bearing on Rohan's life, except when he needed to break up drunken fights over women. The third desire had disrupted his life a lot in the past, dragged him into the disgusting bush, far too often. He did not want it to happen again.

At least one of the young men, known as Mick, was a hunter by way of employment, and a skilled tracker by reputation. Rumour had it he had learnt his skills from a Native servant at his father's station, that he was as good as the Natives, maybe even better. It was not rumour but rather simple fact that his family supplemented their income with the animal hides he collected and sold. It was also fact that often his family were the only Settlers in town who never went completely hungry.

Rohan was glad to have him along; experience had eliminated the illusion that he would ever be able to trust a Native tracker. Other troopers used them, he mused, but they must like being led astray, lost on purpose and then robbed by the trackers who were so good at disappearing just when you were starting to trust them. No, a Settler trained to track by a Native was much better than a Native tracker, at least a Settler would not abscond with a mount and all their supplies in the middle of the night.

The last thing he needed was two Native fugitives to deal with. The one he was ordered to find was bad enough.

The other young men were merely muscle, of the kind you can never have enough of when tracking a Native. Everybody knew the Natives were cunning, and although they were never really organised could be dangerous. More at home in this place than the Settlers, they could attack with surprise and, even armed with their primitive weapons, kill the unprepared. They had survived with nothing but their ancient weapons for a long time before the

Settlers arrived; that should be warning enough that they could be hard to capture.

Still an hour before noon, the scorching yellow sun not yet overhead, it was already hot, too hot for Settlers to be comfortable having come from a much cooler, far damper, place. The Natives had no such limitations, although in their animal intelligence they tended not to travel in the hottest part of the day if they could avoid it. With the sun scorching into their skins and burning into their eyes, Rohan called a halt. The Settler boys gratefully, gracelessly, slumped from their mounts and into the shade of a tree. It was the only sensible, if not clever, thing Rohan had ever learnt from Natives: spend the hottest part of the day under a tree.

A sun like that, heat like that – it bleached the entire sky yellow-white, nothing like the blue sky one was used to from home. It was that sky that was a warning, the yellow light a warning that this was not a hospitable place. It was the glow of pain, the glow of the end of the world. It was not a friendly colour for a sky to be.

Sergeant Rohan had to show more decorum than the younger men so, despite feeling as hot and uncomfortable as the others, he slid from his mount with intent, control and grace. Walking over to the tree he sat down with a calm he did not feel and took a controlled sip from his water bottle. He was thirsty, devilishly so, but it would not do to run out of water when he had no idea where he would next acquire some.

The others – younger, undisciplined, inexperienced at travel and survival, untrained – were taking great slugs from their bottles, seemingly unaware of the risks out there, drinking as if water was not in short supply. Surely they were not that stupid, even in their settlements there would not be limitless water. If you needed proof of their unfitness to survive in this place, he thought, how they and their families used water was surely all you needed.

'Lay off on the water, boys,' Rohan interjected finally, perhaps a trifle too late. 'We are going out there for who knows how long and water will be short, we will run out.' Three of the boys stopped, looking sheepish, stoppered their bottles and put them away.

The fourth felt it was a good time to complain. 'Well, bloody find us water then,' he grumbled, 'you brought us out to this hole, you find us water.'

'I would love to,' the Sergeant's voice was tense with the need for restraint, 'but most likely there will be none to find. We are out here chasing a Native fugitive who knows this environment better than us, is better prepared for it and likely exhibits some of the Native cunning they possess to make up for their lack of intelligence. He is probably smarter than you are acting. For all we know he was not even born in the settlement and was raised wild, then he would be even harder to find. I don't know where we are going, I don't know how long it will take to find him and I don't know where we are going to find water.

'If we had a Native guide he no doubt would find us water. Yet I cannot trust a Native, last time I did he stole all the food and mounts and buggered off.'

He took a deep breath, showing his exasperation despite himself. 'You volunteered for this job, presumably to have an excuse to hunt and kill Natives. It's risky, dangerous, and frankly running out of water is one of those risks but it's a risk you chose to take.' His hand touched his gun lightly, he was barely aware he was doing it. 'You chose to be here, you can do what I say or you can go home to your safe little houses and pray the Natives stay in theirs.

'Any questions?'

There was silence around the tiny group as the boys realised the gravity and danger of the situation. Wind shook the leaves of the ugly Native trees, a light hot wind, bringing thirst, sapping what strength they had left. Despite being in the same situation they were different men and had different thoughts but they all had at least one thing in common.

All of them had relished the thought of the sanctioned killing of one or more Natives. Every one of them passionately hated the Natives. Not one of them had considered that hunting Natives could be dangerous. They had forgotten that Native men, unlike the other despised wildlife, had a tendency to fight back.

Rohan ignored them, deeply engrossed in his map. He alone was completely aware of the danger they were in. Along the track they must take, to hopefully cut off the fugitive Jacky, there were a few waterholes but not many and he knew that the water supplies marked on the maps were often unreliable. Settlers had died looking for water out there, not the Natives though, they must have hidden secret sources of water because they survived where the Settlers died. It was the start of summer, so while there would be no rain, at all, there would still be some water left in waterholes. Soon they would be all dried out and only Native knowledge could keep them alive.

Native knowledge they lacked, for they had no Native tracker.

It was heartbreaking, skin-scorching hot, the white heat that drains your energy, consumes your will to live. When they moved on after a too brief rest, as painful as it was, they did not hide, did not stop. The faster they did what they had to do the quicker they could go home to the settlement.

There was no complaint, no grumbling, not the slightest noise of protest as they rode out into the sun. Rohan thought they must have been cowed by his monologue or they were too tired, too hot to talk. He didn't care in the slightest which was true.

They, like him, would soon learn to hate this place. Nothing like the green and pleasant land from which they came; this land was grey, this land was washed out by the sun. The sky bleached yellow and far too bright. The light like blades of ice in their unprotected eyes.

@

The council were meeting again: for all the good it would do them, it would do the camp even less. Even from her humpy Esperance could see the bobbing of heads, the whooshing of tangled grey hair, the wagging of long beards. It was futile, she knew, but she put on the billy for tea.

Tea was important; not only was it a social activity that did not involve booze, it was also a way to make water safer. She was not sure why but people who drank their water as tea got sick less often than those who did not. Yes, tea was important.

She owned nothing unnecessary, nothing superfluous to her survival except for a spare mug, a tea-mug for Grandfather. The water boiled and, carefully, in silence, Esperance made tea for both of them.

As she suspected, the bobbing of heads, the talking of the old men and fewer old women, stopped as soon as she approached. The group was silent; whatever they had been discussing was not for her, or for anyone outside their circle. Grandfather took the tea, turned and sprayed her with a wide grin, a smile that lit his whole face. Even his beard seemed animated by it.

Esperance stood there a moment too long in the futile hope that someone would talk when she was there, that she would have some inkling of what they were thinking. Turning she strolled away as if nothing mattered, hearing the first muttered return to conversation while she was still in earshot. They had done well, she was not close enough to hear them.

Grandfather indulged them, she thought. He founded the camp, he had always led them, they had pulled together as a community behind him, not the elders. The only criteria for their leadership was age; when they got old enough that the others didn't remove them they got to stay. That was what Esperance thought anyway.

They had just gathered over time, mounded in place like blown sand collecting against the wall of a hut.

Jacky lay in the deepest shadows he could find, flat on his groaning empty belly as he studied the cluster of buildings before him. The shacks, sheds and boxes huddled together in the middle of a cleared space in the forest as if scared of the trees. He knew that place well, it had once been the closest thing he had ever known to a home.

It was not the place where he had grown up, he had grown up at the farm, where he had been a slave. That hadn't been his home either. He could not remember his home, for all he knew he had been born as his parents camped on a riverbank, fleeing from the Settlers. He had heard that story, or stories a lot like it, from many in his life; he had no reason not to believe it true for him as well. He barely remembered arriving at this place, so alien to him at the time; he remembered all the shapes had seemed strange, the buildings bizarre.

There he was to receive an education, and he did if being beaten, locked up, punished, mistreated and controlled and then finally, when broken, trained to be a servant was an education. He learnt to work, learnt to obey, learnt the religion of his captors. Most importantly for the Settlers, he learnt to fear them, to respect them as his betters.

Now again, many years later, the mission did not look any different. There were the clusters of buildings, with smaller clusters of children, all Natives, moving between them. They were herded from behind by beings in robes of charcoal, strange square heads he knew to be hats. He knew they were the nuns, he also knew to fear them.

This, the closest thing he had ever known to a home was also the scene of all his most terrifying nightmares.

He could not risk approaching that place, not in the light of day, yet he could think of no other way if he wished to find his real home, his parents, his family. Somewhere in that place was someone who knew where he had been taken from. In that place, that terrible place, was the information he needed but fear and indecision kept him frozen.

His courage rose with the failing light as if the daylight itself had been sapping it. The knots of children slipped into the barracks. If things were the same as when he was there the doors would be locked. For a time, the slender, taller, robed figures moved about like strange black wading birds, searching before them for tasty morsels of fish. Some time after the departure of the sunlight, under the nearly day-bright light of an almost full moon, they too went inside, into the building of wood and stone, with a roof of slate, rather than tin, next to the stone church.

When the pregnant moon slipped behind a cloud he made a move, steeling himself, fighting his fear, for there was nothing else he could do but give up the hope that he held with his entire soul. Moving silently through the trees, he dumped his shoes under a tree and ran barefoot, for hard soles make too much noise. He slipped over the fence into the compound. The dormitories of tin were a pointless destination, there would be nothing there of use. The building near the church where the nuns lived, to go there would be suicide. That left the church, the school and a third building that he shuddered even to look at.

That smaller building, between the church and the dorms, was the most terrifying of all: the office where punishment was meted out. Nobody was ever taken to that building for a pleasant reason. Shaking with terror he thought, had hoped, he would never feel again, Jacky crouched in the shadow of a silent dormitory, staring. If it was not for the fact that he was certain the building was empty, there was not a force that could have made him move. If there had been any other way at all he would not have moved, except to flee into the woods and at least the feeling of safety.

There was no other choice, in fact no choice at all. He forced himself to stand, forced himself to sprint the short distance to the other building. The door was locked, of course it was, and so were the windows, as they always were in the past, and in his nightmares. Panting, terrified, he hid in the only shadow he could find. In his memory, almost gone, almost there, was something he was missing, if only he could remember it, he was sure it was important.

It came to him in a rush and he crawled and skittered around to where there had been a loose board all those years ago, a loose board he and the other children had used to break into that building. They had always been hungry at the mission; food could be stolen from the building before him. There was a pantry full of the food the nuns ate, food that the Natives never saw. They were all scared of that building, yet in desperation they were always trying to get in.

A miracle, the board was still loose. He pulled it free, wincing at the creaking noise it hadn't made last time he had gone in through there, back when he was a child. The hole it left did not look large enough to squeeze through but, desperate, he lay on his belly and tried.

Jacky was always small. After the abuse of the mission and the settlement, he was visibly malnourished, he was tiny. A larger man would never have made it through such a gap, made by children.

The room through the hole was silent, empty, the only light a watery patch of moonlight cast through the thin curtains covering the window. It was not enough to see by so he crawled in silent caution towards where the door must be. Then a hallway, even darker than the room, the door clicking, almost silently, shut behind him.

The room he wanted, he hoped, was the main office – there must be records there. He remembered paper, lots of paper, there in the great wooden chest of drawers that covered the entire length of one wall. It was difficult but he walked past the locked pantry, ignoring the screaming of his stomach, towards the office.

The office was too dark, he could not see to search, yet a warm glow was cast from the fireplace on the opposite wall. Above it would be the iron kettle – the nuns liked tea, he remembered that. There were papers on the desk in the middle of the room, he could not see to read them but snatched at them in desperation. Twisting a few loose sheets into a rough taper he lit it from a coal in the fireplace.

By the flickering red light he tore into the cabinets looking for some sort of clue – was there a file in his name among all those others? They were in order, the alphabet they had forced him to learn. He dug into the 'Bs'. There he found it, Jacky Barna, that was the name he had used at the settlement, but the rest of the file he could not hope to understand.

Here, in this place, he had learnt to read, he had worked hard at reading so he could better himself, be as good as a Settler, which he never seemed to achieve. The words in the file seemed to flow, to swim in his vision in the flashing light. There were too many words, in a tiny cramped handwriting; he could not begin to decipher them.

His taper ran out, the flame and light disappearing without warning into the room's sickly moonlit glow. He quickly fashioned and ignited another one, and another. So many words in his file were words he did not understand, had never read or even heard. Bent over the file, eyes watering with the attempt to read, he did not hear footsteps in the hall, did not hear doors open, did not notice anything until the doorway behind him was lit with the glow of a lantern.

He dropped the flaming paper in his hand, yet did not stay to watch it make its slow flickering way to the floorboards. In panic he dashed for the closed window but his frightened fingers fumbled at the latch, hampered by the papers he refused to drop. Trapped, he turned to face the light, backing against the window and freedom he could not reach. Backing as far as he could, as if by willpower he could walk backwards right through the wood and glass, he stared at the light as one terrified of fire.

'Wha . . .' a voice stammered. 'Who are you, what are you doing here?' He could not see the face before him, the lantern ruined his night vision, but the voice was female. There was a musical lilt to the voice, the voice of a young woman, surely not much older than him. That he did not expect – when he was a child all the nuns were old. Jacky was silent, unable to force words through his fear.

'Who are you? You are not one of our children, you are too old. There is nothing here but paper, why break in to steal paper?' She paused in thought, staring at Jacky's face. 'This is a school, there is no grog, nothing to drink here, all the food is in the kitchen.' She was circling as she talked as if to give Jacky an opening if he decided to run. Jacky shuddered with the conflict in his mind between the desire to run in terror and the need to find what he needed. The fact that he had nowhere to run without bowling into the nun in the doorway decided it for him. 'Please,' he breathed, barely audible, struggling to find the words to be understood, 'I need to find my home, I don't know where it is. I need to get home to my family.'

'You were here as a child?' The nun sounded nothing but curious. She stared at the papers in his hand. The paper rustled slightly with the force of his uncontrolled shaking.

She moved closer, she seemed less afraid than Jacky thought she should be, less afraid than Jacky was. Reaching out she took the quivering file from his hand. 'Jacky, is that your name?' She opened the file as Jacky backed towards the door. He was prepared to run, the moment she called for help, raised the alarm. He could not understand why he was not running already, yet this woman, this girl was not threatening. 'Terrible handwriting,' she said, 'who wrote this?' She looked up at Jacky, shrugged, then her eyes dropped back to the file. 'It says you were collected from a camp near the town of Jerramungup.' Jacky did not respond, the name meant nothing to him. 'Here, let me show you where,' she said, when he did not move. 'Here, on the map,' she said, pointing, 'here, here it is, east of us.' Jacky stared at the map, at the strange symbols, wishing that it meant something to him, he didn't even know what a map was, he had no way to even begin to read it.

The name 'Jerramungup' and the direction 'east', though, they were burned into his brain. Too nervous even to thank the young nun, he turned to the window and reached again for the latch. It was stuck.

The distant outside door of the building creaked open. Screaming loudly the young nun threw the file on the floor, adding the map and other files from the open drawer. With a terrifying, deafening clatter she swept the contents of the desk onto the floor. Jacky, already standing on the knife edge of his nerves, completely lost any control he had over his fear. Unable to budge the window frame, he dashed to the fireplace and, grabbing the poker, returned to the window. The noise of the glass splashing outwards from his wild swing was breathtaking, it filled the world to overflowing, running over the other noises, leaving silence behind it.

Sound rushed back into the world as Jacky released the breath he wasn't even aware he was holding. The sound of boot heels on the floor came from the hallway, someone was coming, someone was right outside the door. The once comforting yellow light from the lantern, from the flames of the dropped taper catching on the papers on the floor, flickered and flashed a menacing red. He scraped the bottom of the frame with the poker in a desperate attempt to remove all the glass. There was no time, the sound of footfalls in the hallway ceased. When the door opened to the room he bunched up, threw himself headfirst out the window. He stopped midair, for a fraction of a second, levitating as a hand lashed out and grabbed his ankle. He felt the hand slip on his sweat, letting go, but his momentum was already lost.

He landed outside the window, dangling from one foot still hooked around the window frame, the bare dirt and gravel of the ground outside lacerating his face. Blood ran down his leg from an excruciating glass cut in the ankle stuck in the window. He rolled that leg off the window frame, rolling sideways with the motion, scratching himself on the gravel and broken glass. All around him he could hear the mission rousing – shouts, doors banging, children yelling.

Jacky scrambled to his feet, in his panic feeling like all his limbs were too long, his joints too loose. He dashed towards the waiting, familiar forest as behind him the entire mission jolted awake. He knew, although all the teachers were women, nuns, there were always a handyman and a guard, there was a tracker, they would be after him. Although it was dark he knew someone would soon be running to town to tell what troopers were there of the night's excitement. His presence was no longer a secret.

Stumbling over slippery branches, sharp rocks and fallen trees, almost invisible in the darkness, he tried his best to run for it. Half running and half crawling, stumbling and repeatedly falling he scrambled as deep into the woods as he could. The moon went into the clouds again and in the darkness he fell and fell again. He tripped, tripped and tumbled, in the end he crawled, it was too dark even to walk. On hands and knees he crawled under a low scrub, into a scratchy dry thicket, tearing his skin on sharp twigs and thorns that had already torn their way into his clothes.

Pulling his kitchen knife out of his pocket he removed the scraps of cloth he had wrapped around the blade to stop him cutting himself. His empty stomach growled its complaints into the silence; it would be a help in staying awake, watching and listening for the inevitable searchers. Not that there was anything to eat even if he wanted to.

Just before he fell into darkness, he remembered: he had forgotten his shoes.

@

Sergeant Rohan was not far behind. The message had arrived with surprising promptness, he was in the middle of nowhere and would not have expected to be contacted at all. Finally, he felt like he was doing something, doing his job, rather than just getting lost, thirsty, hungry and frustrated. The legendary tracking ability of his tracker, Mick, had turned out to be exactly that – a legend. He could track Jacky when he had, for example, been running over mud leaving tracks that even Rohan could see, but beyond that they were relying on news and hearsay.

The trooper and his little posse arrived at the mission and could not find a single soul. They must have all been at lunch. The Natives had already eaten their morning porridge – the only thing they would be eating before their evening meal near sunset – and without supervision they had reverted to type. Lazy, idle, they were playing in the trees, talking in half whispers or just lying about in scraps of shade. They were lucky to be there, lucky they were being fed at all. When the posse arrived they at least staggered to their feet, meandering over to touch the legs of the men, or examine their mounts.

Approaching the mission office he noticed, with jealousy, it was far better built than the dump where he was forced to live and work. Riding slowly, they were followed by a moving crowd of Native children; they crowded the mounts, dangerously close to getting under foot. Clean – well, at least the nuns took care of that – they were still a disturbance, untidy, unkempt, smelly. They were also loud, talking loudly and without a shred of discipline, a high-pitched riot of voices in a shabby pidgin. Rohan could see clearly the hate, the disgust, radiating from the faces of the young men, his reluctant deputies, as he dismounted and entered the office with the nun who had come out to meet them.

The office, one of the most soundly built buildings he had seen in years, was tidy, clean, far more so than most of the Settler houses. Barely a speck of dust was visible, not a paper out of place, except where they could see the Native had been. Paper had scattered in his wake, ash dusted the floor, his footprints meandering here and there, marked out perfectly in ash on polished wood. Ash evidenced where he had tried to light a fire with the scattered papers.

'I don't know how he got in but he got out through that window –' Sister Bagra indicated with an imperious wave of her hand. 'He threatened one of my sisters with a knife and then tried to burn this building down.'

'Any idea what else he wanted,' Rohan questioned, 'beside the obvious, beside his desire to destroy the building?' It was hard to fathom, usually, the motivations of these savages, if they had motivations at all. They were destructive, seemingly without reason, rebellious to no purpose. Why this building, why such hate, to break in just to seemingly start a destructive frenzy?

Sister Bagra was clearly of the same mind. 'Who knows what they are thinking? It doesn't matter what we do, we try to help them, try to elevate them. They might never be our equals but at least they can be better than they are born.' The calm in her voice gave scant clue to her exasperation. 'We educate them so they can have a place in our society, a place as lowly as they deserve, we even give them faith, give them purpose.' She walked over to the window with a curious stiff walk; Rohan recognised it as the side-effect of her attempt to maintain iron control. 'Their minds, what minds they have, are completely unfathomable.'

'Maybe he just likes fire,' said Sergeant Rohan, with a laugh in his voice. In response to that Sister Bagra merely snorted as if humour was somehow inappropriate, always. There was an uncomfortable, loaded silence both seemed reluctant to break. 'A lot of the Natives like fire,' he amended eventually.

There was a moment of silence, slightly too long.

'You are sure it was the fugitive Jacky?' Rohan finally said, sounding bored and eager to get the distasteful job over with.

'Of course I am sure, he was a student here, and I remember every student.' Her voice rose at the end of the sentence, a sure sign of exasperation.

Rohan doubted that; it would be a truly impressive feat of memory considering there was little to remember, little difference in features from Native to Native. Yet he said nothing, it would not help to antagonise her. 'We will get underway as soon as you find us something to eat and fill our water bottles. We have not had breakfast and we are quite low on water.'

'You cannot eat with us; our dining room is out of bounds to men. We will bring some food to the verandah.' She left, her demeanour almost but not quite covering and controlling her anger. Sergeant Rohan suppressed a laugh, remembering his religious education, the worst time of every week, remembering the nuns and how hard it was to break their composure. Sister Bagra must have been quite close to the edge already to be pushed off it so easily. That he could tell without even knowing her personally.

The Settler boys were outside, leaning lazily against their mounts. Rohan could see their eyes flick from side to side as they studied the Natives while trying not to show it. The contempt they felt for the Natives they were not trying to hide, or if they were trying they were not trying very hard. They were no longer as cocky; instead they looked slightly scared, more nervous, far more cautious. It had not rained where they were for some time, so their mounts and their legs were covered with a thin veneer of dust.

'C'mon, boys, the nuns are going to feed us,' he shouted, holding back a smirk as two of them started. They looked guilty as if they were not proud of the hate for the Natives showing on their faces. The other two, one of them Mick the tracker, were proud of their hate or just didn't care. 'Let's take a seat on the verandah here and see what they bring us; we need to eat and drink whenever we can.'

The day was not getting any longer; it would be well after noon before they could get moving, even if Mick could find a track, which Rohan was beginning to doubt. He had lost almost all faith in the young man's hunting ability. No matter. Jacky would be far away, and it would do no good to run off without eating, without water in their bottles, without packing whatever food they could get their hands on into their bags. Rohan took the least comfortable seat. He would never allow any of the younger men with him to think they were tougher than he was.

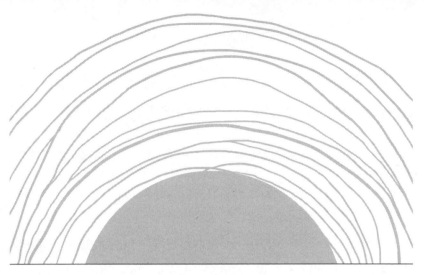

CHAPTER 5

There is nothing more important, to us and to you all, than the economic health of this colony. Without economic independence we can never hope to gain political independence from home; that was a condition that was laid upon us. So long as we are dependent on assistance from home we can never hope to be self-governing. Grazing of livestock and the effective export of the fruits of that labour is the simplest, the fastest, way forward towards that economic power.

The only thing standing in our way, the main limitation to our growth is the depredations of the criminal, aggressive and intransigent Natives. So long as our livestock is not safe from the immoral and illegal actions of these primitives we will not be a real country. We call upon the government of the colony to assist us in the control of this menace. We need more police, with more discretionary powers. All Natives who endanger our livestock must be arrested and tried for that crime.

It does not matter which Native killed the stock, without doubt every Native has joined in on the savage, pagan feasting they are no doubt partaking of at our expense. Every man, woman and child is involved either directly or as accessories to the crime.

If, as we suspect, every Native is involved in livestock killing then every Native must be arrested. The danger must be eliminated at any cost.

– AN OPEN LETTER FROM THE UNITED GRAZIERS ASSOCIATION

THE FIRST MOMENT it was light enough to see, just light enough to avoid walking into the bruised, twisted trunks of the trees, Jacky was away again, this time with a new direction. He kept the light in his face as he wove his way through the trees. There was not much information in as simple an imperative as 'east' but lacking more to go on he took what clues he had. At least at dawn, east was easy; Jacky ran towards the sun.

He had to move fast; they were right behind him. He had to move carefully, leave no tracks, no trace, they were right behind him; he had to run, he couldn't run, they were right behind him. Leaves were soft on his bare feet. If he ran on leaves he would leave almost no tracks but unfortunately there were no leaves on the ground. He dodged between the trees, stepping when he could on fallen wood, on stones, on bark, not on the earth between. It was a bizarre, jinking, looping, staggering run; he swayed and swerved, he constantly changed direction. He was a flittering bird, a scurrying rat, a leaf in a storm; what tracks he left would give scant clue to his direction of movement.

Hungry again, he wished he had taken the time to steal some food, though that would have increased the risk. He knew if he had stopped to break into the pantry he would have never found out what he needed to know, he might have even got caught, but that was no consolation when his stomach was screaming. He had no time to hunt, not much of a chance to gather food when every moment of delay could be costly, every delay an unacceptable risk. He could only run, and watch for food as he did so.

He had not, at first, noticed how the trees had changed as he had run. Jacky did not belong here; the country now was unfamiliar, completely so. It is always possible to identify the country by its trees, and these trees around him, he did not know them. Although he knew in which direction he was running he did not know where he was; he felt lost although he was not.

It was always a problem for him defining 'lost'; he had a vague idea where he was but he had no real idea where he was going. East was a direction, not a destination. Jerramungup was a place but he had no idea where it was. It would be child's play to retrace his steps, to return to the mission, to return from there to the settlement he had escaped from. He was not lost, he just didn't know where he was going; he was not lost, his destination was.

Passing a thicket of blackberries he grabbed handfuls, hunger and fear making him incautious, scratching the hell out of his hands and arms. Slaking his thirst, providing needed calories, they were small, sour and hard to get to but far better than nothing. The meal gave him just enough energy to keep running, running east.

Finding a clean-looking stream, clean enough, he drank until his belly sloshed, until he felt a little ill, until it was almost impossible to keep moving with such a lake inside him. Yet still he moved, no longer even understanding how he kept the will to go on. A bird silly enough to have its nest a short climb above the ground lost its eggs; only tiny morsels but Jacky needed them.

He ran the day through, walking when too tired to run, ignoring the hunger that he was not quite able to satiate, ignoring the fatigue he knew would only get worse from day to day. Trying to ignore the fear, trying to live on hope, he ran on as the sun wheeled overhead, staggering with unacknowledged fatigue. He ran again until it was too dark to keep running. Finding nowhere warm enough or safe enough to sleep, he lay in the bushes at the base of a tree, shivering himself to sleep with fear and the cold.

@

It had been a night of fire and noise, a night of gunshots and screams, of fear, blood and death, mostly death. A glut of death that had ended Johnny Star's life. Following standard tactics, they had arrived at the Native camp a couple of hours before dawn. They were searching for a fugitive, a murderer who had killed a Settler. It did not matter why the Settler had been singled out and killed, although the Native would surely have some story, some pathetic excuse. Murder would not be tolerated.

The Troopers had crept carefully into the scratchy dry bush around the camp until they could see the huts, the humpies, the tents, the coals of dying campfires, and the men, women and children lying asleep in the dirt. There were troopers prone on the ground in the scrub, troopers standing behind trees in the dark, peering around them at the camp. Twenty men in all, likely too many to arrest a single Native but you could never be too sure. They were silent, although they were nervous; they had all heard stories of the sneaky Natives and their tricks.

So silent it was that every trooper was startled when the captain screamed, a blood-chilling wail, a battle cry, a death cry; no words just pure aggression as if he had tapped into the frenzy-killer in his brain and connected it straight to his vocal chords. When he fired his gun in the air for emphasis, the Natives stood almost as one and made to run, lurching up from the ground, surging out of the huts. They tripped and stumbled as they made their ragged way; there was no order, no pattern, no sense to the stampede.

'Fire,' the captain cried and the startled, nervous, half-trained troopers, used to obeying orders without question, did exactly that. They fired into the fleeing crowd. Men, women and children fell among spraying blood. The survivors were sprayed with so much gore they looked like they too might have been shot.

Johnny was with them as they chased the terrified, fleeing survivors, in the almost dark, in the glowing red light of scattered coals from campfires, in the light from burning humpies. Some of the Native men grabbed their primitive arms and tried to fight back but men with ancient weapons cannot stand against men with modern guns. They were gunned down. The flickering, fluttering firelight cast enough light to see the violence but not enough to see the details. Johnny ran with the others of his troop, guns empty – who could be bothered reloading? – running buoyed by their bubbling laughter, knives in hands slitting throats and piercing bellies.

Dancing flames and leaping sparkling coals, leaping running figures and glinting sparkling blades. A red dawn of fire, coals and blood, the blood transforming from black to red where the sunlight hit. People, his people, dancing around the camp holding flaming branches casting fire into the Natives' meagre homes, their meagre Native belongings, their meagre Native flesh.

He saw a babe, taken from its screaming mother's arms, wailing as it was dashed against a rock with a sickening thud, its head spurting blood onto the stone, its still shuddering body cast onto the flames of its burning home. Its wailing mother, falling to her knees, was unable or unwilling – her shaded eyes already blank – to resist as her throat was cut. The father – he assumed it was the father – screamed defiance right until a blade pierced his chest, screamed defiance and pain from bubbling frothing lungs.

He saw a man running, his tattered rags of clothing afire, chased by laughing troopers, trailing smoke and flickering light. He saw a gutted man still living, holding his entrails with desperation as his eyes slowly faded. He saw a woman shot, bent over her child to protect it, then a man shot bending over her to wail for her life. He saw death: death walking and death running, even death dancing. He saw death in the blades and death in fire and smoke.

Running in the terrible light, in the metallic smell of blood, of raw meat, in the noise of death – no longer thinking, blind with unaccustomed emotion – he didn't see the corpse he caught his foot on. When he fell, he landed with his face on something soft; he did not want to know what it was that had saved him. As he rose he had no choice but to look. In the first light of dawn he saw a Native – a child, stomach opened like a hunter's prize, like a corpse on an autopsy table, like a gutted fish, like a pig slaughtered for meat. As he wiped the blood and entrails from his face, he retched; he did not want to vomit on the dying child below him. His mind came close to breaking point as he watched the last light, the last glimmer of life, leaving the child's eyes.

Trying too hard to wipe the blood from his face he bruised, abraded, battered his own skin. Near him another trooper was actually laughing, a cold reptilian snigger, finding something funny in Johnny's face-down fall into a corpse. Johnny's hand twitched towards his handgun, he fought the urge to draw on this stranger who had once been his friend. Surely none of his friends would laugh in that hell.

When it was light enough they piled the corpses to rot, not bothering with burial or even with cleansing fire. They regrouped: many men were grinning; others, abashed, looked like they wanted to be sick. Johnny saw no sign of the horror consuming his soul in anyone else's eyes. There were souvenirs: one man held a spear, others held scalps; one man was told to throw the severed head he was carrying onto the pile of bodies. 'It will only rot and stink,' the captain told him. 'You know that from experience, Captain,' someone quipped, and most of the men laughed.

One man, with more forethought than the rest, held a squirming Native child, less than a year old, too shocked, too tired to wail. 'It will be a great pet for my girl,' he said. The others laughed.

'Wish I had thought of that,' said the man next to him.

The abattoir smell of corpses not yet beginning to rot made Johnny's head swim. The breeze shifted, blowing the smoke from a burning hut in his direction. He smelled the smoke, then his stomach churned; under the smell of smoke was the smell of food, of roasting meat.

In the full light of dawn, the coals of smouldering fire, the blood of Natives, turned the world red. In the silence after the battle, after the massacre, even the last flames that still had something to burn seemed afraid to crackle. There was no noise of footsteps, no noise of bodies pushing through bush, not even the sound of breathing. The grieving world held its breath.

Almost exactly one week later Johnny walked away from camp in the middle of the night. He took nothing with him but his stash, a few notes he had kept in an empty ration tin and his sidearm, for it was dangerous out there. He told nobody he was leaving, gave no explanation, not being certain he could explain it if he tried. He could not tell anyone. He was absent without leave, he had technically stolen his firearm. By leaving he had become a criminal. Leaving behind his old life, leaving behind his old name, only suited to his old life, he became Johnny Star.

A week later, when he collapsed from hunger and thirst, when he closed his eyes knowing he was going to die there, he was surprised to wake to a Native holding his mouth open with a strong hand, pouring cool fresh water down his throat. The water was the most delicious thing he had ever tasted and he moaned in protest when it was withdrawn. Only a moment later his stomach revolted to the water, nearly violently emptying itself as wave upon wave of nausea racked his body.

When he woke again, not even knowing for sure he had slept, the Native was seated, cross-legged, staring intently at him, talking. Johnny didn't speak the language but he assumed that what he was offered next was food; it looked like food, like meat, so he took what was offered and ate it.

It was almost tasteless – an unseasoned hunk of some Native animal, scorched in a fire, but to him at that moment it might have been the food of the gods.

The Native watched him, impassive, as they always seemed to be. Johnny finished the hunk of meat in his hand.

'Thank you,' he said, his voice audibly breaking with emotions he could not begin to express. Johnny, unexpectedly, regretted that he had never bothered to learn the Native language; he had to hope that the Native had learnt his. Had the Native understood his thanks, did the Native know he had saved his life? There was no way to know.

Why was this creature, this Native, this person – he surprised himself with the word – saving his life? A distant relative, maybe even a close relative, of the people he had helped massacre only weeks ago – did he not hold a grudge? Did he not know what sort of man Johnny was? Or was this how Natives behaved, helping the helpless even if those helpless could be their enemy? Were they that stupid, that foolish?

Johnny was not accustomed to this much thinking, it was making his head hurt. Were people like that, kind to others? Certainly his kind would help their own, yet they would be disgustingly, foully cruel to the Natives. Obviously they did not consider Natives people, thought them less than animals maybe. Yet, here was a Native, a wild Native for all he knew, saving his life. Did that mean the Native considered Johnny to be his people, or was he really so stupid it did not occur to him to allow Johnny to die? Did the Natives fail to draw that line, the important line that had driven Johnny's life before, defined all Settlers' lives: the line between 'Us' and 'Them'.

The Native stared at Johnny with his dark, deep-set eyes; stared at him as if to try and read the lines in his face, see the pain in his eyes. Satisfied, or maybe deeply dissatisfied with what he saw, he turned to walk away.

'Please . . .' Johnny's voice was uncertain, fearful. He thought he sounded embarrassingly like a child. 'Don't go.' He could not fathom the reason for his plea – the food and water had given him enough energy to move on, to continue in whatever direction his life was taking him. Maybe he was lonely, wanted someone, anyone to talk to; maybe he wanted to find humanity in the Native before him. Maybe – he hated himself for this thought – he was looking for the humanity in himself.

Was it the tone in his voice? Whatever it was it worked; the Native stopped and turned back. Johnny pointed to himself: 'Me Johnny,' he said slowly, laboriously. The Native stared at him as if he was the stupid one, as if nothing he said was making sense. 'Me Johnny,' he said, even slower and more precisely.

The Native – tall, muscular, dark – stared into Johnny's face with hollow eyes, suddenly flashing a wry smile. 'My name is Tucker,' he said in an intelligent drawl, 'and I will never know why you Settlers always think us so stupid that we can't learn your language.'

@

Sister Bagra was deeply disconcerted and she did not like it. She stood a little too long outside the door where the stupid girl – the one who had found Jacky – was meditating, staring at the door as if by will alone she could render it transparent. She could not be certain – she was certain she could not prove it – yet she believed the girl had helped the Native boy in some way. She did not – could not – believe the girl's protestations. Hence the order to time in contemplation and prayer, hence the closed door, the door that should be locked just in case.

Maybe some time in thought, in meditation, would bring out the truth, or at least make her feel guilty enough to prevent more such lapses.

What was that girl's name again? Certainly the younger sisters tended to merge and blend until they seemed all the same to her. Surely she should be able to remember their names at least. The main difficulty was the tendency of the younger sisters to lose faith. Too many of them left the mission, asked for transfers to other missions; the life at the school was clearly too much for most of them. What, therefore, was the point of getting to know all of them, any of them well? This one, this almost nameless girl was even harder to remember than the rest of the faceless nameless girls. Regardless, she would need watching to ensure she was not losing faith. Mel, that was her name. Sister Mel. Sister Bagra would have to ask the other women to keep an eye on her.

If she could trust anyone else to watch the girl.

The mission was silent as she strode the halls, searching for more security breaches, for more failings of faith. She could not even hear noises from the kitchen; surely someone was preparing the gruel for the children, the more substantial meal for the nuns. Turning on her heels she strode towards the kitchen.

There was a malaise in the mission: the nuns losing faith in the work, beginning to question the teaching of those children. She agreed they would never rise up to the intelligence of the race who now ruled the land but they could surely be risen above what they were before. If they could be improved, it followed that they should be. This is a noble cause – Bagra's belief in that was deeply embedded, unassailable, unshakeable.

The kitchen was indeed empty, cold. Why would she care if everyone ate late? Taking a pad of paper down from a shelf she scrawled a note; it was a good opportunity to ensure the kitchen knew their place, knew that her orders were to be followed. She would also make sure they knew she was displeased in the morning.

She stormed from the kitchen into the deep silence just before dawn.

Maybe the concerns the others were having stemmed from what happened before and after the Natives' time in the mission. Some would say it was not right to take the Native children from their homes, from their families. Sister Bagra had to admit, she had some doubt about that herself – every creature from the lowest animal is happier among its own kind. If you take a puppy from its mother, the mother will wail, mourn. It should not be surprising that the Natives do too.

However, giving these children religion, teaching them to read and write a language far superior to the jabber they talked before, justified rounding them up, keeping them at the mission, imprisoning them, some would say. Those critics were morons. Surely the end justified the means; it really was best for these children that they be educated, that they be raised by civilised people. They were primitives really, living in squalor, living in dirt, living dull, short, pointless lives.

What concerned her, if anything did, was the children being taken or sent, after the mission school, to lives of drudgery as domestic servants, or as low-class farmhands. Surely the school was capable of elevating them further than that: maybe to priests and monks; maybe to menial, but independent, labour of some kind. It would be interesting, she thought, to see how far they are capable of being educated.

She was tempted – it was so tempting – to separate a child from the mob, and give that child a further education, maybe an education as good as the children get back home, see how far it could go. Besides the benefit to the Native, it would be an advantage to have a Native priest, a Native teacher to take the teaching to the others. She had been tempted to try that with Jacky, when he had been a child. That would have been a disaster given his current rebellion. Again, not for the first time, she gave up on the idea. The Natives were too rebellious.

She arrived at the punishment cells, the 'boob'. Silent, as they should be, she was almost glad, almost smiled. The children in there were asleep or were learning the value of silence. She knew they would rebel again, but at least for now they were being silent.

There had been a few children, a special few, who had shown a bit more potential than the others. There had even been star pupils who were almost civilised, almost equal to a Settler child in their knowledge and perceptions, their understanding of the Settlers' world. It was unfortunate, therefore, that those who did best were also those who had been taken from their Native lives, from their parents, at a younger age. The younger the better.

It was such a pity that babies, when they were taken, created so much work for the missionaries. Raising babies was hard but it was worth it. They were much easier to teach, and less rebellious having never been brought up with the Native way. Children raised from infancy made much better servants, they spoke the language better, could read and write better and followed orders better. And they knew their place.

With these thoughts in mind she visited the nursery, just another shed of local wood with a tin roof. There were rows of simple cots and a couple of larger beds where the Native girls, who were learning to be nursemaids by looking after the babies, were sleeping. Every cot was full, with only one baby in each, of course. Babies are too precious a commodity, too hard to replace, to shove them together in a pile.

They were silent, as they tended to only be when asleep, and she was glad of that. The baby of the Native was even uglier than babies usually are, and more ugly even than older Natives. Bagra, despite her duties, hated babies. If they were wailing, when she was so on edge, she might do something that would reflect badly on the mission if anyone found out.

It is so important not to be found out.

Children, but normally not babies, had gone 'missing' before, though not often because she had lost her temper. Most of the deaths in the mission had been acceptable: starvation, disease, disease caused by starvation, accidents, all were acceptable causes of fatalities and could be reported acceptably. The Natives were always sickly and weak anyway, so it was expected that several would die every year, even every week.

It was death through violence that was harder to clear up. The Department for the Protection of Natives tended to want to investigate and there was no way Bagra could tolerate such an investigation, such an invasion. It was lucky that nobody really knew how many Natives there were, and how many there were on the mission. Files are flexible, pages can disappear; and normally their mission file was the only proof that a Native existed.

Who, after all, would bother to record the existence of a Native who was of no use to anyone and certain to die soon. What a waste of paper.

Lucky also, that Natives had such a deplorable tendency to escape, or at least attempt to escape. Many had escaped over the years, disappearing into the Native population outside of the towns, in the forest, in the deep desert. Some had not been found for years, lost for a long time before returning to continue their education, some surprised to be ejected from the mission for being too old. Others had not returned at all. She did not like to admit it but some were better off absconded – better for her, anyway – they were so disruptive. Others were better off reported as 'absconded' – better for her, anyway – than reported as dead.

The department would look for any Natives reported as absconded, she knew they would never find them. At least it would give them something to do other than bother her.

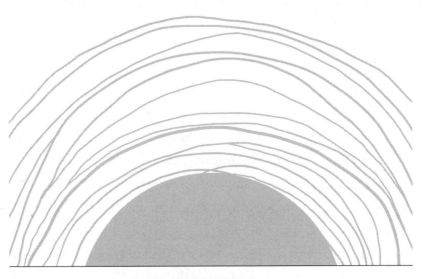

CHAPTER 6

We must continue to attempt to educate these savages. We must try although they will never truly be our equals. They will never be ready to take places among us as citizens. However, if trained and educated they can maybe, one day, find a place among us, as labourers and as servants. It is unlikely they will survive the situation in which they find themselves, a situation of our doing. Frankly I am surprised they survived even before our arrival. If they survive we must find a place for them in our society. We must find for them a place befitting their limited capacities.

– SISTER BAGRA

ROHAN WAS NOT having a good day, consequently neither were the young men helping him on the search. Again and again they had lost the tracks; it was impossible to be certain whether it was the skill of their quarry or the lack of skill from Mick that was the problem. Too many times they had been forced to backtrack in the excruciating dry heat, trying to find the tracks that had disappeared so suddenly it appeared the Native had learnt to fly.

As expected they had run out of water; there were no police or trooper outposts on their trail to resupply them. They rode into a homestead through the choking dust, finding neat buildings and watered gardens in an otherwise parched land. The gardens, wasteful of water as they must have been, were a welcome relief to the posse; the ponds, a disgusting indulgence with a desert all around, were delightful.

Amazingly, given the fish ponds and the lushly watered gardens, there was no water to spare for the bedraggled posse. Appeals to the Settlers' better natures, informing them that giving visitors water was simple hospitality, were met with blank stares; maybe they had no better natures. Even informing them that without the presence of troopers their homestead would be overrun by Natives did not have the desired effect, or any effect at all.

In the end Rohan drew his gun and threatened the Settlers with summary arrest, shocking his deputies as much as he scared the Settlers. The Settlers stared at him with seething defiance as they handed over the water then politely informed Sergeant Rohan that his superiors would hear of this harassment.

Rohan's laugh had nothing in common with an expression of humour; it was disdainful and cold. 'I bet,' he said, pointing to shapes of carved wood decorated with mud and pokerwork designs, 'those Native artefacts have never been declared.' They were worthless – junk – but the Settlers had them on display like they were treasures. 'That cute little servant of yours, I bet she's undeclared too.' His foul mood got incrementally fouler with every word until his voice was dripping with it.

'Let me guess, there are more Native servants . . . maybe a cook, maybe someone to collect the wood. I bet the Department of Natives has no idea you have such servants. I can always tell them.'

It was his opinion that prevention of artefact theft was not and should never be part of his duties; he already had enough, far too much, to do. Who cares if a few Native treasures adorned the local houses, who cares how they were acquired – only seemingly the anthropologists and the Department for the Protection of Natives. The department, from whom he occasionally took orders, were the only people who believed it was his duty to police the trade in stolen Native 'treasures'. He did not care if they had undeclared servants. His threat was idle and empty, but the Settlers didn't need to know that.

He and his men left the homestead without food, but at least carrying the water they needed to survive a little longer, and the growing conviction that it might not have been worth the trouble. In fact the entire, almost certainly futile, search for an absconded Native was quite pointless. Who truly cared if one servant took off, went wherever it is Natives go? Well, frankly only the department cared, apart from the Native's master. If not for the fact that some escaped Natives boasted to their friends that the Settlers can be defied, there would be no need to recapture them.

There were already way too many Natives around anyway; if you lost one you could just get another.

He knew he was at the edge of losing the last of his control when he drew his weapon on Mick, who had again lost the track. Staring at the boy down the sights of his gun, listening to the startled gasps of the other young men, staring deeply into those terrified eyes, so much like his own, he pulled himself together.

The young men had learnt not to complain about the weather, being thirsty, being hungry, being tired, being lost. Rohan would not have noticed if they did; he had long ago stopped listening to them anyway. As a party, keeping pace, they kept relentlessly, stoically on their way, lost or not.

It was close to night, time to look for a camp. Mick, looked up from Jacky's tracks as they disappeared again, fired from the saddle, killing one of the strange Native animals. Rohan was impressed; if it was not luck, such skill would be valuable if they found that Native. Tonight at least they would not have to dip into their dwindling food supplies; this gave Rohan some slight cause for relief.

He did not relish another night under the alien trees, the twisted limbs, the hanging bark, the wrong colour; their waxy grey-green leaves too hard, almost glassy. That afternoon they became unwelcoming, threatening, every growing shadow under their misshapen branches was a potential hiding place for a dangerous Native.

As the sun set upon them, darkness descending like doom, the young men rolling out their bedrolls at the foot of a strange tree, he was consumed with the desire to go home. Not the remote town where he worked, from whence he had been sent on this ludicrous search; that would never be his home. Nor did he want to return to the capital city of this colony, where he had been born, where he always had felt like an uprooted tree planted on alien soil. No, the home he longed for was the land where his parents had been born, the land always in the heart of his people, the land where the trees looked like the trees in books, the homeland he had never seen.

Oh how he hated this place, and the damned, stinking Natives. Oh how he hated his parents for moving here, to this 'land of opportunity', although he could never tell them how he felt. He hated everyone and everything except the precious homeland he had never seen and would likely never get to see. All his money, what little wages he got, had been saved to buy passage back there, and it was still not enough. Maybe it would never be enough. He shuddered at the thought he could be stuck.

Dinner was a disappointment; sure, the meat was fresh but it was tough and tasted like all the other Native meats — quite unappetising, only to be relished by the desperate. Good thing they were desperate then. It was an unpleasant meal even if he ignored the fact that out there in the bush there was nothing that even resembled fresh fruit. All they had was hardtack to the side of their plates, dipped in their dwindling water to soften. The boys were too scared, too threatened by Rohan's temperament, to complain. There was silence as one by one they tried to ignore the alien noises and finally fell asleep.

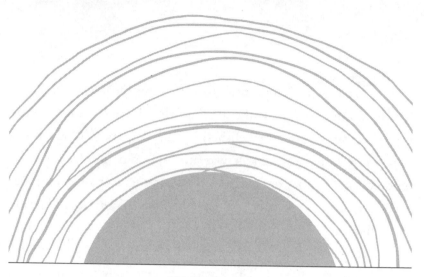

CHAPTER 7

I have walked my feet ragged to try to get home
I have fought my heart broken to try to get home
You took me from home you took me from me
Because all that I am, I am in my country

– 'HOME', ANONYMOUS

JACKY WAS HIDING under the long, scratchy, overhanging needles of a grasstree while he studied the activities of the group of Settlers, troopers and Native slaves before him. Not that it mattered in the slightest what they were doing; all that mattered was that they were in his way. Unless they moved soon he would have to find a way around them. If only they would stay put – stay in the camp they had established for utterly mysterious reasons of their own – he would find it easy to beat a path around them and back to the road.

Unfortunately, the Troopers demonstrated no desire to stay in their camp. Patrols were being sent out in every direction except towards Jacky. He assumed they were not bothering him because that was the way back to what they called 'civilisation'. Nothing bad could be expected to come from that direction. Those patrols, mounted and on foot, spreading everywhere as if they owned the place, were going to be a problem. He could not move while they were out and about.

So Jacky lay on his belly under the grasstree, one of many. Between the rough trunks of the tiny thicket was a tinier clearing, carpeted with their brittle, golden needles that cracked and crackled quietly whenever he moved. There is a smell to grasstrees, a resinous smell; oily yet comforting, it embraced him. Praying nobody would find him there Jacky wriggled down into the litter and dozed. It was hot in the middle of the day – a sweaty fly-infested heat. Surely only the mad and desperate would be out in it.

Lying there he dozed, dozing he fell asleep. Sleeping he dreamed of heat, of hunger.

They were only children, yet they were already enslaved. It was not called that, never called that, rather it was called 'education' or 'training'. Why not call it slavery, though, when the nuns, the teachers never worked, never raised a hand except to point or to punish? All the work in the mission was done by children. How better, the nuns believed, to train someone as a useful servant than to have them working from a young age, the younger the better.

Jacky and the other children were collecting firewood, or at least that was what they had been told to do. No nuns would be out there in the bush, not in that heat, so the children were under the lax supervision of the gardener, who was dozing fitfully under a tree. Paid only room and board, as much a slave as the children, he had little or no reason to do a good job as long as he was not caught. It was too hot to work, too hot to talk, that was his excuse for lying there, yet the younger children, virtually unsupervised for a change, ran and screamed like children.

Streaming with sweat, the older children – teenagers all, Jacky among them – worked as hard, as fast as they could. If they did not have firewood to show for the time spent out there, all the children would suffer equally. They did not want the younger children to be punished so they collected far more than their share. Stomachs groaning with pain and emptiness they piled the wood into wheelbarrows to be taken back to the mission.

It had been a long time since breakfast – a bowl of thin porridge, a cup of weak tea – and working hard they were all hungry. The older children were not much bigger than the younger children. They were all thin having clearly not been fed enough for most of their lives.

'Lookit,' one of the teenagers shouted. Jacky turned to look and all the boys and girls ran, almost as one. It was a lizard – a goanna – longer than the children were tall. Six feet from nose to tail at least, patterns of white on the black making it almost invisible in the dappled light until it ran. Grabbing sticks, grabbing the smaller logs from their woodpiles they chased the lizard to a tree, where it dug sharp curved claws into the narrow trunk and climbed.

'Jacky,' an older boy said, 'you're a good climber, you go.' One of the teens started a chant, 'Jacky, Jacky, Jacky . . .' and all joined in.

Resigned, carried to the tree by the chanting, Jacky scaled the rough bark upwards, the lizard climbed away from him, until it reached a fork in the trunk and went no further. Jacky, sweating even more from the heat and the exertion, climbed to the goanna, grabbed it by the whipping tip of its tail and pulled it off the fork.

It was running almost before it reached the ground but the children were pursuing just as quickly, swinging at it with whatever lengths of wood they were carrying, diving for it with grasping hands. In breathless silence, with disturbing, almost frightening determination far different to the joyful running just minutes before, they caught and killed the animal as Jacky slid carefully to the ground. Calling over the littler kids and motioning them to silence the children moved further from the mission compound.

There was an older child. Jacky in his memories, the Jacky of the dream, had no clue what her name was; maybe he hadn't known back then. She had been in the bush most of her life, had arrived at the mission already a teenager. Her family had long avoided discovery by the Settlers, until the expansion of the settlements surrounded and trapped them. Older than most of the other children and more self-reliant, she was their natural leader. She led them to a hidden dell and got a small fire lit with her supply of stolen matches.

There was not much to go around once they had gutted the goanna and cooked it – not for thirty or so children anyway. They had been hungry so long – for most of them they had always been hungry – it felt like a feast. Every child acted like they had plenty, eating only a little, pretending they needed no more, so the others could have a share. Every child was still hungry when the lizard was nothing except scattered bones and stripped charred skin, yet many theatrically rubbed their bellies.

That night, emboldened by the meal of lizard, and still hungry beyond imagining, six of the older children, Jacky included, escaped from their locked dormitory. Sneaking carefully across the silent mission grounds, each praying all the others would be as quiet as them, they broke into the dining hall. At the back of the silent hall was the kitchen, hard-floored, surprisingly cold and empty at that time of night. They stole through it like cats.

The pantry was locked when they silently and carefully tried the door; it had not been locked last time they had performed a raid. Although they had not been caught, the missing food must have been noticed. In silent agreement they boosted the smallest child up to a grill above the door; it was loose and emitted only a tiny creak like the song of a cricket.

She slipped her head and shoulders through the grill and wriggled until she lay over the sill of the vent on her belly. Her hips disappeared and then she slithered into the hole like a lizard. Too fast, she must not have found anything to hold on to. There was a thump, and then a terrifying clatter, too loud in the silence. Jacky stepped closer to the door, suddenly worried for the girl. A string of whispered profanities he was surprised the girl knew filtered through the door.

The door lock clicked, barely audible through the bitching and moaning, and the door swung open. The girl was lying on the floor, half curled up, a scattering of food containers half covering her. She moaned then, making sure she would be heard.

Helping her to her feet the other children fell upon the bounty before them, shovelling whatever food they could into their mouths. It was simple food: some of the cured meat the Settlers ate so much of, some bland cheese, blander bread, dried fruit that was sometimes, rarely, used to make their porridge more exciting. In determined silence they shoved small amounts of food in frayed pockets and down their tucked-in shirts. So hungry, so intent on filling always empty bellies they were oblivious to anything else, heads empty of all thought.

It was not until they prepared to leave, bellies distended, pockets bulging, that they gave thought to hiding their presence there. It was too late. Jacky turned to leave and saw the silhouette of a nun in the doorway, shadows at her back, blacking out her face.

They had only two sheds in which to lock the children so four of them, including Jacky, were chained to trees at the corners of the mission. Left there for days they were given barely enough water to keep them alive, but no food. 'You have eaten enough,' the nuns would say when the children begged for something to eat. In the end the heat, the thirst, the hunger was too much for Jacky and he blacked out, unconscious, oblivious, near to death under his tree.

When he awoke in a bed in the tiny infirmary he was allowed a small bowl of watery soup, not much more than broth from boiling bones, not even any bones to gnaw. It was water at least, even if it was not a lot to eat. He returned to the dormitory then, hungrier than he had ever been in his life, so sick they allowed him a day off work, a day off classes, a day moping in the dormitory. When the other children returned from class that afternoon nobody wanted to speak to him, nobody wanted to be the one to tell him. The girl who had climbed in through the vent, who had opened the door, had died of starvation and thirst in the 'boob'.

Jacky woke in his nest in the grasstree needles; they rustled and cracked under him as he rolled over to look for the Settlers who had inadvertently trapped him there. It was dark. Jacky had slept and dreamt the whole day through. The Native slaves had stopped working on what he thought must be the start of some sort of building, at the crossroads. Some of the tents glowed with a faint, warm, yellow light; others were dark. A small number of the Settlers sat around a small campfire in the middle of the circle of tents. Jacky could see them there well enough to count them – eleven, and there were no doubt more in the tents – yet not well enough to get any clue what they were doing.

They are probably eating, thought Jacky, as his stomach moaned at him again.

He had no hope of getting to sleep, his unplanned rest taking away too much of his fatigue. His fear of discovery, his long-standing hunger, were conspiring to keep him painfully, annoyingly alert. No matter, it was best that he watch what the Settlers were doing. Lying there he rolled into a more comfortable position, as silently as possible. He needed to pee, yet would not dare move; it was too dangerous.

The moon was directly overhead, casting her silvery-blue light on the world, before the last Settlers wandered off into their tents. Stopping to relieve himself within the cover of the grasstrees, Jacky began a wide skirting path around the camp. It was his hunger that stopped him from simply running. There would surely be food in the camp, could he, should he risk it? Was entering the camp, stealing from the Settlers, more of a risk than going on without any food?

Hunger – desperate, painful hunger – drove him into the camp of people he knew could be nothing other than enemies. There is no greater drive, no greater force in behaviour than hunger; it trumps even sex, the desire to breed, for those desires do not exist in the truly hungry. People will do almost anything if you starve them long enough. Hunger made him careless, hunger made him stupid.

Relying on the scant darkness for cover he silently edged closer to the ring of firelight around the Settler camp. All was still; not even the sound of snoring broke the silence. Not every Settler in the camp had made it inside to sleep; some lay, long cloth-wrapped lumps, around the fire. There was no sign he could see of the Native workers, the slaves, they must be locked up somewhere.

The night was so silent Jacky would have believed he had gone deaf had not a curlew cried out, cried like a restless spirit. 'Weeeooooooooorleeooo,' it cried again, mournful and cautioning.

Jacky knew he was not safe. Maybe half-woken by the alien noise a Settler snorted and rolled over, almost rolling onto Jacky's foot as he skittered away from the Settler's hot breath.

Dashing to the pile of luggage and supplies, momentarily forgetting caution, Jacky climbed up top, feeling the bags and boxes for anything familiar as he went. Here, dried meat; there, something that smelled like dried fruit, finally something he could eat for a long time; a bag of flour. He stuck handfuls of dried fruit in his pocket, and grabbed so much dried meat in his left fist some slipped through his fingers. Raising the heavy sack of flour to his shoulder, a difficult manoeuvre with meat in one hand, Jacky prepared to run.

Unexpectedly, he was startled by a sudden voice.

'What are you doing here?'

Jacky stood up just a little too quickly, a little too carelessly. The mouth of the flour-bag frayed open, showering him and the surrounding area with flour. It filled the air like fog; it filled his nose and mouth, making him choke, making him sneeze; it covered his face. The curlew cried again. Jacky was looking straight into the eyes of a trooper, those eyes were wide with shock, maybe with fear.

'Who-what-are-you?'

Jacky was speechless, was frozen with fear. He stood there making no noise at all. Another night-bird called out, wailing its defiance at the sudden return of silence. He turned too fast towards the noise, flour billowing off his clothes into the still night. The trooper screamed. Jacky ran, stumbling, tumbling down off the hillock of baggage. The clatter and crunch, the screaming and shouts followed him as the rest of the troopers woke. Dashing off, he was too afraid, too desperate to even notice that he was running through a cloud of flour leaving a white, dusty trail, his bare feet marking it clearly. The Settlers were too sleep-fogged, too confused to give pursuit, even those convinced it was not a ghost who had attacked them.

@

Johnny Star was completely and thoroughly sick of the local meat, the stuff the Natives seemed to relish. It was tasteless, it was tough, far tougher than what he had grown up on, tougher than his boots if anyone asked him. Even if it had been better meat, it would still be inedible, charred as it was, by necessity, cooked direct on the flames. His friends, companions, had provided this meal, and many before it so maybe it was time to raid another settlement for food he would find more familiar. They sat around the fire in a rough ring, everyone but him a Native. But they were different to the other Natives he had seen.

These men were rough, rugged, strong, solid and healthy; carved of bone, leather and wiry muscle. They were dressed in a ragged, dirty combination of Native clothes and those they had stolen from Settlers. There was no reason, no intent to their choices except for the desire to cover their bodies in protection from the elements. Johnny had been learning how to read their faces better and under every expression – joy at the food, laughter at a joke, sleepiness, a shallow constant fear – simmered an underlying anger and fierce determination.

They were all, to a man, armed with weapons they had stolen from Settlers. This was what the Settlers feared; the Natives were already cunning, violent, dangerous. Their skills had kept them alive with no modern weapons for thousands of years. The addition of better weapons had made them extremely, even terrifyingly, dangerous. They were his friends, the only friends he had, having deserted from the Troopers. Maybe they were the best friends he had ever known. He admired them, trusted them, even loved them. Years of fighting and escaping together had forged bonds stronger than he could have imagined. Despite that, even Johnny was scared of them; he was too sensible not to be.

Above all, what made them different to all the other Natives was that they still had pride. He remembered the Natives from his old life: those he policed, those he arrested, those he injured and killed in the process of arresting them. Those he injured and killed for no reason. They had no fight left in them; they lacked life, they lacked energy, seeming to want little more than to make it through their remaining days with as little energy spent as possible. His friends were different: they stood straight and tall, unbent; they were strong.

He had learnt, through his friends, that the bent, broken drugged and drunk state of those surviving near the settlements was not the habitual state of Natives. The truth was, it was a sort of depression brought on by what they had lost, brought on by being dominated and controlled by another people. Who could not be depressed, being treated like animals in a land that had once been theirs alone.

His friends were only five, but with those five he had terrified the Settler communities.

Tucker, the man who had found him half-starved and nearly completely dehydrated, was his right-hand man, and most importantly his best friend. He would be the leader of the group were it not for Johnny's training as a trooper. It was that training that had kept them alive so far, kept them free. He had taught them the Settler ways, taught them Settler guns and the brutal tactics that had made the Troopers so feared. Perhaps more importantly, he had taught them to show no mercy.

Only the Natives' respect for his abilities, abilities learnt to fight their countrymen, kept him in charge, not his status as a member of the Settler race. Which was fine for Johnny. He was no longer convinced his people had any right to control the Natives, or even that they deserved to continue living in this place.

The truth was, were it not for Tucker they would all be long dead. His ability to find food in the most barren of environments, his ability to hunt game, both small and large, had earned the respect of Johnny and the other Natives. He was not, however, the best fighter. That title belonged to Crow Joe. They had found him when he ran away from a Native circus owned by a Settler. There he had entertained the Settlers with an unearthly ability to throw an axe with pinpoint accuracy. There he also got in constant trouble for brawling.

Deadeye was the best shot in the group. Before he absconded, running for his life after refusing to hunt down a countryman, he had been a Native tracker working for the Troopers. His employers, who relied upon him at every moment they were out in the desert, had foolishly taught him how to fire a rifle. So impressed they were with his skill they had bet against others on his accuracy. It had not occurred to them, then, that a Native who could outshoot them would be dangerous.

Brothers Dip and Dap were almost silent and completely unassuming, almost impossible to notice unless they wanted you to notice them. They had escaped from a mission when still quite young, eking out a living in towns and on the fringes. Somehow they had avoided being recaptured, becoming almost invisible, hiding in plain sight among the servants and workers of their race. Making a living as thieves they survived that way from childhood, developing a devious cunning intelligence and an uncanny ability to fade into the background.

It was unpleasant out there, where they were camping, where they were hiding from his former friends. Near the settlements was simply not safe. He had been declared outlaw, his life forfeit, after he was recognised on their last raid. So they were out on the edge of the desert where, without his Native friends, he would have almost no chance of survival.

His Native friends thought it beautiful – this place he was forced to tolerate, this hot dry desert, the twisted grey trees, grey trunks and grey leaves. He was trying, always trying to see it their way. If he could appreciate the beauty, his life would be more pleasant. No matter how much he wished it, this place was not beautiful.

Not for the first time, not even for the hundredth time since that fateful, excruciatingly horrific night when he lost his faith, lost everything he had, Johnny wondered why they were even there, why the Settlers had taken this place. It was not like the other places they had colonised. It was drier, more alien an environment than any they had been to before. It was less hospitable here than any other they had conquered.

Why did I come? That was the thought that never left his overburdened mind. Why did he travel to the colony to join the Troopers? Certainly home was not the land of opportunity; there was nothing for him there. But here, this place . . . what a shithole. Why did I not, he thought, tell them all to bugger off when the choice to come here and join the Troopers was offered?

Now he was declared outlaw, he could never go home; he would be lucky to be sent home in a box once he was dead. A lonely unmarked grave, never to be visited by mourners, never to be mourned, for nobody would even care. That was what happened to the other outlaws after their execution – he had seen it, he had helped catch those same outlaws. That would be his fate. All he could do was live as long as he could then hope for the afterlife he had been promised.

He didn't deserve the afterlife, none of his people did. Murder is a sin, he had been taught that so many times, yet murder was the way of life throughout the colony. How could people be so blind, so ignorant to believe that killing the Natives was in some way an exception to the rule?

They might not even bury him. His bleached bones would lie forever, long after his soul had left, long after his flesh had rotted. He had seen the places where the Natives had been buried after his people had attacked; where rivers had flooded and eroded, cutting through the mass graves, scattering the bones. He had seen where burial had been too much effort, where wild dogs had scattered bones in their squabbles over the last scraps of flesh.

It was a land of bones he walked, a land of death and bones and pain. He had helped make it that way, had added bones to the soil. He was as guilty as any other. He knew now though, that when you plant bones, nothing grows from them. Nothing but pain.

As much as his homesickness racked at his soul there was no use thinking about it. This camp in the bush was his home – a series of camps in the bush would be his home until they planted his bones.

The blue-grey of the desert trees, stunted and dry, matched the blue-grey sky better than the green of trees from a wetter place. Jacky was at home there, for a short time. Even the sun was not too hot for him. He was home, not the home he knew, or even the home he did not remember. Instead he felt the touch of home in the scorching fire of the sun.

He stopped running; there was no longer any need, or so he felt. They were still after him, but they were no longer close, he hoped. Freedom, something he could not remember ever feeling before, lifted and cradled his wounded heart.

Weeping, he staggered to a stop; the sky, the leaves, the cloud-grey bark, blurring from the tears until he could no longer place his feet. Falling to his knees he lost himself in his loss, his hope, he could not know if his tears were happy or despairing. All he knew was that he could no longer stand, no longer even try to walk.

Even if he could stand he would be going nowhere; he was no more lost than ever before. This was not the issue, was not what blocked his path, he simply could not move. Despair and hope pulled him in opposite directions until there was no impetus towards either.

Swaying in a breeze that did not move the trees he stood, breathing in air that was too heavy for his lungs he stood. There was nothing he could do, no way to move, he would stand there until he starved, until he fell, until his bones were painted brown by the dust of his flesh. Or at least that was how he felt.

'Ghosts don't steal flour,' one man said. 'It was just a Native, look at the footprints,' said another. Yet the argument continued. The trooper who had seen the apparition refused to give up his theory; there was no way he would accept being scared by a Native. The sides when they formed were more along friendship or grudge lines than based on knowledge or logic. Most of the civilians – the engineers, the builders were on the 'it's a ghost' side, surprised to find the Natives siding with them, though it was impossible to know whether they took that side just to frighten the Settlers.

Sergeant Rohan smirked. So like engineers, builders, shop-keepers – everybody who has little contact with Natives. Civilians. He wanted to spit the word, spit in their faces.

'Why did you not pursue?' He loved asking that question, loved the terrified, embarrassed, ashamed expressions on their pathetic faces. There was no answer that was not embarrassing.

'How did the ghost, or Native,' Sergeant Rohan smirked, 'get into the middle of your camp anyway?' He was not pleased; another message had dragged him to the crossroads when he should have been looking for Jacky.

'That's why it must have been a ghost,' exclaimed the man who had discovered the looting. 'No Native would have, could have slipped in here!'

'Could it have been the Native known as Jacky?' That was a more interesting question: Jacky was almost a ghost, they had read about him in the news, everyone was talking of him yet nobody had seen him. If nobody could catch Jacky he was a perfect excuse; being robbed by Jacky was not so embarrassing. Potential fame, certain forgiveness for the incident awaited.

'Yes,' the trooper replied with a half-coy, half-smug smile, 'it could have been Jacky.'

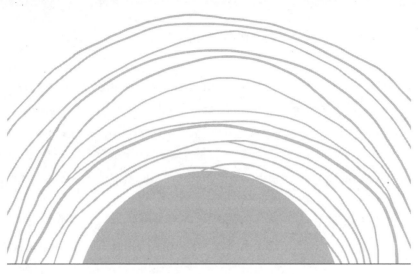

CHAPTER 8

The gun and the word
The word and the gun
They cannot stand alone, for each is only half
Each leans on the other
And their tower is made strong.

– ANONYMOUS

BAGRA READ THE letter from home feeling her anger rise, feeling the heat of it. Showing her anger was a luxury she allowed only now, safe and alone, isolated in the comfortable quiet of her room. How could they, how dare they criticise her work, her mission, these men who had never even been here, who had doubtlessly never even left home? How could they believe they even had the right? How could they think they knew what was going on? They had never even set foot on the hot dry ground here let alone actually met and spoken to a Native.

Nevertheless, they had written and they clearly believed they had the right to complain.

'Most esteemed Sister Bagra,' the letter began, 'we have received reports from your mission that have filled us with grave concerns, not only for its future, but indeed for its very fitness to continue. We can only continue to hope such claims are spurious; we believe such claims cannot possibly be true but unfortunately we have an obligation to investigate.

'We might have simply taken your word in your reply to this letter that we await anxiously, yet we cannot as questions have been asked of us by the government back here, questions that suggest they have received reports similar to what we received.'

She stared at the letter with disgust. She did not know who had sent these excremental reports to the Church and to the government back home but she would find out. She could not send them home when she found them, but she could make them so uncomfortable, the situation so intolerable that they would beg to leave. When, finally, their torment was complete, when they begged in tears to go home, she would not give in to their wishes.

She would keep them there, where they no longer wanted to be once she had made them hate the place even more than she did.

'There have been complaints,' the disgusting letter continued, 'of the systematic use of unacceptably cruel punishment by your nuns and especially by you. It has also been said, in those same complaints, that Natives have been tortured and starved to death, deaths which have been covered up as a matter of course. These complaints surely cannot be true, yet because the government is now involved, we have an obligation to investigate fully.

'We are confident that these complaints are unfounded, that an investigation will prove this to be true. A senior member of the Church has been dispatched on the same ship as this letter to perform such an investigation. There will likely be delay in his arrival at your mission as the information we received also suggested a tradition of cruelty towards Natives, across the entire colony. Additionally, it is believed that some mission schools in the colony are preparing their students for nothing more than a life of servitude, of slavery.'

Sister Bagra hissed like a reptile into the silence of her room before she could stop herself.

'The Church, as you know, stands adamantly with the government against the enslavement of any member of an intelligent race. Evidence suggests that the Natives there indeed have enough intelligence to preclude their slavery under our law. If indeed slavery exists in the colony everybody here would be most disappointed. Our laws and morality would demand we take some sort of appropriate action.

'We are confident our investigator will find no evidence of slavery; surely such claims must be untrue. He will leave the city after his investigation in the Colonial Administration offices and arrive there at the mission to clear this up as soon as safe transportation across the colony can be arranged.'

For a moment it seemed like Bagra was going to give in to an Earth-shattering rage, throw the letter to the pristine floorboards and storm around the mission buildings. How dare they? If they only set one foot down in this place, lived here a day even, they would discover as she had that the savages here were completely and utterly unsuited to civilisation. She wanted to scream insults into the air, in the hope they would make it home, but that would never do. She must not be seen to lose her temper.

Instead she forced herself to be calm, to think.

Who could have managed to send a letter to the Church back home, to the government, without her getting an inkling? She was again forced to fight back her rage at the thought. Cruelty? How could it be cruelty? Anyone who has trained animals would surely know that only a firm hand can teach them, that there is no use reasoning with animals. Even little children must be disciplined – a slap was so much more effective than any number of reasoned explanations. The Natives, never willingly growing away from their savagery, were animals. At most they were children. The only way to help them was to use training methods appropriate to what they were.

Who could it have been? She dragged her thoughts back there, somewhere they would be useful, somewhere she could do her sanity some good. If she could find who reported to home she could at least take her consternation out on them. She smiled at that, a small tight smile.

They would certainly have a long time to regret what they had done.

@

Jacky was used to hunger, had been hungry before, but always before there had been a chance of something to eat, something to steal from the kitchens. He did not really know how to survive out there in the wilds. Maybe that was why so many people ended up at the mission, there was not enough food there but at least there was some.

The food he had stolen from the camp had fed him for a couple of days, only because he had stayed hungry, never quite eating his fill. The flour had turned out to be a disappointment, a ridiculous mistake. He had lost more than half of it in his mad, panicked run, leaving a flour trail even a blind Settler could follow in the dark. What was left was useless without water, and without the fire he could not risk lighting. The dried meat, overly salty, had done nothing more than make him unbearably thirsty, and water was, as always, in short supply. Only the dried fruit was really worth the effort, the risk. He chewed some slowly, to make it last longer, as he walked.

It had been a long couple of days, knowing he had made such a commotion, knowing the Settlers had even more reason to hunt him down once he robbed them so brazenly, knowing that the trail of flour had made it easier to find him. His terror had been constant and almost crippling. He had, in the end, been forced to shake himself, to slow down so he could travel as carefully as he knew he should. When he had left such an obvious trail it was important to ensure that trail ended somewhere. It had taken all his skill, all his instinct to ensure the obvious trail would become a dead end.

Care made him slower, care used more energy per mile, care was tiring. That was why care made him hungrier, made it all harder. In the end he had walked himself to a standstill; this place was as good as any.

He was outside a small Settler town, though it looked big enough to him, hiding in the shadows of the stunted trees, avoiding everybody. He was even hiding from the sprawling, untidy Native camp and the campies within it. He watched all day, in the shade, not moving as the sun wheeled overhead, keeping cool, barely avoiding dehydration. There was no safe way in that he could see, no way to the food or water. Everywhere he looked were Settlers going about their business, alert, prepared, paranoid.

All day he lay there, most of the night he lay there; at least the night brought some relief, cooler than it was in the day. He was still just as thirsty but at least it was no longer getting rapidly worse; it was almost bearable. There was, however, no relief from the gnawing, relentless hunger. Now, also, he was feeling the cold. Barely dressed, running away with nothing, he had no protection from the weather.

In the cold the hungry get even hungrier, the starving starve to death.

Lights moved slowly around the township like embers; not many but enough to inform Jacky that the Settlers were alert. Somewhere in there a guard, a sentry, a trooper, or a police officer, a sheriff – who knows, hopefully not more than one of them – was keeping his eye out for interlopers, was arresting the drunk and the destitute, keeping the campies in their camp out of the town. All the buildings were well lit, as if by keeping lights on they could keep the Natives out of their town. It was working. Jacky could see no way in.

Moving carefully in the dark, there was no light to see by but desperation drove him on. Jacky navigated his way around the town, searching for a way in. He came finally upon a shallow depression in his path, a shallow depression filled with the trash of the town. On the far side he could see the fires and moving figures of a Native camp – just beyond, adjacent to and almost within the garbage dump. There, within the putrid smell of the town's garbage, lived the last dispirited Natives in that area; their shabby dwellings almost inseparable to the eye from the garbage heap. Jacky picked his careful way down into the garbage, trying, fearfully, not to alert anyone, even those in the Native camp. His own people lived there but there was no way to know whether or not they would be inclined to help him. So destitute, they might even betray him to the Settlers for a reward as small as a scrap of bread. They might even betray him for as little as the dream of a scrap of bread. They were probably desperate enough.

He wished he could approach the camp, talk to the campies but he could not risk betrayal. He was desperate for the company of his own people – that desire tore at his gut as much as the hunger did. Yet he did not, could not, approach them. His fear might have been unfounded but it was his fear, and all his life his fears had kept him alive.

The moon had risen, a yellow half-moon that would not be enough to see by except that Jacky had been lying in complete darkness and his eyes had adjusted. Even then it was a slow dangerous crawl, over who knew what disgusting trash – over rotting food, over sharp, fragmented, broken goods.

The smell was a constant, unwelcome companion. Jacky hoped it would not stick to him too badly; he almost laughed at the idea of the Settlers tracking him by the smell of their refuse. His nose wrinkled until his sense of smell started to shut down, like an eye blinded by too much light. The stench was strong but no longer unbearable.

In the faintly blue darkness he found the newest trash, the part of the tip closest to the town. Someone had dumped a sack of who knew what, not yet putrid, or at least relatively low in stench. The sack was not even torn. Jacky opened it, emptied it, hoping there would be no noise, nothing to reveal his presence. There was a bottle, unbroken, empty, a treasure beyond the imagining of anyone who had never been thirsty. Jacky slipped it into the hungry open mouth of his new-old sack.

His sense of smell, heightened by hunger and the darkness, started his mouth watering, despite the pervading smell of rot that surrounded him. His mouth dripped before he was consciously aware of what his stomach was smelling. There, in the trash tumbling around his knees, was a bone – remains of someone's dinner, with a few scraps of meat still on it. So hungry, so desperate he gnawed the meat off that bone and swallowed a half-rotten piece of fruit right where he was kneeling in that aromatic mess.

There were noises out there, in the trash. Jacky's fears rose at the knowledge there was something unknown, unseen, in there with him; something that might or might not be dangerous. Whatever it was, it too was eating; he could hear trash tumble as it searched, hear what sounded like licking and slurping and the sharp crunch of bird bones splintering. With a will he didn't even know he possessed he pushed down his fear to at least a manageable level.

Hopefully it would be nothing more than a cat, or a feral dog, maybe a large lizard of some sort. He had seen all three of those animals, along with rats and crows, in the trash pits at the station where he had been too long a slave. Once he had even seen a wild, escaped pig; that was the most dangerous thing that would dig through trash, besides humans. Pigs were uncommon – Jacky hoped like hell it was not one. It was coming closer, rummaging in the filth, crunching more bones. Rather than risk a confrontation, Jacky grabbed a hunk of mouldy bread lying right next to his hand, and ran.

It was still too dark to run, even attempting it was a mistake, one that was almost fatal for poor Jacky. He stumbled and tripped over something large, inanimate and immovable, falling on his face then rolling over something even more putrid-smelling than the things around it. Something broke underneath him as he rolled, something that cracked like shattering glass, unpleasantly reminding him of the window at the school. The bread fell from his hand, something indescribably foul-smelling and sticky glued itself onto his face.

There was a sudden outcry from the Natives' camp; lights, torches and fires flared on, voices yelled. It filled the dreadful silence, the void left when Jacky stopped tumbling. Voices were coming his way from the camp, clattering and crunching through the mess, shouting, crying out when they tripped, when they stumbled. They were speaking the language of his parents; he recognised the tone of it even though he could not identify words in that jumble.

From the adjacent town came the sound of people rousing, either woken by his dangerous, noisy tumble or by the cries from the Native camp. It didn't matter which – it was almost too late to run. Jacky scrambled for his sack, thankfully close at hand, and desperately, hungrily searched for the dropped bread.

Finding it, he wiped the disgusting, sticky goo from it, and shouldering his sack, Jacky ran as if his life was the prize in a race. Fear made him careless, being chased made him careless; luck, or something else unfathomable kept him, for that moment, safe. He sprinted, staggered and stumbled, almost fell, found his feet, again and again yet somehow this time kept his feet under him. Behind him he could hear the shouts, jeers and swearing of the Natives from the camp. Further behind them and to the left could be heard the shouts of the Settlers, awakened and not happy about it.

Some time later – it might have been an hour – he lay on his belly on the pushed-down reeds at the edge of a dam, washing his intolerably filthy face, trying to remove the stink, drinking his fill. Remarkably the bottle in his sack had survived his fall, his mad dash. Relieved, he lowered it into the water, letting it fill.

Behind him the hue and cry must have been continuing but there in the cool reeds, screened from searchers by the growth, he felt safe. Hearing no voices, seeing no lights, he had to assume the pursuers had given up or had gone the wrong way.

He fell asleep there, after eating the bread, mould and all. It tasted disgusting but he was far too hungry not to eat it. Finally, he felt safe enough to sleep, and for a time he was more tired than he was hungry, more tired than he was thirsty. He did not even notice the cold that night. He had been cold before, and cold was nowhere near as intolerable as cold and hungry.

@

Before Johnny Star, a small fire flickered, no wood there to burn. They had run out of wood days ago, even run out of the tiny sticks that burn too fast throwing a lot of light but not near enough heat. Fortunately, dry dung burns well, producing adequate heat with little flame, once you waste some sticks to get it burning. They could still boil the foul, muddy water from the dam, make it safe to drink, or safer at least.

It was no use at night, though; there was nowhere near enough light to see by, only a pale warm glow. Fire and water, two things that loomed greatest in the lives of the Natives. They were the sacraments, the bible of the bush, they were life itself as much as they were death to each other.

Water had an importance to the Settlers too, yet to them it was not yet a sacred commodity, for to them, where they had come from, water was much too common. Settlers had come to this land in search of wealth, in search of gold. Most of them never learnt, often dying from the lack of knowledge, that water is far more valuable. You can live without money.

You would have thought that a dung fire would smell but for some reason it did not, or at least not as much as a wood fire. Strange that a fire of manure, filthy and foul-smelling when fresh, would smell less than a fire of clean wood. Not the only mystery in the world, and not worth wasting much thought on, but a mystery nevertheless.

The main problem with a fire of dung was that the fuel – best to think of it as simply fuel – did not collapse when burned away. After a time there was a pile of ash, still dung-shaped, still the same size as it was. Anyone moving the dung, if they managed to not burn themselves, for red-hot dung coals looked as dead as spent coals, would discover they were almost weightless.

Yet you had to move the dung lest its ashes smother the fire, fill and strangle the fire pit. If you piled more dung on top all you got in the end was a huge pile of smouldering dung.

Several turns of bad luck had led Johnny and his band to this place, this dry paddock in the middle of nowhere. Needing food, water, ammunition, other supplies, he had entered a small town, pretending he had no reason not to be there, trying to give no clue he was outlawed. He was, after all, a Settler; he could just go shopping. He could take one of the Natives with him, as long as the Native was happy pretending to be a servant, a tracker, an assistant, and – most importantly – obedient.

It was a game they called master and servant; they had played it before, more than once, shopping with their stolen money for legitimate goods. How strange, to have plenty of money, which was easy to steal, yet nothing to eat, for you could never steal enough food.

It was all going well until they walked out of the general store with their purchases – Tucker, loaded up with groceries. All faces looked their way. Everyone in the street – under the verandahs, in the shade of the few emaciated trees – was staring at them. Even the Natives, silent and dressed in rags, stared or was that a smirk on one of their faces? Beside Johnny on the wall of the store, where he had somehow missed seeing it on the way in, was his face, staring expressionlessly from a wanted poster.

It was not the first time they had fought their way out of a town, though it was the first time there had been only two of them. Only the fact that nobody expected Tucker to be armed, to be a damned fine shot with a pistol, saved them. They ran from that town, guns blazing, slippery and quick.

Tucker had needed both hands to fight their way out; the groceries were unwieldy, he dropped them. Their wild risk came to nought – they ended the day with as much food as they had started it. Ammunition had been wasted in the desperate escape, and they had not yet managed to purchase any. They were even worse off than they were before.

More desperate than ever – or at least hungrier, which was much the same thing – they had executed a ridiculous armed raid on a homestead not far from town. The Settlers, husband and wife, could have no idea that the gang could not spare the ammo to make good on their threats, even if they actually wanted to. This time there was no wanted poster, no armed response, no danger to the raiders. Neither was there any food.

Running headlong from that town Johnny's gang had become acutely aware that they had become a bit too conspicuous. The raid on the farm had not helped matters in the slightest. There was no doubt the Troopers would be looking for them, looking hard this time. They had to run and run, further away from civilisation than ever before. Not for the first time the gang had to fall back on the hunting and gathering skills of the Natives, making Johnny feel useless, making Johnny paranoid that one day they would decide they wouldn't need him.

They had run, and run, further from the towns, further from Johnny's comfort zone, further into the alien, Native landscape. The trees of his homeland – spreading slowly from the towns and homesteads – disappeared, leaving nothing but the alien, Native bush. Deeper and deeper into the woodlands and prairies they moved. None of them had made it that far before, not even the Natives. Eventually even the trees had thinned; rocks and sand and grass – that was all they had to look at besides sky.

Everything was alien: the people around him, the trees, the prickling grasses, even the soil and rock itself. The rock was a deep carmine, the sand was redder – a beautiful yet disturbing earthy scarlet. The overlay of grey-brown and golden yellow plants somehow cast a purplish tinge upon the land.

The dung fire was surprisingly comforting, giving emotional comfort to his friends as always, yet this time it was working on him as well. To his Native friends fire meant home, one was not really at home until a fire was lit. Sitting by the burning dung, for the first time he understood: fire gave a sense of place, a feeling of home. Or, at least, his Native friends were his home, and fire was home for them, which was near enough. Tucker and the others, as lost as him, had taken him home.

Even Tucker, who had an almost supernatural ability to find food, had been unlucky on the last hunt, capturing nothing but a single starving rabbit – all bones under its mangy, soft fur. It provided them nothing but some flavour for a weak broth, some meat to gnaw off the bones, eating slowly so it felt like more. Yet soup was better than water again, water and nothing, boiled muddy water from a collapsed dam. It is generally understood that people can survive about three weeks without food, and only three days without water. He felt he would not last even that long.

It would therefore be a couple of weeks, at least, before the gang would come close to death. Close to death from starvation at any rate; there were other less expected, less well-scheduled ways to die.

Johnny's quality of life, on a downhill slide for years, had reached almost rock bottom; he could see little way it could get worse. His spiritual life, on the other hand, had been looking up; he had friends, closer than he had ever experienced before, and for the first time in his life he did not hate himself. Their poor condition, the lack of food, had brought them closer together. They were a team, even a family, more than ever before.

Small consolation for the roaring in his belly.

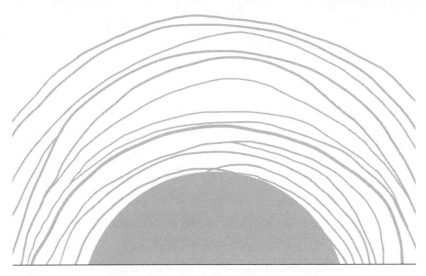

CHAPTER 9

We have always been here
We are still here
We are not going anywhere

– ANONYMOUS

JACKY KNEW THE Troopers were right behind him. He could almost hear their heavy booted footfalls, expected any moment to hear the 'You are under arrest', or the shot in the back that might come instead. He knew there was only a matter of time before they found him; felt little hope by then that he would continue to avoid them. He could already feel the shackles on his wrists and his ankles, the cold steel ring around his neck. He had been in shackles before – punishment for small infractions. They would take him to prison; he had met people who had been there, broken and bent by years of hard labour. He actually hoped they would take him to prison if he was caught, otherwise they would take him back to the settlement, where his master, unrestrained by the law or by witnesses, would punish him far more vigorously than the Troopers, than the law could. There was no time to scavenge, no time to hunt or to gather food. There was only time left to steal.

Nobody was home at the silent homestead as he riffled through their relatively empty pantry. The buildings had been built with skill using local materials but age was beginning to show: there were cracks in the wall hastily caulked, and there was no doubt the roof would leak in heavy rains. Unfortunately, the lock on the door had been sound – strong even – and the windows also locked.

Inserting a stout branch into a tiny gap, Jacky had been able to lever a loose plank out from the wall. At least the mission had taught him something useful. It was a tight fit but he had just enough room to crawl in, to drag himself in sideways.

He needed food that would travel well. Flour was good, he still believed that despite the evidence, even after his last experience with it. Grabbing half a small sack of it, he threw it in his bag. Bacon – that would travel better than other meats – he grabbed that too, hoping it was less salty than last time. Having no idea how long he had before the Settlers came home, he ate everything he could that would not carry well – fresh fruits he did not completely recognise, cheese, cold cooked meat. He would, he thought, eat until his stomach hurt.

Eating fast, without care, without his habitual survivor's paranoia, he did not notice the Settlers were home until he heard the click of the door opening behind him. Turning, mouth and both hands full of food, he would have cut a comic figure if things were not so desperate, the danger not so severe. The Settler woman did not react for a moment, so surprised to see a Native in her normally inviolate kitchen, how does one react to such an invasion?

She screamed, a formless wail, a screech without words, a reaction without any thought. His way of entry forgotten, Jacky, terrified, blinded by the sound of screaming, the fear of being caught, headed for the only open door he could see. The Settler woman was in his way; in the narrow doorway, she bounced off the doorframe, leaving a smear of blood where her face had collided. Jacky bolted through as she fell to see a man moving towards him, carrying a small axe.

Jacky was as surprised as the Settler was when he grabbed the axe handle just below the head and pulled the weapon free. There was no thought, no skill displayed by either of them. Swinging wildly, holding the axe awkwardly, it was not a surprise that he missed. The Settler dived, almost fell, desperate to escape the axe, fear stripping him of all grace. There was nothing in his way so Jacky again ran for it, heedless of the hue and cry behind him.

The food, too much food, sat heavy in his stomach as he ran; he nearly vomited with the breathless effort of running with his stomach so overladen. His sack was heavy, and it fell repeatedly from his hands. He slung it over his shoulder, a shoulder that still hurt from the impact with the Settler woman. The axe was a useful thing but in his panic, its weight, its size, the length of the handle getting caught in the bushes was more of a hindrance than anything else. He dropped it, not even noticing where it fell.

Not for the first time he ran.

@

Tonight Johnny and his gang would eat. Tucker had appeared out of the blinding light of the setting sun, with the limp carcass of a kangaroo, larger than Johnny had ever seen, draped across his shoulder. This was proof, surely, that they were far from the Settlers; large roos did not live long near towns. What it was, more than proof they were far from the town, was something substantial to eat.

None of the standard, expected complaints of 'roo again', in a hundred variations, emitted from anyone's lips that night. 'Stupid kangaroo saved my life again,' Tucker drawled unexpectedly, leaning back against the tree as he swallowed a satiating mouthful.

His face turned in the campfire light as his deep-set dark eyes absorbed the confused and startled looks on his companions' faces. He chuckled and closed his eyes, looked ready to sleep, not to say any more, when suddenly he spoke again.

'We did not know of the arrival of the Settlers, not at first. It took them a long time to come to the place where we lived, and we never left there, not by choice.' His drawl gained a dreamlike tone; he was elsewhere as he spoke. None of the others wanted to interrupt him, so rarely did he speak. 'We were out hunting, my brother and I, in the bush. We were walking home – I was carrying a kangaroo, a big kangaroo. I was slower than my brother because of that kangaroo.

'My brother shouted, I didn't hear his words, then there was a loud noise. I had never heard it before, and his shouting stopped suddenly. I was worried. I put down the kangaroo, carefully under a tree, walked quietly to where my brother was. He was on the ground, dead, I suppose. He was surrounded by Settlers. I had never seen Settlers, never seen anyone but my own people. He was lying on the ground; they stood all around him holding long things. I had never seen them guns before neither.

'He must have stumbled into them, musta not been looking where he was going, idiot. We'd never seen Settlers before. How could he know to look out for them? I hid in the bushes; I was alone and there were more of them than there was of me. They left my brother there. I didn't watch where they were going; they were not going to my home, so I guess it didn't matter.

'My brother, he was dead, there was nothing I could do, I needed help, I went home. I was only a kid at the time, not yet a man, I needed my parents. Leaving my brother, leaving the stupid kangaroo, I ran home. When I got there –' for a moment his pained breathing was all they could hear '– bodies everywhere, broken, burned, bleeding.

'They were all dead, everyone there, all my family, all my friends, everyone I knew. The Settlers must have killed them. They didn't even bury them, pile them up, burn them, nothing, they just left them there, everywhere, wherever they fell. I kept tripping over them.' Tears ran down Tucker's lined face; he seemed not to notice them, not to care. 'I was alone a long time then – couldn't even bury my family, my brother, not alone, too many . . . they would hate that, not even being buried. It was too much for me, I was just a kid and those Settlers might have come back.'

He laughed unexpectedly, a pained laughter, intermixed with tears, deep, heavy tears. 'That stupid kangaroo was heavy. It saved my life making me walk so slow.'

Silence descended and held on. But for the crackling, the yellow light of the fire you could believe that there was nothing out there but darkness. Then Crow Joe broke the silence.

'The only way I could find something to eat was in the circus.' His voice sounded pained, unusual to hear for those who had known him so long. He was almost defined, normally, by his lack of emotion. 'More of a zoo it was, my parents and I were all there; not my sister, she was already dead, raped and dead, left for dead, maybe not dead, how would I know, I was only a kid.

'Yeah, probably dead.

'Daddy taught me to throw an axe, throw a knife, throw a stick, throw anything and hit anything. Then they killed him – they paid him in drink until his liver died. Mummy died too – working for them, it just wore her out. I was there alone, entertaining the monsters, like a performing pet,' he spat the word, nobody dared flinch back from the spray of spittle.

'Hated myself, hated everyone, fought everyone because I couldn't fight myself. Got in trouble, so much trouble for fighting. One day I was sharpening an axe when the circus boss yelled at me for fighting. I didn't mean to hit him with it, I just lost my temper, I threw it to scare him. Then I had to run, and I will always be running now.'

'I shot my sergeant,' Deadeye interjected, 'when he had me guarding some of my own people. We arrested my people, who knows what they did. I could not stand them in chains like that.'

The group fell into a tense silence, each trapped in their unpleasant memories, each unprepared to traumatise the others with questions. Dip and Dap had not spoken, they seldom did at all. The weighted glances they gave each other said it all – there were too many bad stories to tell. They did not even remember when they had been taken to the city.

Sparks and embers flew lazily from their fire, flying up to join the stars slowly marching overhead. Each man stayed lost in his memories until one by one, staring at the night, they fell asleep.

@

Rohan and his posse could move faster now they had a real tracker to follow. Many days of travel, many days of searching and he had allowed himself to come to the conclusion that Mick was completely useless. How he had managed to make a living from hunting, from tracking, was a complete mystery.

They had picked up a tracker in a settlement. The Settler who had provided him, his master, assured Rohan that the man was good, exceptional even. 'He will take care of you,' he said. 'He's the best, used to work for the coppers.'

He was the darkest Native Rohan had ever seen: carved from mahogany, with black curly hair and deep-set black eyes. He certainly looked like a tracker; his eyes seemed to simultaneously stare into the distance and watch the ground. It was doubtful that anything useful, any information, would ever escape those eyes. Rohan wanted to trust him, needed to trust him, because what he needed more than anything was to find Jacky.

A day later saw Rohan riding behind the Native who, seemingly terrified of the mounts, was refusing to ride. The trooper and his deputies were limited to the walking pace of the Native. However, they were doing well; he had found the track immediately once they returned to where they had lost it last, and since then they had not lost it once. It was a winding trail, heading vaguely east.

Rohan, for all that the tracker's appearance made him uneasy, found himself warming to the Native. Maybe if all Natives were like this he would have less cause to hate them.

It was hot, it was always hot, and the Native was the only one not suffering. Rohan shared out the last of the water. When that ran out they would be in deep trouble unless they could find more. 'Tracker,' he shouted as he rode, then spurred his mount forward to ride beside the Native, 'is there any water around here?'

'There's water everywhere,' the Native said, 'you just have to know where.'

'We need water.'

The Native's shoulders flinched up and down in an almost imperceptible shrug and he walked off to the side of their path while Rohan followed. Selecting a tree that looked no different to any other the tracker stopped.

'Water there.'

'Water where?' Sergeant Rohan was incredulous. It was just a tree.

'Need axe.'

When Rohan returned with the axe and his deputies, the tracker took a swing at the tree, chopping into it in a place that looked the same as any other. Again and again he swung, cutting a hole in the trunk of the tree. Dropping the axe and cupping his hands he caught the water that dripped out and drank it.

Rohan was right behind him with a bottle, the dripping was painfully slow but after an eternity standing there his bottle filled. They were there for some time, by that tree with the dripping wound. All of them filled their bottles, all of them drank their fill. There was a faint taste to the water – Rohan couldn't identify it – the taste of tree, he supposed.

Rohan, despite himself, was beginning to almost like this Native.

For two days Rohan and his deputies followed their Native tracker through a tight, claustrophobic labyrinth of rock and trees. How he followed the track, when there was nothing on the ground but rocks and leaves, continued to be a mystery. He never got lost, never backtracked. If the tracks they were following went into a dead end he knew about it and didn't follow.

They would never have lived through it without him. Totally reliant, they were beginning to trust him; they almost forgot what they thought of Natives. Other Natives could not be trusted, but this was 'their' Native.

Rohan watched the younger men interacting with the Native. No longer did they question the direction, no longer did they treat him like an animal, they still treated him like he was barely better than an animal but that was an improvement. He felt himself warming to their Native.

It was a complete surprise, therefore, when they woke on the fifth morning since they entered that maze. The patch of ground where they had last seen the tracker was empty, his blanket gone. They searched the camp and there was nothing, no evidence he had been there at all. There was no sign of him, no sign of a track, he was just gone. He had not even taken their supplies, he had just disappeared.

The only thing he had taken was their map, basic as it was.

Rohan screamed in frustration and anger, a wild formless cry aimed at the heavens, at the hills around him. Mick swore and cursed, continuing after Rohan's cry faded to silence. The other deputies frantically packed their things, their fear and panic written on their faces, and in the way they moved. It had taken all of the tracker's skill to get them into that maze of rock, and they could not remember the way out again.

'We gotta find the tracker,' Mick said, his voice frantic. 'We'll never find Jacky without him, we're going to die.'

'Don't be stupid.' Rohan's reply sounded like he had walked through rage and found a deep pool of cold calm on the other side. 'If we look for him we will just get more lost.' He paused, deep in thought, staring into the cloudless sky. 'We have to go on, we will follow compasses, follow the sun, go east, wait for news of Jacky.

'The tracker led us here, left us to die in this mess. We will see him again and when we do, I will kill him.'

Bagra sat, silent, in the cool comforting darkness of her cell, relishing the empty silence that allowed her to finally think. Again she could not get the letter, the filthy accusations from home out of her mind. She had become obsessed with the accusations, with the betrayal implicit in them; she could not clear her head, could not stop thinking about it, no matter what she tried. She must determine who it was, must identify who betrayed her, the mission.

There was, of course, one obvious choice. That stupid child, Mel, had questioned her duties, questioned their entire mission, questioned the great, important work they were doing, argued with Bagra. Nobody else doubted what they were trying to do here; all the other sisters believed, wholeheartedly, in the good they were doing the Natives. If they did not believe in the work, they believed in their Order, did not question and simply did what they had to do, what they were told to do, without complaint. Bagra had little doubt that some of them must have their doubts, though she could never tell who; they were so good at not showing it. They were too clever to let her see it.

Mel, on the other hand – you could tell she had doubts. The silly girl even had the audacity to directly question her elders and betters, even questioning the purposes of the mission at the dinner table where such discussions have no place.

Then there was the incident of the fugitive: the girl was the one who found the man known as Jacky, and even without evidence Bagra had doubts about the events of that night. What if, and the thought made her cold, the girl had not just found him and screamed? What if she had found him earlier and was in some way helping him fulfil whatever his inexplicable purpose was?

These doubts, ruining the peace inside Bagra's head, fuelling a rising paranoia, had to be managed some way. It seemed most obvious that the traitor who had written home must be Mel: she was newest, she was youngest, and therefore most prone to a silly girlish, thoughtless sensitivity. Not only that, she had also questioned Bagra. That was no proof she had informed home, but she had questioned the mission in front of all the nuns.

It would not do, however, to simply confront the girl. What if she was innocent – foolish but innocent? There was also no way to just get rid of her, send her elsewhere. If she was silly enough, was willing to send a letter of complaint back home, surely there was no limit to what she would do. Bagra would not inflict such difficulties, such thoughtless action on another mission; she would have to deal with it internally.

There was a faint rustle, quieter than the fluttering of dragonfly wings, as she pulled a piece of paper out of a pocket in her habit. As dark as night in the cell, she could not see the letter. That did not matter, she knew every word already. Sooner or later she must reveal the letter, and its contents, to the other nuns in the mission, but later would be better. She worried, though. If she waited too long it would inspire whoever had instigated this mess to wonder why they had no response to their letter. Who knew what they would do then?

Telling the others too quickly would warn the traitor she knew, warn them she was watching; doing it too slowly would likely lead to more letters being sent home. If the other sisters knew she was hiding a letter from home, such an important letter, they would be angry; they too might turn traitor. It is impossible to find a balance when you don't even know the weights.

Mel would have to be watched, to find more evidence that it was she who had betrayed the mission. It would have to be done carefully, secretly, and Bagra would have to do it alone. She was not certain enough that there was nobody else involved.

She could do nothing but watch, and wait, for something to change – for the silly girl to make a mistake. She was waiting anyway, for this excremental inspector who was meant to be on his way. A part of her wished he would just hurry up and get there, get it over with; the other parts all hoped he was not coming at all.

A cacophony of children's voices from the distant dormitory broke her concentration. Opening the door with a bang, she was out of her cell and moving at a brisk walk before she was even consciously aware she was standing. It would not do to be seen running, so she strode as fast as she could down the dark hallway. She needed no light; she had walked these halls so long they were burned into her brain, and light would be an extravagance. The nunnery buildings were still silent, though she could hear the faint sounds of others stirring, the slippery rustle of hard blankets sliding off a bed here, a bare foot hitting the floorboards there.

It was still deep dark, and the noise rather than abating was still waxing, too loud to differentiate individual voices. She was not the first there, though she had no doubt she was the first to arrive, for she had not even been asleep. Mel was already there, she must have been there before the noise began, or arrived just after – impossible – nobody would have been moving faster than Sister Bagra.

Why Mel was there was a mystery. With her was another of the younger girls, though not quite as young and stupid. This, too, was mysterious. She taught mathematics, counting and addition – just enough for the Natives to be able to do simple chores. They seemed to have little aptitude for counting. They learnt that just like they learnt everything: by rote, by singsong. There seemed little point in trying to teach them more.

It did not even occur to Bagra that a girl who had no experience at teaching would be terrible at teaching mathematics. Bagra wouldn't have cared anyway. The law said they had to be taught mathematics, so the mission was careful to hold mathematics classes. Nobody official bothered to check how well it was taught, or what was taught.

Bagra suspected they could just have the children sit and do nothing as long as the classes were scheduled.

Behind her she heard the door swing open as somebody went through it at about the same pace she had. Her staff, the other nuns, everybody, had better learn to respect the building more, before someone tore the door right off. She made a mental note to ensure that people were aware of the proper way to open a door. Everybody was now awake it seemed, and it was time to discover what was causing such a noise.

The door to the dormitory was open a crack. Bagra led the two girls through to investigate. She could not tell if that was confusion or guilt on their sleepy faces. The mission's Native tracker was standing in the middle of the dormitory holding a squirming child by the scruff of his neck and shouting at the children to hush.

'What is going on here?' Bagra was forced to roar to be heard over the noise; the bubbling of her temper made that easier. It was not good to shout too often, though this time it felt justifiable.

The tracker gulped. 'Ma'am, I found this girl in the camp, she was sneaking about, I am sure she was up to no good.' Bagra realised then that the child thrashing and writhing like a fish on a hook was a teenage girl. The child – the right age to be sent off into service if she was more disciplined – was screaming and wailing. If there were words in all that noise, there was little doubt from their tone that they were profane and probably blasphemous.

'And why did you not bring her to the office, why did you not inform me rather than bring her here, unleashing all this noise and ruckus? You seem to have woken the entire mission, surely it would have been better to just wake me?'

'Was very late, ma'am,' he shouted over the barely subsiding noise, his Native accent almost rendering him unintelligible. Behind her there were faint rustlings and quiet grunts as the two younger women fielded children at the door. More nuns were arriving, more escapes were unlikely. 'I din't want to wake up anyone.'

'And you did not want to get the child in trouble,' Bagra said in a cold voice, loud in the spreading silence as children discovered their chance of escape was over and began to understand they were in big trouble. 'Otherwise you would have done the sensible thing and chucked that thing in the "boob". That would have let us sleep and prevented the creation of all this chaos and noise.' If she had shouted the last word it would have been less frightening than the cold-blooded hiss she used.

'No,' she said, her voice so cold it could have formed icicles, 'I believe you were attempting to clean up this mess without me finding out about it.'

Was that a significant glance he cast towards the two young nuns in the doorway? What did it mean if it was?

'Let us discuss this outside, away from the ears of these little darlings.' Her tone turned the word 'darlings' into 'monsters'. 'Bring the child.'

Turning she strutted out the door, gesturing to Mel and the other girl to come with her too, trusting the tracker, chastised, would follow with the child. She led them to the 'boob' and opened one. The tracker, knowing better than to argue, threw in the Native and closed, then bolted the door.

Nearer to the nunnery building she stopped and, trusting her ability to control the others, spoke without turning. 'How long has this been going on?'

''Scuse me, ma'am?'

She was gratified the tracker had followed; he seemed sufficiently obedient, or scared enough to obey if not. 'How many children have you captured trying to escape and returned to the dormitory without informing me?'

'Ma'am?'

She whirled suddenly, seeking the faces of the two younger nuns, hoping to catch an uncontrolled expression. 'You two,' she snapped, 'how long has this been going on? How many times have you helped this Native,' she spat the word, 'hide escapes from me?' She was disappointed with their blank looks. For a moment she stared into their eyes, daring them to rebel, to give her some excuse for a more vigorous punishment.

There was no rebellion in their faces, only terror in their eyes. Bagra finally turned away and looked to the dormitory, thankful that the other nuns, awakened by all the noise, had the sense to be standing guard around the building. Two had taken the initiative and were silently searching around the dormitory for any clue how the Native girl had escaped. That was a good idea; Bagra made a note to quietly commend them later.

'No matter,' she said after waiting long enough for an answer, 'however long it has been happening it must stop immediately. If Natives who attempt to escape are not disciplined for it they will never learn to obey orders, they will escape again. If I discover again that escapes have gone unreported there will be consequences.'

Turning, she took two steps and then stopped. 'I will discover how long this has been happening, it must be reported.' She turned to face the women but her eyes only met Mel's. 'Disobedience to the dictates of our Order will not be tolerated. I am the senior here, I represent the Order here. I am the Order here. If you don't understand or agree with the rules here it doesn't matter, you still must obey.

'If you can't obey my orders you have no place here.

'You will spend the rest of the week in your rooms thinking about what you have done and praying for guidance. You will only emerge −' she let it sink in '− to eat and visit the necessary.'

The wind was comfortingly cold; in her rage she had not noticed that, and a slight drizzle had started to fall. She always loved rain. It was rain that brought all good to the world. It mattered not what other people said, it was through rain that the hand of God was most visible.

'Tracker,' she said more kindly, the drizzle mitigating her anger, 'go back to your camp, but report to me tomorrow. It is late now, we are all tired, but I must know how long you and these ladies have been hiding these things from me.'

'Ma'am,' he said in an obedient and remorseful tone and slipped away.

'Mother,' said Mel, 'I . . .' she petered off.

'Stop dithering,' Bagra snapped, 'get to bed, get to sleep, if you have any more to say on the matter I might be ready to hear it in the morning.'

Mel was staring down at Bagra's hands. Too late she realised the note from home was still there. She had forgotten she was holding it, had run out holding it, was still holding it. It was too dark to read, but surely the others would be curious.

'Mother?' The girl said nothing as Bagra waited, only her tone informed Bagra there was a question.

'Tomorrow,' she snapped, covering her uncertainty with more anger. 'Get the others to bed, except two. Two volunteers to watch first. We need to take turns watching the children, make sure there are no more escapes.' She wished she could trust the tracker to watch the dormitory, or that she could trust Mel and her friend enough to make them guard the children as punishment.

Bagra was certain: if she left those two alone watching the Natives the dorm would be empty by morning, whether through incompetence or malice towards the mission, towards her. 'We will get the handyman to find their rat-hole in the morning.' With that final word, Bagra stormed off, hoping her display of anger would be enough reason to be almost running. It was not a good time to have them ask about the damned letter.

@

Never had someone come from that direction, north and east, from the deeper desert, where surely nobody could be living. So silent he was that none of the lookouts, none of the keen listeners, none of the sleepless watchers, had seen or heard him coming until he stepped into camp and crouched down, sat on his heels, in the middle of the open space. He seemed to have been born from the sand and scrub; nobody from the camp would have believed there was enough cover to hide someone until he appeared. Esperance, belatedly alerted, ran from her hut, hand on the knife on her belt. Grandfather was smart enough to stay inside when there was a stranger around.

He was almost naked, this stranger, his ancient pants cut off at the knee, or torn off – who could tell, the hems were so ragged. His torso was naked, muscle standing out as if carved; tall and strong he was clearly half-starved, yet not weak. His black skin was covered with patterns of dust – red on white on brown. His eyes, deep-set, were displaying an expression that could be anger, could be something else Esperance could not read.

The camp was sluggishly awakening, clawing its way to alertness. Those who were armed and ready stepping from their tents and huts, walking out from their fragments of shade, hands on whatever weapons they had. Those who were slower to react, those whose weapons were harder to lay hands on, hid in their dwellings, there to be a surprise reserve if needed. There was no need, yet, to reveal all their strength.

Esperance signalled rapidly with her left hand – 'stay, be alert, no violence yet' – then stepped forward to talk.

'Who are you? What are you doing here? We offer you no violence but if you have brought it with you we will retaliate. We are armed.'

'My people, over there,' he gestured north-east – the direction from which he had walked, the direction the refugees had long refused to take knowing it was inhospitable – 'they are gone, they came, killed so many, everyone who lived ran away.'

Nobody should have come from the deep desert, Esperance knew that. She had heard rumours there were people, maybe many people, out there hiding from the settlements, where no Settlers could possibly survive. So rarely did they come out of the desert that the rumours seemed exactly that; she had long ago ceased believing in them. Anyone out there would be safe far away from the Settler camps and towns if they could find a way to survive.

Why then, if it was so safe, would they ever leave?

Once again she signalled, a series of rapid hand signs that she had no idea whether the stranger could read. 'Stay alert, bring water.' She looked at the stranger. 'We had no idea the Settlers had made it inland past us, thank you for telling us. What happened?'

Squatting on his dirty heels, drinking the mug of water handed to him by a tall woman armed with a wood-cutting hatchet, he told his story.

'Don't think they were settling there, in my Country, they can't live there, no water –' He paused then, seeming thoughtful, '– no water they know about. They were not looking for a camp, maybe they were looking for water, dunno. They were just looking, looking for something.' Again he stood there, sipping water, thinking, mulling over his words. 'Maybe they were looking at nothing.

'They would say there is plenty of nothing out there in Country.

'We had heard of them Settlers. People had come into our Country running from them, they told us about the Settlers. They never got to us before, we never seen them.

'We followed them, watching what they doing. We didn't even know after watching but they went towards camp. We knew Country better than them we got in front stopped them.' He turned then to look back the way he had come, as if trying to catch a glimpse of his distant country. Maybe, thought Esperance, looking that way would help him remember. Was that a tear in his eye?

'We had no weapons, except for hunting, we needed no weapons except for hunting. It not matter. Their weapons, better than ours, they make a loud noise, and we die, simple as that. We had to hide, then kill whoever we could catch —' something like a mix of pride and despair was written on his face, if Esperance could read it right '— we caught some, they went away, for a while, then others came. They killed the camp, whoever could, ran away, I ran away, we cannot go home, they can't live there but they camp there at our waterhole. My people are everywhere, every direction, I hope we will find each other again one day.

'We survived, have always survived,' he said with pride, 'that Country where I belong, where my family belong, we have walked it forever, we belong there. It looks after us, and anyone else who tries to go there, it doesn't look after them so well.' Esperance could tell from his tone that he saw it as fact: the Country chooses who can live there, it punishes those who don't belong.

'People from other places came before, those white fellas, they came before, long time ago, but they couldn't live there, in that country. The white fellas let us have our Country because they couldn't live there. These grey fellas, they don't much like the hot and the dry, they like it less even than the white fella do.'

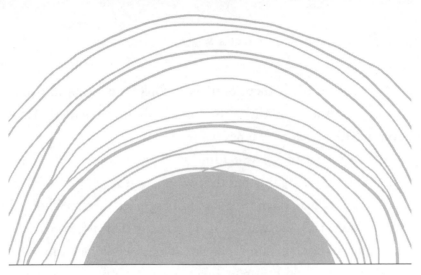

CHAPTER 10

This is Not an Invasion

I am writing this report from under a camouflage tarp somewhere north and west of the Murray River, in what once I would have called the desert. Which is the only reason I am able to write it at all.

We are not being invaded, we are being colonised, and there is absolutely nothing we can do about it.

When they first arrived we did not know whether they would be coming to invade or coming in peace. Having never left our planet, indeed not even having made contact with life from outside our atmosphere, we had no context in which to understand them when they arrived suddenly, without preamble. How could we have expected the total disregard with which we would be treated?

Bear in mind, they do not fear us, they do not hate us, we simply do not conform to their narrow definition of 'people'. Rather they look upon us as merely part of the fauna of this planet they are settling and intending to tame. We are animals, to them, and thus to them this is an empty planet ripe for their settlement.

There is no use appealing to them person to person; they will ignore it as the terrified bleating of sheep, the aggressive yapping of dogs. They will ignore us as the Colonial powers of the eighteenth and nineteenth centuries ignored the Natives in the lands they invaded.

There is nothing we can do but fight them, although we will almost certainly lose; many would say we have lost already. I am one of that many. Not since Europeans armed with guns, with cannons, and with complete conviction that settling in Australia was their right, has a Native population been as hopeless and relatively unarmed as we are now. Our most powerful weapons are to them what wooden spears were to men with muskets. Certainly if we catch them unprepared in the right situation we can kill one or two, but that is the anomaly.

Our larger weapons, all of the technology of the world – missiles, cannon, even our terrifying nuclear arsenal – are reliant on our primitive understanding of electronics and electromagnetic fields. In their superior knowledge, their seemingly infinitely superior technology, they can simply switch our machines, our bombs, even our nukes off, remotely.

Now only a few places remain where humans are free, and those all have one thing in common: they are all dry and hot. The Sahara Desert surely still has some free humans – heavily armed Arabs and Bedouins, returned to a nomadic existence, trying simply to survive in certain knowledge that confronting the enemy would be death. In the hottest parts of the desert in the USA there are militia, built up from survivalists and Native Americans alike, who surely finally have a common enemy. Kenya, Ethiopia, Mexico – surely they have free people, hiding in their paucity of cover from the invader's aircraft.

Surely the Afghans, experienced as they are at resisting better equipped armies and overwhelming odds, a people whose homeland is intolerably dry, are still living a similar life to the one they always have. Well, a similar life to that they lived under Soviet occupation, and under every other attempted occupation throughout their long and unpleasant history.

How do I know this? I don't for certain – there is no longer any long-range communication system under human control at all. Those places were the last places we had contact with before contact was lost. We do know one thing. The aliens don't tolerate heat and dry air well; the most heat-intolerant humans love heat compared to them. That is why Australia, the hottest, driest continent in the world, was the last to be taken by them. That is why we still have a resistance at all. That is why this newspaper is still being published and you can read my words.

All is not well, though. The cities of the east coast, most of the east coast country and all of the Australian Alps are theirs now. Tasmania is crawling with them – it is after all our coolest, wettest state – and the cities of Melbourne, Sydney, Canberra and Brisbane, previously home to eighty per cent of the continent's human population, are now subjugated and the population exterminated or in 'reservations'.

The last human city to fall in Australia, maybe in the world, was Alice Springs, being so deep in the desert they did not, could not, settle there. Even Alice must have died, though; fearing a city they did not understand, where they could not live, they would have bombed it flat. We have lost contact with Alice Springs but we can hope people survived, we can hope humanity has a city somewhere.

This paper survives and we will continue to write and distribute it the best we can for we fear this could be the last free human voice. I will not tell you exactly where I am, where we have printing presses – the last free human press. They cannot survive where I am, where we are, but if they find us they will surely attack from the air.

They came in peace, their peace.

– *HERALD SUN*, 21 SEPTEMBER 2041

AUTHOR UNKNOWN

ESPERANCE'S GRANDFATHER WAS old enough to remember the Invasion, the colonisation, well and he was therefore sought after as a storyteller. For all her childhood she had sat around the fire listening to his stories as he told the entire camp, and visitors from other camps, about the world before the Invasion, about the arrival of amphibious invaders from the stars. She knew the story better than almost anyone.

That was when people could still have a fire at camp; they had learnt early that you could only have fires in summer, when it was so hot the fire was unnecessary, or during the day in winter. Winter nights were the only time the Settlers would overfly the desert. Their fliers were noisy but fast; by the time you heard them there was no longer time to quench the fire. By the time you heard them you were under attack.

Fires could not be risked.

It seemed quite unlikely that the Settlers were still looking for the camp, still seeking out any humans, looking for resistance. It was almost as if they had decided that any Natives left, any humans, any earthling animals, were safely contained in land the Settlers didn't want and couldn't use. Surely they must believe most of the human remnants to be harmless. The humans had lost the war – what little fighting there was – years ago.

Maybe the aliens, the Settlers, were right – maybe they were harmless. They had done nothing to prove otherwise, had not fought, had not taken back land, had not even killed a noticeable number of Settlers once the first flush of invasion was over. What they were not was subjugated; they remembered, they kept the stories alive, they knew what humans were and one day could be. Everybody in the camp agreed with Esperance and her grandfather: they would die before they gave up their freedom. If anyone disagreed they had never spoken to Esperance about it.

Then one day, maybe they would fight back. There was no way at all they were going to be able to fight back any time soon, and unless something changed it was only going to get worse. Most of the men were drunk whenever they could get the grog, high when they could get their hands on the strange alien psychoactive substances the Settlers used. Those little red pills, they were a scourge, they were deadly, though it was surprising they worked on humans at all. The women, those who did not join the men in destroying their brains, were dispirited and sick. If the chance came tomorrow to fight, they would miss it. How do you fight when you have already lost, when your world has been taken from you? This long after colonisation it was hard to find a way to keep spirits up. Out-gunned when not outnumbered, there was little hope.

She tried to hold as many people together as she could, tried to keep people hoping. The older generations – they had less spirit, less life left than the younger. The longer someone had been oppressed by the Toads, the longer one had lived without hope, the deeper the quagmire became. Therefore she worked harder on the younger generations, those who had little or no memory of any life but hiding from the Settlers. She took their hands, pulled them out of the depression, for to them it was not so deep.

Esperance hated the Toads – the Settlers – and tried to remember, always, what her grandfather told her whenever she felt useless. Humans are as good as the Toads – it was like a mantra – humans are as good as the Toads.

They had taken Earth for reasons of their own, for reasons that were opaque to Esperance. Why could they not be comfortable on their own planet? They hated it on Earth so why did they want it so badly? Maybe they had used up too many resources at the place she had heard they just called 'home', refused to live on what they had, 'like a child spending their pocket money too fast' was what

Grandfather always said. Esperance was not sure what he meant: money was too rare and precious to be given to children.

Maybe it was like when the hunting ran out at the camp, and they had to go further and further afield looking for food. If they hunted too hard, too successfully, they would have to move camp. That might be it – they moved camp a long way, these Toads. Maybe it was like when they cooked a feral sheep and ate it all rather than saving some meat for the next breakfast. A feast then hunger, that is what can happen if you are careless.

It was the middle of what winter they had and not yet dawn – there was still a chance of a fly-by. Listening carefully for the sound of a flier, for the skittering whirr of its engines, she checked over the camp. Everyone was camped in the scrub, under mallee, in depressions in the ground covered with tarps, twigs and debris. Hopefully here was nothing that could betray them to an overflying Settler.

It was only a couple of days ago they had finished their last move, after a flier crossed over them and then banked and returned. There was no certainty that it had seen them but something had made it turn back. The council had decided it was better to be safe, so they moved, they ran. They were still settling in, still hiding all traces of their meagre food stores. Their sanitary arrangements, little more than holes, were not yet camouflaged.

It had been a rough move, a long walk in the scorching heat for many, as the braver souls searched before the group in their few battered old cars. Nobody wanted to walk at all but the vehicles were too risky, too noisy; whoever was driving them would be lost if Settlers heard or saw them. It had been decided they would lead the Settlers in a chase away from the main group of travellers if spotted. Better to sacrifice volunteers and the cars than have everyone captured. If such a move was necessary, it would be unlikely any would return.

The cars were treasures as much as they were hard work. Hunters found them from time to time, abandoned, almost never working. Father had taught son, mother had taught daughter, the skills needed to keep them running. It was fuel that was hard to obtain.

Their only method of communication was outdated even before the Invasion – UHF radio, a medium that Settlers were certainly capable of listening in to but that they seemed to have, so far, ignored. For those on foot – waiting for the crackle of the radio, baking in the heat that was the only thing protecting them from the Settlers, dry and hot yet maintaining a forced silence – it was not a good day.

Most of them, in the camp, had white skin. As good as they were in the heat when compared to Settlers they were still poorly adapted to the scorching sun. All of them were tanned from years of outdoor living, and yet, that day, they burned red then peeled. The agony of the raw skin, the dehydration, the pain of the excruciating heat . . . There should have been moaning, screaming, yet they travelled, they hid, in silence.

Everyone was far too tired to complain, to moan, to scream.

That was only the first day; they had bivouacked at night in the trees, in the dark and the cold, too terrified to start a fire. It was a long night, that first night on the run, everybody cold and scared, huddled in groups under not enough blankets. Men, women and children lay in desperate silence. The trees that normally brought comfort, that hid them from the roaming Settlers, loomed like silent monsters in the feeble moonlight. Above the group fliers could be heard quartering the woodland, searching for any sign of them. No one could understand why the Settlers were, this time, so interested in finding the refugees.

Led by their new friend Paddy, the stranger from the desert, they went further inland, into the desert, than ever before. They were relatively safe there but only during the scorching, deadly heat of the day, when it was so hot not even humans could tolerate it well. At night it was even cooler than it was closer to the coast, which would have been a relief if not for the Settlers. It was still too dry for them but they seemed to manage better in the cool and dry than they did in the hot and dry.

Moving at the pace of the slowest, the humans took a week of painfully hot days to get deep enough into the desert to feel safe. It was the fifth night when the alien sound of the fliers ceased passing overhead. Five nights of the same tiredness, the same fear, the same cold, the same impenetrable darkness.

When the radio Esperance held crackled on, when a forward scout informed the group they had found a potential safe camp, she had no water, no energy left to cry in relief even if her eyes could have spared water for tears. Two days they had been in that camp, she hoped it was safe enough. With meagre supplies and little water many would not survive another move if the Settlers came again.

Paddy from the desert had decided to stay with them; he would have relative safety, company and security there while he waited until it was safe to look for his people. He had travelled lightest of the group, carrying only his blanket – someone had spared him a blanket – hunting rifle and knife. Accustomed to living rough he had not even built a shelter when they stopped. 'It's not gunna rain,' he had said. He was a better hunter than the rest of the group, teaching them to catch the game of the desert.

Tireless, indomitable, he had gone out every day to learn the country around them, finding more water, finding materials to build shacks. Taking out other men he had taught them to find the food he knew better than they. The food out there in the desert was different to what they were used to, nobody wanted to eat lizards, nobody understood the desert plants. In the end hunger and desperation had converted even the most resistant.

Esperance moved carefully, keeping to the trees whenever possible, just in case there was a silent flier above. The Settlers seemingly had no such thing as a silent flier. Maybe they didn't feel the need for stealth so had never developed quieter engines. However, years under occupation had taught caution. The last weeks of frantic flight after flight on foot deeper into the desert had encouraged, enforced, outright paranoia.

It was Grandfather who had taught them how to hide their camp, how to build the sanitary, yet hidden, latrines. Grandfather had been leading them for so long, teaching them how to survive, and finally his health was failing. He was an old man, nobody knew quite how old, yet if he remembered before the Invasion he had to be ancient. Nobody expected him to live long and when he died there would be a problem. The fight over leadership might tear the camp apart. Why would they stay together in a group without him anyway?

Survivors had arrived more than once from other groups, groups that had died, had fallen apart over leadership squabbles. Her group had no leadership as such, just a council of elders who ruled by respect, and all deferred to Grandfather as the eldest, the wisest, their natural leader. So old, everyone merely called him Grandfather, he had no need for a name in their mob.

Even visitors from other groups, even ragged refugees arriving half dead, nearly starved, on the run, called him 'Grandfather'. Some had even heard of him before arriving; some came looking for him.

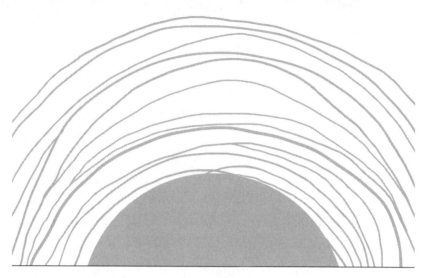

CHAPTER 11

Terra Nullius was a legal fiction, a declaration used to justify the invasion of Australia and subjugation of its people hundreds of years ago by the United Kingdom, a more technologically advanced people. In translation from the long-dead language Latin it means 'Nobody's Land' or 'Empty Earth'. There were people in Australia when the United Kingdom came; there had been for tens of thousands of years. The declaration of Terra Nullius had the direct effect of defining the Native inhabitants as non-people. I use that term now because in your colonisation you have done that exact same thing.

Since the invasion, you call it the settlement, of this planet you have acted as if humans do not exist. If you acknowledge at all that we were here before your arrival you believe we were rendered extinct by your expansion. This has happened before: the English believed they had exterminated all of the Tasmanian Aborigines, the Palawa; in fact they survived the invasion, they still exist now. You act as if humans are extinct: that is news to me.

– DOCTOR ROBERT BLACK, LEADER OF THE NATIVE DELEGATION TO THE SETTLER PARLIAMENT

THE SOUND OF hammering on sheet metal was drilling its slow, relentless way into Bagra's head, erasing her sense of peace as she walked the corridors of her mission. It was everywhere, although she knew it was only coming from one direction. She knew exactly where it was coming from, yet it echoed and crashed, working its way into every corner of the building. If she was going to have to listen to it, no matter where she went in the mission, she may as well go inspect the work.

Outside, closer to the hammering, you would have expected it to be louder yet the nearby alien forest appeared to absorb it, unlike the familiar walls inside. If they had been built to amplify the sound it would be hard to imagine them doing a better job. So, for one of the first times since arriving on this planet, Bagra was glad, even delighted, to be outside. It was a cool day, the air damp and the infernal sun hidden behind a comforting solid grey sky. She could even hope, she would always hope, it might rain.

The work outside was progressing well. Where there had been two metal boxes, good places to lock up the little monsters when they were disobedient, when they resisted their lessons, when they acted like the animals they were, there were now four, and a fifth being built. She was delighted the work was nearly completed, the noise would soon end, but she was also worried that five boxes would not be enough, but it was at least more than two.

Since that fugitive, Jacky, had broken into the office, the Natives had been restless, almost impossible to control. Most of them seemed to believe what the Department for the Protection of Natives believed, that the small pile of excrement was looking for a way home.

Surely that was impossible: the Natives were not particularly intelligent, when they were taken from their parents for education they soon forgot their early life. His home was there, in the mission or in the settlement that had taken him in, surely he would dream of no other.

Maybe he was trying to return home, to whatever slum, whatever filthy camp he had been collected from. It seemed more likely he was taking revenge for some poorly understood slight, for something that had occurred in the mission. Wherever he was the Troopers would get him.

Turning without warning she looked at the windows of the schoolroom. There they were again, the ugly, contemptible faces of the children staring out at the work, staring out at the scrub, staring at her. When they noticed she was looking they all went back to their work. She could imagine their whispering, like the hissing of snakes.

They would have to be disciplined, that entire lot, the entire class would have no lunch today. She could not identify the individual children involved, they all looked the same to her.

Their teacher would hear about it too; there had been a lapse in discipline for the nuns as well, they were getting lazy, more proof they were losing faith in the work. Bagra alone seemed to be maintaining the rules, maintaining discipline, keeping the faith, doing it for all of them. The younger nuns, after Jacky's break-in, were starting to doubt that the children could be trained to become reliable servants. Some had even begun to question whether the children should be trained to service at all.

It was all that Jacky's fault. Somehow rumours of his continued freedom kept reaching the Natives. Somehow the children knew that after absconding, after breaking into and trashing her office, he was still free. 'Looking for home,' they said, the word 'home' said more times in the mission in the past weeks than it had been for years combined. There had been more attempted escapes lately, children believing they could go home. Surely they could not even remember what 'home' was, where their homes could be. 'Home' became a battle cry, a touchstone.

'There are always escapes, have always been escapes, it is one of the Native's basest drives, to escape,' Bagra told the other nuns that night over dinner.

'Why, if we are trying to help them, are they so desperate to escape?' asked Mel's stupid friend, the other young nun.

'Before Jacky broke in,' Bagra said with false calm, with affected boredom, 'the attempts had always been for pathetic, shallow, selfish reasons, a desire,' she was hissing, losing her temper, 'a constant urge to escape their work, plain laziness, a desire for whatever animalistic pleasure they were searching for when the tracker caught them.'

'They are escaping more, or trying more,' said one of the nuns, old and decrepit.

'The others cover for them,' Mel interjected, 'hide the fact they have run, wanting to give another the chance to "go home".'

Bagra agreed even though the silly girl's attempt at getting into her good books was transparent. Escapes were taking longer to be discovered, the children getting further before the tracker started. Tracks were getting lost.

The brats had a stronger desire to run now, trying so much harder to stay free, to avoid the trackers, to avoid recapture. There had even recently been a little monster who had escaped, and been recaptured but who would not submit. She was dragged back kicking and screaming, injuring the tracker, kicking the walls of her prison box all night, keeping everyone awake.

Nothing could stop the rebellion, end the noise – even beatings, even withholding food and water. Suddenly after days of screaming it had stopped: the child was unconscious, near to death from lack of water. One of the older sisters had collected the child and taken her to the infirmary to recover. Bagra wished they had just buried it, not saved its life. The very next night, having shown no sign of waking all day, it escaped from the infirmary and disappeared.

They had laughed at her, dared to actually laugh at her; she heard their giggling, their horrible twittering, always behind her when she walked. She never caught them at it – by the time she turned they were always silent, always looking the other way. She never knew which one it was. The laughter followed her everywhere, even seemingly empty corridors could erupt into childish, monstrous giggles.

She lacked the resources, even the will to punish every child in the mission, not when the other nuns might resist. Punishment would need to be handed out arbitrarily. Could she get away with doing it randomly?

It was all that Jacky's fault.

Turning from the noise of hammering she would have run into the schoolhouse if her sense of propriety had allowed it. Restoring discipline to that classroom would certainly help to restore her equilibrium. If not, it would certainly cheer her up, especially the disciplining of whoever was supposed to be teaching.

'I have contacted that man they call "Devil", the Chief Protector of Natives, personally,' Sister Bagra said as the older nuns nodded sagely. 'I did not ask much, merely that he hurry up and capture the fugitive so peace can be restored.'

There was murmuring around the table. Bagra spoke again to quiet them. 'There was no answer, that terrible man with no respect, so I wrote him again, told him that there would be no peace from the Natives until Jacky was caught.'

Bagra believed that soon it would be too late; as more and more escaped others would get the courage to try. One day all of her charges would believe they could 'go home'. She had heard of trouble in the surrounding settlements, servants taking Jacky's example, disappearing in the middle of the night. Soon they would lose control completely.

What was it about this particular fugitive that everyone was so interested in, that the Natives would not ignore? There had been escapes before, many of them; whether or not the Native was captured was irrelevant to keeping order. Yet this man, barely more than a child kept everyone excited. He was not even particularly interesting, barely memorable.

'Until Jacky is captured we will soldier on as usual,' she stated in a tone that left no room for argument.

At least until the inspector came, which seemed to be delayed again and again with no explanation, nobody even deigning to inform the mission. There was a ready excuse, the communication satellites were useless, they had travelled across the stars to this godforsaken planet, yet they had no modern communications most of the time. Half the time they sent messages not knowing if they would arrive, the other half they did not even trust the system that much and relied on a courier.

This could not do, this waiting for a guillotine blade that never fell. He had arrived on the planet, that much seemed likely; the trip to this planet was no longer difficult.

Travelling across land, that was more dangerous – there was the heat, the dry and the depredations of the Natives. Anyone who did not rate a flier was in real danger travelling anywhere, maybe something had happened to him on the way. Bagra was not certain whether or not to hope he had met some disaster. If he died on the way it would not end their problems, instead it would simply delay them as another inspector was dispatched.

A new inspector was no more likely to be forgiving, and the administration back home less so once they had lost an inspector from the Church. The next inspector could instead be a 'hatchet man', sent to clean up rather than investigate the mess. If they had been kind with their choice of inspector there was still a hope she could convince him there was nothing to worry about.

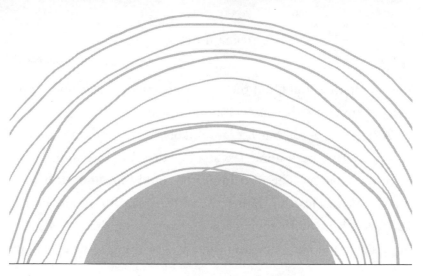

CHAPTER 12

Person to person we are stronger than them, faster than them and we have the advantage of local knowledge. We are no less intelligent than them, might even be smarter on an individual level. Where they beat us consistently is in technology and the unrelenting, merciless, largely impersonal, application of force. Our species is also as ancient as theirs; when we were climbing down from the trees they were taking their first upright steps from the swamp, so there is no age advantage. It seems all their advantages developed because they come from a part of space where populated planets are more numerous.

Stated simply, their interstellar enemies and friends are right next door.

While we have developed in isolation, until they came, they developed in a society of constant interstellar contact, trade and war. They have traded technology with their near neighbours, they have stolen technology from their neighbours, they have had the need to develop that technology for defence and assault against those same neighbours.

We have had no reason to develop the technology of conflict to the level they have, because until this point we have known of nobody offplanet to fight. We did not develop the technology of interstellar space flight because we had nowhere to go, and no competition for getting there first.

We always thought we were an aggressive people, warlike and violent. On contact with other species from the other side of the galaxy we discovered that we are not. They are to us as a lion is to a lamb.

An analogy that would help us understand is western Europe on our planet. A tightly packed mass of small kingdoms with relatively high population densities they have, since prehistory, always traded technology when they were not fighting over land and resources. The competition, the drive to develop the technology of travel and war was intense leading to the technological advantage that Europe developed.

Distant countries, perhaps less warlike than those in Europe and, importantly, with lower population densities, developed complex social systems that enabled them to survive in their environment. They did not travel and invade, they did not go to war like the Europeans did. Importantly they had everything they needed and did not invade other people to steal their resources. People of those countries did not even need to defend themselves against populous warlike neighbours until the Europeans came, by which time it was, for them, too late.

Now Earth is the isolated country that has a relatively low population, lower technology and a culture relatively un-warlike. In the history of the world, when Europeans landed in Australia, the most isolated continent on the planet, the people there had no context in which to understand the new more powerful, warlike enemy. The mental and emotional technology of the Australian Aboriginals taught them to live in peace and harmony, to survive in the toughest natural environment in the world. It did not equip them to defend against an attacker from outside. In interstellar terms we, the people of Earth, are the Australian Aboriginals.

We have fought wars, we have killed, we were killing each other right until the invasion but do not believe in killing indiscriminately;

we fight but deep down we believe that peace is better for society. We sometimes fail to act brutally enough, a collection of ethics we call 'humanity' tempers our reactions. They have no such compulsion, we are not their equals; to them, we are merely a part of the inhospitable environment they are trying to tame.

I had always thought humans were brutal in war, merciless in combat, but that was before the Settlers arrived. In the early days of our resistance, starting immediately after their arrival on our planet, we had some success in destroying them, in fighting back. This success came at a cost we were unwilling or unable to keep paying. If one of them were killed, ambushed or slaughtered (there were no actual battles) their retaliation was swift and decisive.

When Europeans 'colonised' the lands of the so-called primitive peoples we were brutal. The 'murder' of an Englishman in Australia, for example, could lead to the death of an entire tribe. This had the effect of terrorising the people whose lands we had colonised. They could not, for the most part, understand that sort of brutality.

Similarly we could not have imagined the violence with which the invaders of Earth, the colonisers of our planet, would react. When a Settler was mobbed and killed in London, after beating a human child in the street, the city was 'sanitised' and not a single human was left alive. The entire south of England was enslaved and the island we called Britain was turned slowly into a fortified camp, their greatest stronghold.

– REAR ADMIRAL (RETIRED) MARTIN FREEMAN
(REPRINTED WITH PERMISSION COURTESY OF THE INSTITUTE FOR HUMAN STUDIES)

JOHNNY STAR WAS utterly helpless, if Johnny Star had the strength left to move he would be writhing in pain. Johnny Star knew he was about to die. His soft moist skin, so like that of an amphibian, poorly adapted to the heat and dry, was so parched it was starting to crack. If he didn't find water soon he was doomed, cooked.

His friends, the Natives, had taken off, either certain he was going to die and abandoning him to his fate, or, as he hoped, on a desperate search for water. He had been delirious with the heat when they left, he had no idea if they had told him why they were leaving.

If they were looking for water they would in their humanity show, by contrast, exactly how compassionate his own people were. Which was, in his opinion, not at all. His own people would have left him there to die. He just wished his friends had left someone with him; he hated being alone.

He had heard before what it was like to die from the dehydration – the 'dry death' they called it. More than once, when he was a trooper, he had joined the search for Settlers missing from their settlements. When they were found at all they were often dead under whatever pathetic shade they could find. If the searchers were lucky they found a corpse, skin cracked and dry eyes sunken into the sockets. Otherwise what they found was a terrifying, mummified 'thing', skin like paper stretched over brittle bones, the remains contorted by the dry heat. The eyes, the windows of the soul, would be dehydrated to almost non-existence, leaving nothing but a leather-wrapped skull.

Many troopers, once they had seen mummified victims of the heat, vowed this would never be their fate, they would take their own lives first. Sometimes lost troopers were found dead, shot with their own guns well before the dry death could occur. Maybe some of them could have been saved if they had just waited.

Johnny had fought for his life for far too long to take that quick, relatively painless option. As long as there was hope that somebody would come, as long as there was hope that it might rain, he held on. It had gone well past the point where there was genuine hope; Johnny was holding on through pure, bloody-minded stubbornness. Dying of the heat and the dry was one experience he could live without.

In the middle of the day, when the sun was highest, it was too hot to survive in the open. Even in shade the heat felt like a blowtorch blasting against his skin. Desperate, he buried himself deeper into the litter of fallen bark, sticks and leaves knowing it would be slightly cooler there, hoping for some moisture, any moisture to absorb through his desiccating skin.

Out in this desert though, even the leaves were desiccated; there was not even enough rain, enough moisture to rot them. The litter would stay there until the inevitable fire, the fire that always comes, turns it to ash. When cleansing fire came it would burn his corpse too, a cremation, his ashes fertilising the trees, far better than following stupid orders to a fool's death, buried in a bone yard, murdering humans who did not deserve to die.

There were species of frogs and toads on this planet that were capable of hibernating when there was not enough water for them to survive. Before the water ran out completely they formed a cocoon of slime filled with water. Within that they would sleep through the dry, sleep until the rain came. What magic, what beautiful, unbelievable magic, surely this cannot be possible. Johnny wished so hard his people had that ability, or at least that he had that power. Screw the rest of his people, let them die. It would have been more useful to him right now than the intelligence and industry that had enabled them to build spaceships, to colonise other planets. He could sleep through the heat, where none of his people would find him, return when the rain came to a new world, maybe a world where he would be forgiven, where he could forgive his people for the massacres of the Natives.

This time he was out of luck; he was going to die here under a tree, in the heat, die of the heat and the parched oven-hot air. He would die and in this grey-green pile of leaves and bark, so close in colour to his skin, he would be perfectly camouflaged, invisible. In death he would disappear. He realised, too late, when he had no strength left to move, his friends, if they returned, might not be able to find him, already buried as he was.

In his most optimistic dreams he survived and even thrived on this strange planet, maybe one day finding a way to make it home. More likely and a death he could accept would be going down in a blaze of plasma fire, in the song and light of a gun battle, shot down by his own people. His own people would hunt him down like an animal, slaughter him. He understood that, didn't even really blame them.

If they did not, if they tried to take him alive, he would make them fight to the death. He would not be captured, he would fight until they killed him. If they captured him he would die of old age in a prison, or be publicly executed. His people were cruel, in execution doubly so. The death chamber is nothing more than a giant dehydrator, not that different to how he was feeling except in an execution faces would be jeering at him through the glass walls.

Even in his nightmares he could not have imagined it would end this way, alone and lost, dying of the heat and dry. Not long, if help, if his friends did not come, not long and all they would find was a papery-skinned corpse, as dry, brittle and faded as the leaves, fallen bark and twigs he lay in. If they found him at all.

Passing out from exhaustion Johnny dreamed of cool water, of cold swamps, of air so humid it dripped at the slightest provocation and condensed on your skin. He dreamed of home. Home, where your skin was never dry, where the moisture of the air was enough to stay wet. There were forests on this planet where it was like that, never dry, the air dripping. Those places were the most sought by his people, used as luxury estates, for luxury hotels. He had never been there and could never go there now he was outlawed.

He had been miserable as a child, back at home, hated the restriction, the religious strictures, the mentally inflexible people. He had hated the school where they had been educated almost from birth. A disobedient child, he had grown up into a surly, rebellious youth in his third decade, the time many of his people go a bit wild. It was everybody else's fault; he would not have had troubles if everyone else was not so bloody boring. Boring, controlling, stuck-up, mindless drones, he did not hate his people back home, he pitied them. It seemed inevitable that with his native intelligence and disrespect for the restrictive culture he was born into he would get in trouble with the law.

It had started minor – a habit of trespass, a disbelief that there should be restrictions on where he could walk. Arrests for brawling followed, though he was never responsible for starting fights, always seeming to get caught up in violence. He always, however, ended the fights, and it was hard to profess his innocence when after almost every fight he was the only man left standing.

With almost complete disrespect for the law and a firm under-standing of the unfairness of a society with haves and have-nots he had moved on to minor thefts, not to make money from crime but rather because he did not believe he should be denied something he wanted. It really didn't matter to him who owned something when he wanted it.

More and more brushes with the law and he lost all faith in the laws of his people. No longer caring for the strictures of his society, unable to tolerate the strictness of life in the city he turned vagrant, disappearing into the deep swamp.

He was happiest then, better suited to the life of a wanderer and outcast, hunting and gathering, carrying only the technology that suited his lifestyle. It was a lonely existence – nearly all the people in his advanced culture lived in cities and towns. Only a few tramps, poorly adjusted to modern life, still lived in the swamps in which their people had evolved.

Every society in the galaxy seemed to create people like him: throwbacks who could not tolerate the urban life, who were happier with a more primitive way of life. Most of those people were loners, they would help each other in need, they were friendly when they happened upon others, but otherwise they had no desire to seek others out. Every society in the galaxy drove the people like him out.

Solitude had not bothered him then; he was happiest in his own company. The swamp, the small flopping, wriggling things living around his shack, the wet hanging trees – these were his friends, his family. His communicator was useless out there in the swamp, out of range, but that was okay, he needed nobody, even his family, even his old friends were surplus to requirements. They had been no help when he needed them to get him out of trouble with the police. If he needed them he knew where to find them.

The end to his freedom, to his relatively idyllic existence came suddenly and with no warning. A dead animal in the swamp – a large amphibian, good hunting, good to eat – had alerted him that something was wrong, then he found another and another. In the vast miles upon miles of trackless swamp in which he had made his home the life started dying. Fish, amphibians, even the worms, the small skittering things, died. Soon there was nothing to eat. The swamp was surely not dead, it was the size of one of the big oceans on Earth, but all the food animals within reasonable travelling range were dead or dying.

Johnny had been hungry before; when he first ran from the city it had taken him some time to regain the skills his people had lost, skills that he needed to survive. There were some lean times then, with between little and nothing to eat, but he had lived through it, eventually learning the skills he needed to find food. This was different, there was simply no food, no end in sight to the hunger.

With no other choice possible he swam the many miles to the camp of a family he knew, a family who had walked into the swamp so long ago they had children in their second decade who had been born out there. Surely they would know what to do.

They were not there, not in their camp of ramshackle huts in the swamp, not out hunting in the water nearby, just gone, even the mother and children. There was nothing to eat, no stored food, no hanging meat, no drying fish. Presumably they had wandered off looking for better hunting, though their tracks in the mud led in the direction of the nearest city.

Johnny had been left with only one choice: he too turned towards the nearest city and started walking, following their tracks. His meagre possessions were already in the ancient, mud-stained backpack he had carried into the swamp all those years ago. When the mud ran out he entered the water; tangled with tree roots and reeds it was hard to swim through. Luckily, though it was not a good sign for the health of the swamp, the large predators that might have made it difficult were not in evidence.

A week later, exhausted and half-starved, he came upon a wide, clear, marked canal – a highway through the swamp, where civil engineers had made a deep cutting and kept it clear of mud, plant life and debris. Normally boats carrying goods into the city, and between cities, moved up and down the canals while family transports zigged and zagged, swirling, splashing, dodging between them in a rush to get somewhere else.

The canals were bustling, noisy places.

This canal was impossibly silent. Confused and disconcerted Johnny swam just outside of the markers where he would be safe if a boat came speeding along. It would be another couple of days swim to the edge of the city; he had hoped to hitch a ride but there was simply nobody passing.

His hunger was almost intolerable. There was still nothing to eat, he had nothing left but prayer – prayer to a deity he no longer believed in, to the god of the religion they had hammered, beaten into him at school, prayer he would find food.

A few miles from the city, when you could hear the hum of it but not yet see it through the swamp trees, his personal communicator chirped. So shocked by the unaccustomed sound – the long-silent, forgotten, disregarded device – he inhaled water, choking and spluttering as he took it out of his bag. It was a warning, a warning that the canal he was swimming in was closed to traffic due to an accident. How bad was it?

Johnny stared at the suddenly unfamiliar device; had he forgotten how to use it so quickly? He pushed another control and down-loaded a news feed: a couple of freighters had collided in the canal and others had been moving so fast they had added their wreckage to the tangled mess that was already there. One of the trucks had been carrying an agricultural chemical, deadly to fish and most other swamp life.

There was no use trying to escape it – he had been poisoned already, had been swimming in it for days, weeks even, for as long as it had been leaching into the water. If it was going to cause Johnny harm it was going to anyway, it probably already had. He may as well keep swimming to the city.

A day later he came upon the canal-block, a string of boat-sized floats right across the canal. It was posted with signs in bright purple, 'NO ENTRY', 'TRAFFIC HAZARD', 'HEALTH HAZARD', 'BIOHAZARD' and other similarly dire warnings. What was missing was a 'DETOUR' sign as there was no other path, no other canal to take.

The swamp forest here was thick, thicker than anything Johnny could remember seeing, almost completely impassable. There was a drift of dead fish floating against the buoys, ranging in size from minnows, the length of a finger joint, right up to a single monstrous beast as large as a canal freighter.

Paranoid, terrified if he could admit it, he returned to the edges of the swamp, as far away from the cleared canal as he could manage. The thickets were genuinely impassable, though at the edge running along the length of the canal was a reed bed with a few scattered shrubs. Keeping in the reeds, there to be virtually invisible, hiding behind small trees and smaller bushes Johnny began to skirt past the disaster.

There, among the wreckage, the sunken ships, the dead fish, were workmen, wearing bright colours, wearing what seemed to be environmental suits if they were in the water. Johnny was no expert, so he had no way to identify the heavy machinery they were using to clear the canal. There were also police, dressed in their yellow, heavily armed, standing on barges and speedboats. There were fast boats parked near the wreckage, plain-clothed police or government inspectors, maybe both. None of them saw Johnny as he swam past in the shadows among tangled trees and hanging vines, his face above the water and that barely.

When he finally reached the outskirts of the city he was weak, barely able to crawl out of the water onto the mud and sludge at the edge of the island. Certainly some of that weakness was hunger and a long swim, but a part of him, the part more aware, less exhausted, was worried that such long exposure to the poison in the swamp had harmed him in some way.

He was pained and tired, barely able to lift his face from the mud at the edge of the water, unable to sweep away leaves that tickled his nose and eyelids. Slipping in and out of consciousness he had no idea how long he lay like that, breathing but only just, not moving, not awake yet not sleeping. The thin mist from the jungle of the city-island, the damp of the mud, the water in which he half lay, that was what kept him alive in the thin watery sun of that season. Waking, if it is waking when you have no memory of sleep, when collapse leads to sudden wakefulness with nothing but a gap between, he crawled under the cover of the trees. Half delirious with starvation, exhaustion and poison, he could not think, his only remaining drive was the hunger that had driven him from the swamp. There were houses on the edge of the trees, larger than most but still built to the open, water-loving plan as the rest of the city – lily pads of ceramic and steel, wet drooping foliage of glass and aluminium, sculpted fronds and dripping moisture.

So hungry, he was barely conscious of the alarm that went off as he raided the refrigerated food stores in the first house he found. Too tired and too sick he was too slow in getting away, unable even to turn a door latch with his hands full of food. All his blood had run to his stomach; he was sluggish, sleepy, ill and he didn't even resist when the law officers cuffed him and led him to their boat.

Some days later, well fed and rested in the lock-up, treated for the poisoning by the police doctors, it occurred to him how stupid he had been, how unlucky. He didn't even have someone to contact – he had no numbers for old friends and family, nobody would even know he was alive after so long in the swamp. The numbers in his communicator didn't work, everybody must have changed them in the years he had been away. There was nobody to get him free, nobody to find him legal representation. Alone by choice in the swamp, he was alone when he needed help.

The judge had taken pity on him, lost and alone, starving and sick as he had been when he was picked up. He was given a choice. Jail or the Colonial Troopers.

There was no way he could have known then that jail would have been the easier fate.

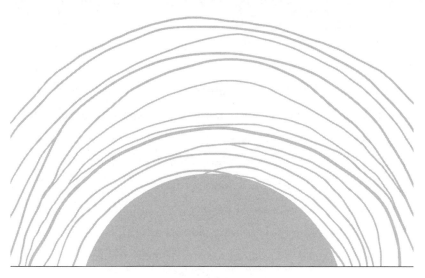

CHAPTER 13

They are not like us, these arrivals from another planet, these beings who have decided to colonise our world. Evolving, coming to being on a different planet to ours, they have very few direct similarities in physiology to any life on our world. This is despite the fact that the basic building blocks of life – DNA, RNA and protein – are essentially the same. We were surprised when finally able to examine a sample that although the cell structure is completely alien their biology is built of the same sixteen essential amino acids and they have the same four bases in their DNA as we have.

Their biochemistry is in fact similar enough to ours that they can digest the protein and fat that we do, can in fact live on our food. The main difference in digestion and metabolism is that they eat far less carbohydrates than we do. It is not known whether or not there are fewer carbohydrate sources on their planet or their position on the food chain caused them to evolve into almost obligate carnivores. Until we study other species from their world we can never know.

While biochemically they are similar, almost identical, to us, morphologically they are almost entirely alien. As stated before, their cell structure is completely alien with no organelles or structure we would recognise. This has the unintended effect of causing some confusion, as they don't look as alien as we would expect them to. In fact, they look so similar to life on this planet people without a scientific background would have no idea how alien their biology is.

Superficially they appear to have similarities with the amphibians of our world; essentially they look like great humanoid salamanders. They have the same moist, slimy skin as amphibians and there is evidence they are as tolerant of heat and dryness as most amphibians, which is not at all.

This would explain, for instance, why our base, the last military science base controlled by the US army, has been moved to the middle of the desert in Afghanistan. The invaders that the military have begun to derogatorily refer to as 'Toads' are reluctant to move into the deserts, if they are capable of it at all.

There is much we still don't know. We have absolutely no clue as to the morphology of the other life on their home world, except for assumptions we can make that their animal life will likely be as related to them as ours is to us. Despite their obvious intent to settle here they have not yet unloaded livestock from their ships and are living on rations or from hunting. We also have no idea as to the manner of their reproduction. Do they have two sexes as we do? That seems likely as this is the most expedient manner in which to guarantee genetic diversity and the survival of the species. Are their children born live or from eggs? Do they undergo a metamorphosis as do amphibians from our world?

We may never know, because before we can study them they may very well have completely wiped us out.

– CARLY BOYLE PHD.

DOCUMENT RECOVERED FROM HARD DRIVE IN THE REMAINS OF BASE DELTA, DATE UNKNOWN

THE PEOPLE IN the Settler town where Perth used to be, on the continent that was once called Australia, did not know how lucky they were that Father Grark of the First Church had been sent to the planet unarmed. For days he had been moving from pathetic colonial office to more pathetic colonial office, attempting to request, then later to requisition a flier. He had been told by the Trooper Office that it was unsafe to travel by land, especially for someone inexperienced and unadapted to the local climate.

He was far too important, they said, to risk himself on a surface journey, by boat, on foot or mounted. Besides, they said, it was too far, would take too many days, maybe even weeks. They were forced by policy, unbreakable policy that disallowed exceptions, to deny him the right to travel overland. He would need a flier, they said.

Then they told him they had none available. Even if there was one not currently being used, they said, it would still be unavailable. It did not matter who he was, who he knew, why he was there or who sent him, he was still a civilian and had no right to access their scarce air support. If he had only intended to make a short trip they might have been able to incorporate his travel into existing patrols, as a favour to the Church, but at the distance he wished to travel this was impossible.

There were private taxi services, of course, but all of them said where he wanted to go was too far, too dangerous. One driver, when informed where Grark intended to travel, coughed into his drink, spraying himself and collapsing back into his seat in a fit of choking. He was still choking when Grark walked away, half glad he was unarmed, half wishing he could shoot the idiot. Maybe he was still choking, or dead. Grark's ability to care about whether he had accidentally killed the idiot was rapidly fading.

He even tried to hire a flier, take himself there. He walked to the flier rental agency, filled in the requisite forms, handed them over to the agent who filed them in the trash. They then showed him the clause in the contract; no fliers would be rented to anyone travelling to the outback, it was still too unsafe. It did not matter that the government said there was no Native problem, the rental company thought different.

The Church owned no fliers; he even resorted to contacting the Department for the Protection of Natives, which apparently had no budget to buy fliers either. Everybody but the Church, who paid no taxes, complained constantly of the extreme height of the tax rate both at home and in the colonies. While trying to get a flier out of department after department, Father Grark wondered where all that money went.

Briefly he even considered stealing a vehicle, a thoroughly illegal act which would also be totally pointless. For some reason he could not sufficiently explain, he had never learned to fly and learning over somewhere as dangerous as the deserts of the driest continent on the driest inhabited planet in the galaxy would be worse than foolhardy. He could hijack a flier and pilot but he was unarmed. Adding the purchase of an illegal firearm to the crimes of hijack and kidnap would certainly make his superiors back home more than a little upset.

There was no transportation to have for love, which he was out of, or money, which he never had, having long ago taken a vow of poverty. The Church, however, had plenty of both. For that reason Grark decided that it was high time the Church bought a flier and hired a driver.

He had reached the limit of his patience; after his time in the city, after all the investigations he lacked the will to find a driver, buy a flier. He did what he had always done; he dropped unsubtle hints while making it clear he was short on patience, until the Church made an underling do it. In the meantime he explored the city, the luxury hotels where every hall, every room had a misting sprinkler, cooling and humidifying the air in an attempt to make the patrons forget they were on Earth.

They had servants there, all Natives. From his enquiries, despite the evasions, Grark believed it quite unlikely that such servants were being paid. That defined them as slaves no matter what their masters wanted to call them. This could not be tolerated: the Church and the state had abolished slavery at home and, they thought, every colony. Grark was ashamed of what he saw, yet there was little he could do about it. All he could do was report it to home, let them handle it.

His people had long been a slave-keeping race, having even raided other countries on their own planet for slaves before their planet united under one government to fight the enemies who had come from the stars. They had taken slaves from the whole galaxy as soon as they could reach out to take them. Recent cultural developments, mostly instituted by the Church, had led to the abolition of slavery and the liberation of the slaves. They had all been sent back to where they came from.

Grark had seen the correspondence, had seen the news reports, the comments, he had studied the issue on the ship. 'There is no slavery,' said the officials of the colony when asked by the government back home, 'we are perfectly aware that slavery is illegal.' That was their official stance, 'no slavery here'. The reports from the media on this planet were different, even those he managed to read on the ship; Natives were not allowed to have money yet they were forced to work. The Natives cannot be slaves, the reports read, because they are not people. Slavery will not be tolerated.

All throughout the city Grark heard and saw the same thing. Whenever he mentioned that home considered Natives to be people, to be citizens of the Empire and therefore not to be slaves they looked at him like he was crazy. His words fell on deaf ears, to the people of this planet there was no debate: Natives are animals and to be used as you would use any other animal.

He dreaded what he would find when he left the city; he had heard that the slavery was worse the further you head out from civilisation. In the city they were aware that slavery was illegal in every colony of the Empire yet did it anyway in plain view of the administration. Surely in the desert, where nobody was watching, where they could claim they were not aware of the law, things must be far worse.

So he lay under a misting sprinkler in an embarrassingly expensive hotel room, all muted greens and clear plastic, dark green, large-leaved plants from home and water, water everywhere. He was grateful for the cooling water, keeping his thin soft skin moist, though he wondered where in this desert planet they got all that water. There was plenty of it in the oceans; they must desalinate it.

The depth of water in the waterbed – it filled only four inches before draining off – was perfect. It helped his mood, it kept him comfortable, though he would love to have a swim later if his car and driver didn't appear first.

Jacky was lost; he had absolutely no idea where he was, and no clue where he was going. 'East' had been a deceptively simple instruction: he had travelled towards the rising sun, or at least as close as he could get to that direction. Unfortunately, it is hard with very poor bearings, no landmarks and little experience to find the same direction every time. In the morning it was easy – walk towards the sun. In the evening it was easy – walk away from the sun. In the middle of the day it was virtually impossible to keep a completely straight bearing.

He was sure, however, he was not going in circles, as bearings from the sun would surely stop him from veering west. He had to be going mostly east, for finding approximate east is laughably easy as long as you can see the sun. Unfortunately, approximate east leaves too much room for failure. From north-east to south-east there is an arc of exactly ninety degrees. With no other directions, no more information, he had virtually no chance of reaching his goal.

The real problem was he was too scared to ask anyone where Jerramungup was. Settlers would ask too many questions, would want to know who he was, where he was going, who was his master . . . they would ask who gave him permission to travel.

Most of the humans he saw were slaves – destroyed, broken, little more than empty shells. Initiative was no use to the Settlers; everyone left with willpower had it beaten out of them. Those who could not be punished into submission were killed. Once he had tried to ask one for directions. The look he got was blank, as if the human could no longer speak his own human language.

The young man, bent and scarred, had rambled in pidgin Toad – a monologue that, most likely, would have made little sense in any language. Jacky could speak Settler, he could still speak the human language a bit and being away from the settlement was bringing more back, yet this mix of both seemed to carry no meaning or its meaning was opaque.

Nor could he ask the few free humans he saw – the campies, the outlaws – those who avoided Settler control or were useless to the Settlers. Most were drunks, or strung out on the new drugs the Toads had brought onto the planet; drugs humans seemed to have no tolerance for. Those who were not actually drunk, or stoned, were broken-hearted, heartsick. They had lost their homes, their families, their children, and they were second-class citizens where once they had ruled. They had lost everything; having no hope they had slipped into a deep depression. That mood was everywhere – there was nothing positive, nothing left to hope for. How can you hope when everything, even your future, has already been taken away?

Everybody despaired, or was paralysed by fear. Many were consumed by both fear and despair, so tired, so depressed they were not even of use to the Settlers anymore. They lived on handouts of rations from friends and family, from anyone who could still work, still bring in something to eat, only if those friends and family had some to spare.

People died, or lay down ready to die, resigned to ending their lives in filth, in squalor. How do you clean up your life with nothing to live for? How do you build a future when everything tells you there is no future for your people?

An old man at the settlement where they were slaves had told Jacky that his people, the humans, had once created a great society, built great cities, farmed, engineered. Once his people, the humans, had controlled this entire planet as the Toads had for Jacky's entire memory. Looking at the world you could see the remains of the human presence: the old roads, the ruined buildings, traces of farms. Despite all that it was hard for him to believe that the humans he was seeing were capable of such things, of building worlds.

Humans had once enslaved other humans, deciding their fate based on the colour of their skin. Racism, the old man had called it. When he described it Jacky was shocked. Humans were not nice people, humans had war and despair and theft even before the Toads arrived. The very land he walked on, the continent of

Australia had been home to one of the oldest cultures on the planet, maybe even in the galaxy. Then a younger warlike culture had come and stolen their land, enslaved the people, killed thousands.

The arrival of the Toads had eliminated all racism and hate within the human species. It was not that with a common enemy the humans decided to work together – humans never made a decision to no longer fight between themselves. Instead the colonisation by the Settlers simply ended all discrimination within the human race by taking away all the imbalance. There was no caste or class within humans; to the Toads who now owned the planet and everyone on it all humans had the same low status. To the Toads, all humans were nothing more than animals.

With no distinction between humans, no rights, no countries, the human race was in the process of homogenisation. A slave is a slave is a slave. Humans had in the past sought to assimilate all humans into one group – to breed out colour, destroy other cultures. Where they had failed the Toads had been successful.

He was still lost.

He could have already passed Jerramungup, or it could still be hundreds of miles away. It might not even exist, might not have ever existed. It could be north of him, south of him, there was no way for him to know. After many days, more than a month of walking, he lacked even the faintest idea. He needed directions, or a map. He had never read a map, never even seen one until the nun had shown him where his home was; they knew of maps in the settlement but the Toads never let the human slaves see one. Jacky knew from experience, and from logic, that it would be impossible to keep slaves if they knew the way home or maybe if they even knew where they were.

Despair polluted his every thought. Lacking his usual energy, lacking direction and impetus, he had slowed to a purposeless walk, almost stopped. He had seen humans with broken hearts, broken minds, in the Native camp near the settlement. They paced slowly and aimlessly, no energy, no direction. Jacky recognised the first signs of their soulless walk in his own.

Stopping through complete lack of impetus as much as for a rest, he leaned against an ancient gum tree, its bark rough and soft, almost padded, its foliage mysteriously the colour of Settler skin. A strange sound reached his ears – not something that belonged there under the trees, not an animal sound but still something he did not understand. Again it came, a scraping rustling sound, almost but not quite the sound of a small animal running for cover through the leaves.

'Water.' With a start he understood it – not a mysterious sound at all but a voice, a word, a single word in the Settler tongue. Again he heard it, then again, the third time in Jacky's own human language. Speech implied a speaker, unless he was going mad. He had seen it before on the farm – one of his people lost his mind, talking of the voices in his head. Talking to the voices in his head.

Unlike the other broken souls in the camp – those who paced and circled, eyes so closed it was hard to imagine how they didn't walk into things, those who just lay down to die – the madman was loud, would not shut up. The Settlers had killed him, mocking him as he ranted, mocking him, laughing at him, even as they shot him then claimed he had tried to escape. They drove him mad, then he was no use to them anymore.

If Jacky could find the voice it would mean he had not lost his mind. He searched, in no organised way, letting his eyes fall wherever his thoughts took them. It was some time before he found it, and even longer to work out what it was – all wrinkled skin, the colour of dead gum leaves. A mouth opened, twisted by the wrinkles; how could there be a mouth in that mass of wrinkled paper? How could it be a face when it looked like someone had screwed up a ball of correspondence and thrown it under a tree?

The mouth gaped red, in startling contrast to the pale white ruin of a face surrounding it. Red, white, red, white, it flashed, like the opening and closing of butterfly wings, like blood dripping into water.

He studied the thing before him, mouth now opening and closing with no more sound coming out, whatever it was lacked the strength to talk. It could be a Settler, dying from the heat and the dry as everyone said they did, soon to be nothing more than a squashed frog. He should leave it there to die, it certainly deserved a painful death, like most of its species it had taken his land, taken him from his home, taken his family. Jacky needed his water, needed it more, he believed, than a dying Toad. He turned to walk away, took one step into the sun and stopped. He needed directions, he needed a Settler to help him find his home. Here was a Settler in a rare position of disadvantage.

Water is heavy – a litre of water weighs a kilogram, the two litres humans need daily for survival is two kilograms, Toads need even more. Therefore Jacky didn't carry much of it, just his old crinkled plastic water bottle, fortunately, for the Toad, full. He had been walking all day, conserving his water, living on the sloshing mass in his stomach. The mouth before him was clicking open and closed, with a sound like someone turning the pages of a bible. Uncapping his precious water Jacky poured some into the dry, dust-red mouth.

The water disappeared into that flaking dry hole and he knew it would not be enough. He knew a Settler finding him on the verge of death would walk away, leaving him to die, not even taking the time to end his pain. Was he so concerned for this Toad because he had been trained to respect the Toads, to call them master, to be concerned for their wellbeing? Jacky hoped, instead, that it was a vestige of humanity, of human kindness. Carefully, knowing his actions might lead to his own death, he poured more water into the parched mouth.

Would he even have enough? It seemed pointless to pour so much life into someone who would die anyway; if there was not enough water to save the Toad they might both die. No matter, Jacky had little hope left anyway. He carefully poured water into the desiccated Settler until his precious water was gone.

With a rustle, with a rattle like the wind through scrub, the Toad tried to speak. 'Thank you,' was all he managed to say but it struck Jacky like lightning into his mind, his soul. Never before had he been thanked by a Settler.

In heavily accented Settler, Jacky spoke. 'Can you get up?' He successfully resisted the conditioned urge to call the Toad 'Master'. 'I don't have enough water for you, I have to find more.'

'My friends,' the Settler coughed – a sound loud enough to make Jacky jump – then he paused, then moaned, 'my friends are looking for water, I hope.' His voice was quiet, not much more than a hiss, 'They were looking for water.' It was such a struggle for him to speak that Jacky was filled with profound pity, a feeling he had only felt before for himself, and for the new children brought as slaves into the homestead. 'I don't have any more,' he said, 'I have to find some more. Don't know if I can, if your friends are not back, have not found some I dunno how I can.' Jacky had no idea why he was so worried, he simply was. Maybe it was the thanks, the gratitude he could not remember ever having received before. Now there was no way that he could leave the Settler to die.

'I will look.'

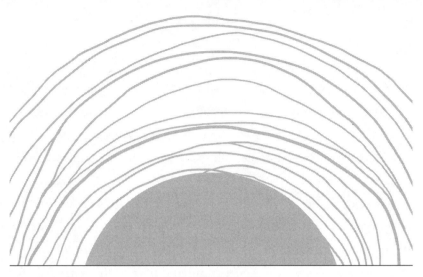

CHAPTER 14

Hundreds of years ago the empires of what was then called Europe were driven by a strong, some would say insatiable, desire to expand. Using their superior technology they invaded the land of peoples less technologically advanced than them. They did not always call it invasion yet that is exactly what it was.

Being armed with spears, with bows and arrows, having never invented firearms, sometimes having not even discovered metal-working, they were an easy target. These so-called primitive people had learnt to live in peace for the most part, and in harmony with their environments. Europeans colonised, they killed and destroyed, they enslaved. It took centuries for the majority of humans to abandon these habits, these traditions, of invasion and slavery, to realise that the people they had colonised had rights, that the people they had enslaved had something more to offer.

Now you Settlers have come with a vastly superior technology to colonise, to invade our world. We were just learning to live in harmony with our fellow man, most of us had learnt to hate war, slavery was abolished and discrimination was decreasing. We could not fight you, our technology was to yours what sticks were to guns in our past.

You came here, you conquered us like Europe conquered other countries, you are trying to exterminate us, to destroy our culture, just as Europe did to other countries long ago. We learnt the folly of our ways, we hope you do as well, before our unique human culture is destroyed.

We ask you, beg of you, that you learn to live in harmony with us as Europe once learnt to live in harmony with the rest of the world. We have something to offer you, if nothing else you can learn from our difference, as we can learn from you. It would be a tragedy for you, and for us, if you discovered there is or was something that we knew, something human culture could offer, after everyone who knew of it was dead.

Rather than thinking of what you can take, I beg you to consider what our two peoples can offer each other.

– VERITY JONES IN A SPEECH OUTSIDE COLONIAL ADMINISTRATION AT THE 75TH
ANNIVERSARY INVASION DAY PROTESTS.

ESPERANCE STOOD ALONE among the trees, listening to her favourite song – the complex warbling, the heartbreaking chorus of the magpies. She had heard that the magpies of the Australian continent were the only species of bird on the planet that did this: sung in chorus, in harmony, every bird in the flock, in the family, singing its part. She could not imagine living away from them, never hearing them again.

They are like us, she thought – interwoven, interdependent, the mob unable to survive as individuals. No matter where they had come from before, whatever culture or ancient human race they had been part of, Esperance's people were one mob, one people, now. For all intents and purposes they were all family.

They had to learn to sing in harmony like the magpies.

Like any family they had their fights, over little things mostly. They squabbled over the best morsels of food, fought over blankets and shelters, had fist fights over booze and drugs. Most disturbingly they argued over status and rank. You see that in all of nature, even the beloved magpies fought, not adverse to jumping on a family member and giving a good show of an attempt to peck them to death.

Grandfather was fond of telling them about families in the days, in the many years, before the Invasion. Families fought, he said, many times, sometimes unfriendly almost to the edge of hatred. Sometimes they went even further than that, past hatred to find a new supply of it when everyone thought it had run out. Yet when assaulted, or even just insulted, by outsiders, families had always turned their aggression outwards, defending each other, fighting the common foe. An external foe of one member of the family almost always became an enemy of everybody.

In an old book they had found there was a photo, faded and spotted with black mould, of a mob of large horned animals. They were being harangued by a mob of smaller animals like long-haired dogs; Grandfather called them wolves. The large herbivores were in a tight group, the larger ones turned towards their foes together, building a wall of flesh and horns to protect the young from the surrounding teeth.

He always said when their people fought among themselves that he hoped his family, his mob, would be like that.

Alone, momentarily at peace, bathing in the song of the magpie, Esperance checked the load in her handgun. Things had become far more dangerous of late and almost everybody was armed, although few were lucky enough to have a small light gun. Most of the rest of the mob were armed with knives, axes, improvised weapons – a bow here and there, spears made of aluminium pipe. Only a select, fortunate few had hunting rifles or shotguns. .

The gun in her hand was the pinnacle of human firearm technology, yet compared to Settler weapons it was as effective as bad language. When her meagre ammo inevitably ran out bad language was all she would have. Bad language and a knife.

Esperance had only one magazine of ammo, and that was in her gun. No spare, there wasn't any spare ammo to get. She checked, as she did every morning now the Settlers were on the warpath, that all was well, the gun was well maintained and loaded. Count your shots, she reminded herself, count your shots. This was essential. If they were overrun by the Settlers, by the Toads, the last shot was for her.

She hoped the decades hadn't deteriorated the ammo to the point it would not work.

There was a woman among them, her soul, her heart broken, so lost from herself she had barely any sense, any humanity left. Hiding among them, always ready to run, she lived in constant morbid fear that the Toads would get her, take her back. So scared was she, so damaged by her ordeal before escaping to the desert, to the camp, her screams were almost unbearable to those living around her. On those days they moved camp she did so gagged, so that her screams would not alert the searching Settlers. She lacked the impetus to move; when they moved they had to carry her.

Yet, no matter how much her screams endangered everybody else, not one soul in the camp ever considered abandoning her.

One of the hunters had found her, scratched and bleeding, unconscious and half-dead with hypothermia from the freezing desert night. She was so still he had almost tripped over her as he tracked a goat through the thorny scrub. She was so cold he had thought her dead.

Her name was Livia. They had pieced together her tale from the words between the screams, between the bouts of unconsciousness. It was a laborious task, to understand her story.

'They took me to a place of theirs, a prison, a hospital, a factory, I don't know what to call it,' she had said in a terrified flurry of words. 'I didn't even know what they called it; they never spoke to me, never spoke to any of us. There were hundreds of us in the same room, all women, all strapped to beds, all tied with our legs in stirrups, pulled apart like a woman having a baby in the olden days.

'They put babies in us, made us have babies, they didn't put them in us the normal way, like a man does it; they did it with machines. There was a needle in my arm, for injections; a machine would hiss and pour more something into my arm.

'I was there for I don't know how long, as soon as we had babies they would take them and put more babies in us. I don't even know how many babies I had, why do they need so many babies anyway?'

After that they knew why the Toads always took the women, especially the young women, the girls. There was one thing Esperance was sure of: she would not be taken to a baby factory. She had her suspicions, thought she knew why they needed babies. Her and her mob were intractable, uncontrollable, aggressive. Humans everywhere when left to grow free were hard to control – they thought and therefore they fought.

She had heard that even humans born in a settlement, born to slavery had a deplorable tendency towards small acts of pointless rebellion. Deplorable to the Settlers that is, amusing to the Natives. The Settlers wanted slaves: if they couldn't capture them and control them they would have to breed them.

They had started with the children. When they destroyed a camp, destroyed a town, they would always take the children, the younger the better. There were schools and camps somewhere, everywhere, where the children were trained into biddable slaves and servants. It could work if they could get children early enough, but where would they get enough small children?

Every year a child lived and grew free, lived not enslaved, would teach that child too much independence. As the human numbers had fallen, the free humans had begun to die off, it must have gotten harder to find children to train. Breeding humans must have been a solution or at least part of a solution to the problem of a lack of slaves.

Esperance had seen the children who came out of the baby factories. She had lain on a hillside staring at a Settler's homestead, watching her own people work for the aliens. Some of the children were as unreliable, as human, as you would expect. They were teenagers, or at least looked like teenagers, a bunch of them with all sorts of skin and hair colours – at least the Invasion had eliminated the racism between human groups that had existed before. She could not see what they were doing exactly but the furtive glances towards the house, the particular way they moved and stood, told her they were up to no good. She wanted to cheer them on.

Near them was a scattering of other children, clearly human there was nevertheless something different, even wrong, disturbing about them. There was a robotic, mechanical cast to their movements. Nothing they did was unnecessary to the task they were doing. If they were carrying something they carried it, they did not wander, they did not stop and stare, did not speak, did not drag their feet.

They were silent; not silent like the older, more normal-looking kids who giggled lightly while trying to be silent. Rather they were completely silent like they had nothing to say, no thoughts inspiring their mouths to move. What was more disturbing than that was their appearance: all the same age they seemed to have grown almost exactly the same amount; there were probably boys and girls although it was hard to tell as they looked about six years old.

Esperance had shuddered when she realised they were all almost identical. In the camps where humans were enslaved there was normally a mixture, a spectrum of skin colours from a pale pinkish cream right through to almost black. These were all-white kids: they were whiter than a natural white, their skin not even the transparent pink of white human skin; it had the colour of porcelain. Their hair too was white, like the bleached hair she had seen from time to time in ancient magazines; white and perfectly straight.

Profoundly disturbed, unsettled, even frightened, she had returned to camp.

When he heard Livia's story, Grandfather took Esperance to his hut and carefully unwrapped the oilcloth that had protected the pistol from damp and time. He taught her to use it, firing only dry, learning with an unloaded gun, as there was no ammunition to spare for training. He had told her to wait as long as possible to fire as she hadn't trained her aim, he told her to conceal the gun until she had to shoot so the enemy wouldn't know she had it. He told her to shoot point-blank, into the face of the enemy so she could not miss, or to hold it against the heart before pulling the trigger, if Toads had hearts. He had told her to save the last shot for herself, to run if she could, to always run if she could but if she couldn't, then it was best to die cleanly.

There were sick children in the camp, and after her brief time alone Esperance returned to nurse them as best she could. It was the water, most likely, because it was always the water or some disease the Settlers brought with them from whatever distant rock they arose from. Children had died the past few days, from a scouring diarrhoea that more often than not left its victim too weak to survive.

They had been as careful as they could be with the water but there was little they could do, all they had was another muddy hole in another parched bone-dry riverbed. If you were careful when you collected the water you could get it without too much mud but maybe whatever was killing the children was not even in the mud. It was in the water.

Tracks revealed the problem, or so she thought. In the sand around the camp strange tracks had appeared; she had no doubt they had been left by the soft, clawed feet of the Settlers' livestock. Nobody had seen the animal yet but there was obviously a stray, or more than one, sharing their water. Whatever it was had clearly fouled where it drank.

When the Settlers had first come they had brought many things, not least of which was diseases the Natives had never contacted. People, Esperance's people, most of the humans, had died in droves before the Settlers even got to them. It had not hurt the Invasion when millions died before you even had to kill them, when soldiers on the other side were too sick to fight.

A stray animal was extremely dangerous. Not only was it adding disease to their water that none of the children seemed capable of fighting, but Settlers valued their livestock and would no doubt be looking for the stray before long. The obvious solution presented itself: kill the damned thing and eat it, which would feed them for a while and remove the danger, unless the Settlers were looking for it, tracking it. If they had any tracking ability at all they could find it.

No choices were good. Taking the animal back to the settlement would work if they knew where the settlement was, and if they could return the animal without being caught, without being seen. Before they returned it they would have to catch it, which would not be easy. Killing it and eating it would still be better, but then they would have to move camp, the Settlers might track it to near their camp and then the whole camp would be at risk. The only advantage would be that they would be well fed when they moved on. They were going to have to move no matter what.

It was clear that the Settlers valued, even overvalued, their animals, more than they valued the lives of Natives. Many Natives had died, hunted down and executed for the crime of stealing livestock. If they didn't steal livestock what else was there to eat?

Esperance had been told, more than once so she believed it, that before the Settlers came the fertile land was all dedicated to growing food for humans, her own people. Then the Settlers came and brought their own crops, their own animals, slaughtering the Native animals and leaving them to rot, to make room for their own. Human, Native, earthling livestock had been killed to leave room for the Settler animals, and that left nothing to eat other than Settler animals.

Settlers called it stealing.

@

It was dry country, but there was always water to be found if Jacky could just work out where it was. Scratching and scraping through the scrub, moving with care but with as much speed as he could manage he headed downhill. Always before when he had found water it had been downhill: there might be a creek down there, or a waterhole, a billabong, there might be mud, a damp gully where he could dig.

If nothing else, there might be a puddle.

The scrub got thicker the further down the valley he scrambled, thorn trees and brambles catching on his clothes, adding their own lines to the history of catches, pulled threads and ragged tears. His skin was not spared – his clothes were not enough to protect him from the thorns and sharp sticks – and he was soon covered with a network of tiny cuts and scratches.

Further down he reached a thicket of alien vines. Brought to Earth by the Settlers, they had escaped the settlements and were crawling their relentless way up the rivers and creeks from the coasts. Deep-rooted and water-hungry, they sucked the land drier, filling their thick leathery leaves with precious water, leaving nothing for the other plants. Where they grew nothing else could, such was their insatiable desire for water and space.

There was fruit sometimes, on this vine, although it was normally in the middle of the thicket and protected with poisoned thorns. Jacky loved the vine fruit; of all the supplements to their meagre rations, all the foraged foods, they were his favourite.

There was also a good chance, Jacky knew, that there was water in the middle of that tangled poisonous mess. The vine could suck the land dry but it normally needed water to get established. He could see no easy way in, no simple way to tackle this problem; it was rare that he had ever found a way into the thickets uninjured.

He remembered well the last time he had been scratched by those thorns. He had lay thrashing in bed for two whole days, delirious with the pain of it. It would have taken his mind if it had gone on any longer, he could not bear it. When it ended, when he was barely strong enough to stand, the pain still there in the background of everything he did, weak from hunger and thirst, for there was nobody to nurse him, he was beaten for missing two days work.

There was nobody to treat his scratches if he got injured, nobody to drag him out of the thicket, he could die in there. He would have to be laboriously careful. Lying on his belly in the dust, the sand, the fallen leaves and the parched remains of native plants he looked through watering eyes for a way in.

As always there were fewer thorns low down in the old wood. If he could crawl flat enough on his belly, if he was slow, meticulous and careful, if he dug down into the mud and muck when he needed to, if he was lucky, he might make it into the gully the vine was strangling.

Or he might get poked, poisoned and trapped.

Hiding his sack in the leaves at the base of a tree he slipped his water bottle into the back of his shirt and took his kitchen knife in hand. It was not much of a weapon but it was sharp; he had scraped the edge against a handy stone only hours ago. He needed something to cut his way in and out if the vines got too thick. He needed some small protection against the inevitable snakes.

It was a dark and horrific crawl, on his stomach in the dark, dry, hot thicket. Sometimes there was not even room to crawl on his belly. Those times he pulled himself through gripping tightly to the vine trunks, using them like the rungs of a ladder. Other times there was not even room to do that much and he had to reverse, a task even harder than moving forward.

Little light filtered through the vines and it got darker and darker in there, until even acclimatised to the dark he could barely see. When finally there was no way further he sawed through the leathery, ropey plants by feel.

He felt the water rather than saw it, his hand squelching into mud where before there had been nothing but sand. He could smell the damp, a comforting smell in parched nostrils. There were vines in the puddle, all that remained of a creek. His hand could feel a tangled mat of roots and stalks leaving barely enough room to slip his water bottle into the filth.

Lying on his belly he drank, face in the water, not caring if the water was poisoned or diseased, knowing one bottle would not be enough, yet that was all he had. He drank until his belly was sloshing. It was purely by luck, in the complete darkness, that he placed his hand on the leathery skin of a vine fruit, fallen from the vine into the damp sand. He needed both hands and there was little chance of it surviving the crawl so he ate it there, relishing the sweet, tart, nutritious flesh.

The crawl out was just as difficult, just as slow, just as painful, and this time he had no water as a reward at the end of it. His mind nearly broke in the darkness; trapped beneath the deadly vines, he fought his way out on stubbornness.

He escaped and ran up the hillside yet night fell before he made it back to where he had left the Toad, who he had inexplicably saved. There was not enough light to see so he crawled into a hollow at the base of a tree and collapsed into a pained sleep.

As soon as sunlight glowed through his closed eyelids he moved again, not quite at a run. Worried for the man he had left there – although he did not know why – tired and hurrying, he was for a moment insufficiently paranoid. He stepped into the clearing to find himself staring down the barrel of an antique human–made rifle.

There were humans everywhere, five of them, all armed with rifles, shotguns, one even with a long rifle of plasticky ceramic. Worried for himself and for the Settler who could be dying, he froze, making no move for his pathetic weapon, knowing it would not be enough, knowing it would accelerate his death if he put his hand on it.

'There was a Toad here,' he spluttered, 'I need him, I need his help, is he still here?'

The humans stood silently, as if frozen, not lowering their weapons. For some reason they did not shoot. Where there were readable expressions they seemed mostly to be of puzzlement. Jacky could not fathom the situation, nothing about it made sense.

A gentlemanly drawl came from behind him, dropping into the silence like a stone into a muddy lake. 'Why would you care about a Toad, little man?' The voice was confident, almost arrogant. If it was a walk it would be a swagger.

'I need his help, I need to find my home and he might be able to help me.'

'He was helpless,' the voice snapped, 'you could have killed him and there would be one less pestilent Settler in the world. Actually, you could have just left him there to die, that would also mean one less Settler for little effort on your part. I just can't understand why you would not want one less Settler.' The mysterious voice was circling around past Jacky's left though he was too scared, too cautious to turn and look.

'Yes,' Jacky replied after what seemed like too short a moment's thought, 'he was helpless, I could've killed him easy, that was why I couldn't kill him.'

A Settler, dressed in a mix of human and Settler clothes, still showing the after-effects of his brush with death, stepped into view. His grey-green face had deep dry wrinkles, white like old scars, where the water had not quite penetrated his flesh, yet he was alive. 'That is what I thought,' the Settler said. He raised his hand and lowered it again. The humans around him lowered their guns.

'I am Johnny Star,' the Toad said, his wide mouth stretching in an attempt at a human smile, 'you saved my life.'

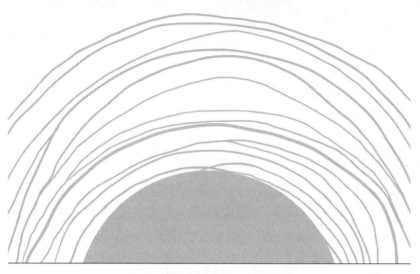

CHAPTER 15

When the British Empire spread across the world, when other empires from Europe fought them for space, they didn't just take with them their technology and their culture. Diseases the Natives had never contacted, and had no immunity or resistance to, hitchhiked with the invaders.

Europe had long been in contact with other continents; it was possible to travel overland across three continents, and this facilitated the spread of disease. Through deaths, through natural selection people developed immunity and resistance to that cocktail of germs. On other continents, long isolated from other people by wide seas, people developed who had not contacted these diseases of Europe, Asia and Africa. Whole communities, whole nations of previously strong people were destroyed by the introduction of these diseases.

When the invading forces from Britain made it into the interior of the country they later named Australia they sometimes found a country as empty as they could have wished. They also found abandoned camps and plenty of dead Aborigines. Their diseases, travelling at the speed of bad news, had beaten them to that first contact.

So it was when the Settler Empire arrived on the planet the locals called Earth. From aeons of contact with other planets the citizens of that empire had developed immunity to virulent, multi-species diseases that had spread across all known life in the galaxy. Humanity, isolated on one planet for their entire existence, had not developed that resistance. The toll of human lives was uncountable.

In the ancient human novel *War of the Worlds* by H. G. Wells, an alien invader from their nearest planet invaded Earth. The human defenders were all but defeated when human diseases, that humans had developed resistance to simply by surviving them, eliminated the threat by infecting the invaders. The reality here is vastly different. Compared to us, the Settlers who have an immune system trained by fighting galaxy-wide pandemics, the humans have a paltry resistance. That is why so many were eliminated by our diseases.

We could have colonised their planet without the aid of nature but we would have had to be more firm in our taking control.

– PROF. KALEK HUSS

GRANDFATHER WAS IN an unusual mood. This story, if Esperance had heard it before, was starting different.

'None of us wanted to admit it, shameful it was, but we were losing. The Toads had kicked us out of the city, killed most of us, routed the army, none of our weapons worked, we had no way to win a conventional war.' His eyes closed, face pained like the story itself was a wound. 'I don't know whether someone high up made the decision or just our captain, but the decision was made to disband the unit, give us all the choice – the chance to fight or run.'

'You were a soldier, Grandfather?' Esperance hated interrupting – the shock forced the words out before she could think.

'I was a soldier then, before we were beaten, but I was not beaten, not ever. You are never really beaten until you give up –' he paused then with a snort of laughter '– or die, I guess. Some of us – the stronger, the angrier, and those who had little to lose – we decided to keep fighting on. All the fancy weapons, the missiles and stuff, that stuff all didn't work right, the Toads could stop it all – all but guns.' There was a smile on his wrinkled face when he paused, one nobody in the camp had ever seen; not the smile of a tired old man but the smile of a younger man, a soldier, a predator. It was almost dangerous.

'Guns, knives, they still worked,' he continued, 'guns, knives, axes, spears, bows –' he laughed, though Esperance had no idea what was funny '– rocks and sharp sticks and human brains. That was all we had left to fight with against Toads with ray-guns, machines we could never have imagined and real bad attitudes. Me and six others, we took what we could carry and took off into the hills. If they were going to wipe us out we were going to cause them some hurt as they did so.

'Back then we called it guerrilla war.'

Esperance didn't want to lose this story, this thread that Grandfather had never traced, and neither did the crowd who were slowly gathering. 'What happened then, Grandfather?' Showing the strongest look of concentrated interest she could muster on her face she sat before him, cross-legged, and stared at his ancient face.

'Ch-shh-shh . . .' It was not so much a shush as it was an impatient exhalation. 'You don't want to listen to an old man, I'm even boring myself.'

Esperance leaned over and placed a patient hand on his shoulder. 'I would say you are not an old man, Grandfather, but then you would know I was lying. You are an old man, you are the oldest man here but that is why we want to listen. Age has given you wisdom, you have seen things I have only heard of. If you don't tell me your story, how will I know what happened?'

Grandfather reached out, without seeming to look, and took the mug of tea one of the men wordlessly handed him. Esperance looked over and nodded in thanks, glad someone had thought to give him tea rather than grog. Studying the ring of intent faces around him like he had never seen them before he nodded with what looked like resignation.

Sipping from the mug he continued. 'We didn't have much success, we killed a Toad or two, blew up a couple of their buildings, nothing much considering what we thought we were capable of, who we thought we were. They nearly caught up with us a couple times, both those times we lost someone: Robbo, when he stayed back to delay them while the rest of us ran like cowards; Andy, poor bastard, just wasn't fast enough.

'They aren't really warriors, the Toads. Given a chance and equal weapons we coulda wiped them out. They love a fight, that's for sure, but take away their guns and they are useless. I could kill a man, a Toad with a spoon; hell any of you could, no way a Toad could. It was like their technology had made them weak. They didn't need skills to survive – they were so advanced and in being advanced they were weak. Unfortunately we never had equal weapons, never had a chance.

'Most of the time that was what we tried to do – make the fight more equal, as equal as we could, catch them unarmed or steal their guns. A couple times, a few times, we succeeded at the first, caught them unprepared and took them down hand-to-hand, knives, spears even sticks and clubs. Catch them unarmed and alone and you can kill them caveman style . . .' At that a sound like a strangled giggle escaped his throat but didn't reach his lips. 'Only twice did we manage the second, manage to steal their guns.

'When I first fired that gun of theirs – you just squeeze this handle and it fires – I knew why we were losing. One squeeze and a tank disappears – one of our tanks, not theirs, they have shielding on theirs. That handgun of theirs I got, smaller than a cellphone, smaller than a walkie-talkie, could do more damage than an anti-tank rocket. They have other guns the size of an anti-tank rocket. I hate to even imagine what they could do.' He paused in thought and once again, for a moment, had the expressions and manner of a much younger man. 'I would love to get me one of those.

'The other weapon of theirs, it was, dunno, about the size of a rifle. I never fired that one but Dave did, and it took down one of their fliers – "thwap" and it was falling from the sky. Only other times I saw one of them go down it was in a dogfight with at least six of our planes. Sure, we can out-fly them but their fliers are armoured like a tank and armed like a battleship.

'We fought our way across the country, fought and hid and ran. We were tired of the war and wanted to get back to our families, those of us who had families . . . we were trying to get home, see if there was anything left of it. Those who didn't have anybody, well they came anyway. Everyone we knew of was in Perth. The city had fallen but everyone was probably alive and enslaved. We would free our families and head to the deep desert where the Toads couldn't live. We couldn't hide there forever but we might be able to for a bit.

'Maybe we could die of old age before they caught up with us.

'Crossing a ridge, carefully between some trees, we saw lights, a scattering, not many, but more than we would have expected in the middle of nowhere. There is a difference between the lights humans like and what the Toads like. When we still had electricity we made lights slightly yellow, like a candle, or a little bit cool blue. The Toads – they like their light a watery blue-green, maybe the light where they come from is like that, who knows. Anyway we were crossing this ridge and there were so many lights below us, like the land was a mirror reflecting the sky and they were the colour of human lights.'

Despite his being obviously tired from the telling, the story seemed to be taking decades off Grandfather's age. 'There was no real way to tell for sure what the lights were, so we were real careful going down the slope, real careful. It was an old camp area, old rest spot on the highway – our highway, not the canals the Toads build. Stupid Toads even build canals here where there is not even enough water to drink. There must have been a couple of hundred of them – caravans, motorhomes, families sleeping in cars, even a few tents, shelters made of tarps. Refugees camped. They must have got out of the city any way they could – a great moving village, heading inland where the Toads didn't go.

'We must have scared them half to death. Dirty, ragged from sleeping under trees, in ditches, we were armed, that must have scared them a bit. None of them would listen – I told them to kill their lights, douse their campfires, told them that the Toads might not be able to live there, they could still overfly it. They thought they were safe.

'Or they didn't want to think how unsafe they were.

'I lost two more of the guys getting out of there when the fliers strafed the camp. I still remember the screams, the guns like eighties synthesiser music. Dave copped it when his Toad rifle failed – probably out of ammo – as a flier flashed towards him. Smitty, well he was just unlucky, caught some shrapnel from an exploding motorhome – it went up like a bomb . . . they had fuel and a couple of gas bottles I guess.' Tears were pouring down his cheeks, unregarded, even unnoticed. 'The other two guys copped it trying to get back into the city. I could run faster and I was lucky I guess, I was lucky a lot I reckon.'

Looking Esperance straight in the eye he continued, 'I got your grandmother out; your auntie, your grandmother's sister – well, she didn't make it. I couldn't save your mother's brothers and sister, they were so little – the Toads had already taken them. Your grandmother was pregnant with your mother. I couldn't save her, not out here.

'I'm so sorry, she died giving birth to your mother. Now you are all I have.'

Esperance was so shocked by the unnecessary apology that Grandfather disappeared into the scrub before she could stop him. He had nothing to apologise for. A better woodsman than her, even at his age, she could not find him.

Sister Bagra was only pretending to read. Although she stared intently at her plaque computer, although she made the thumb movements that one would make to turn pages, she was not reading. Secretly, illegally, she had installed the software on her plaque that gave her almost complete control over the security cameras in the mission buildings.

She was using her plaque to watch Mel.

It was hard work, this secret investigation, watching one of her nuns while ensuring none of them became aware she was doing it, while covering her tracks so nobody in authority would find out. Briefly she contemplated asking someone else to help, finding someone she was more sure was loyal and getting them to assist watching, but in the end she rejected that thought. How could she be certain that whoever she asked was not part of it? There was also the chance that seeing Bagra act paranoid, or seem to act paranoid might stop whoever she asked from trusting her.

Right now she could only really trust herself.

The worst thing about this all was that she could find no proof. The damned girl did nothing on camera that could be regarded as treachery, nothing Bagra could complain about. Bagra stared and stared at the camera feed on her plaque. She spent so long watching, and the silly girl did not even send out any correspondence, not even the inevitable letters home to family that girls like her could not resist.

She was kinder to the Native children than any of the others were, but that was no proof. She could be nothing more than a soft-hearted fool.

It was suspicious, this kindness. Surely someone that soft-hearted would be tempted to complain of cruelty to the Natives.

It had been a highly illegal hack, and entirely unethical, but Bagra had been in the email system reading Mel's mail. Or she would have been reading Mel's mail if there had been any. There was nothing, no communication at all. Bagra didn't know what had alerted the girl to the possibility of an internal investigation, but someone had. She was clearly keeping her head down.

Bagra had been forced to inform the other sisters, all of them, of the upcoming official investigation. If she had not, she could be certain that they would be furious, suspicious when the inspector came. Her chances of passing the inspection without any complaints were minimal if the other nuns believed she had hidden the note.

So Bagra had told them, told them all at once, first thing the morning after she caught them hiding the escape attempt. She had hoped that Mel, who must have been tired that morning, would have her guard down. When she heard, it would show something on her face. You would have expected triumph at her success, or guilt if her complaints had gone further than expected, or fear if she thought she would get caught. There might have been something, but it was almost invisible. The girl had clearly steeled herself for this information when it came. Bagra simply couldn't prove even to her own satisfaction that Mel had done it.

Feigning illness, Bagra spent days upon days in her cell. It was possible, if she was careful, to face her plaque in such a way that what was on the screen would not show on the security camera that was in her room. There was no way to tamper with the permanent record kept of the camera footage so it was best to leave no footage in the first place. It would not do to leave any record of her illegal hacks of the surveillance.

Finally, there was what she had been waiting for: all the nuns, but her, were out working in the mission, in the schoolrooms, outside among the children. She was alone in the building. Quickly she tapped a command into her plaque. Nothing happened that she could see but she hoped the hack she had cajoled, then finally bribed, out of a security department technician had switched off cameras in the entire building for half an hour. He told her it would and the gap in the footage would look, to any investigators, like nothing but a computer glitch. She waited a few moments before moving just in case the hack did not work immediately. Gliding silently down the hallway of cells she made it quickly to the door behind which the girl Mel lived. There was no lock – nobody believed there was any reason for a lock on the door of a nun's cell – so she walked straight in.

All the rooms were the same: a bed with a simple coverlet, and a dresser that contained all the nun's personal belongings. Bagra started there. The guilt she felt riffling through another's personal space was useless to her – she ignored it. In the dresser she found nothing with which to condemn Mel, no evidence that it was her who had contacted home.

The contents of the drawers were completely acceptable, completely conventional. Nothing, even, that the most conservative sister would find unacceptable. She appeared to have accepted the doctrine of simplicity, the vow of poverty completely. There was nothing there to suggest she had any life outside of the Order.

If it was not for her soft heart, for the fact that her soft heart led to her betraying her sisters, contacting home with those accusations, Bagra might have thought her a fitting protégé.

Bagra slipped her hand under the mattress – nothing; then bent down to look under the simple bed – nothing there either. The evidence she needed must be in the girl's plaque, where Bagra would never get it. The privacy of plaques was sacrosanct; they were also almost impossible to hack. Checking she had left no evidence of her violation of the room, she slipped out and closed the door carefully.

There was very little time left. She walked swiftly – but with due decorum just in case someone came in – to her cell, and closed the door. The timer on her plaque said she had returned early enough. If the tech who had given her that hack could be trusted – and she would condemn him to unimaginable·torment in the afterlife if he could not – she had not been recorded on camera. Sighing she lay back on her hard bed staring, again, into her plaque as if reading.

There was nobody else in the building. Maybe just for something different she should actually read. She would find the evidence she needed soon, she was sure of it – the girl would make a mistake.

The book she was reading, a study of the Native, was satisfyingly ridiculous. People who had never worked with the creatures had no clue what they were like, some of them even believed the Native intelligent. She was glad she had taken the moment to download the book from the library. She knew the authors intended it as a serious essay but to her it was the most delightful of comedies. She needed a good laugh. She was still reading the book many hours later when the others returned and collected her for the evening meal.

©

They moved fast – Jacky, Johnny and his gang – though not without care, care verging on paranoia, driven by fear stronger than their urgency. Nobody had any idea where Jerramungup was, nobody had even heard of the place, except for Jacky who had no more information than just the name, a name that to him had reached mythical proportions.

'I wish you would shut the bloody hell up about bloody Jerramungup,' laughed Johnny Star after another tedious monologue from Jacky. This was not sufficient to shut him up.

'My parents will be there, that is why I want to go. I have not seen them for so long, I can't even remember them, not really but I am sure they remember me.' Jacky sighed to the heartfelt moans of everybody else. 'I was taken from there and they would be waiting there for me to come back.'

'It is nothing but a name,' inserted a frustrated Johnny Star. 'If it ever existed it might not anymore. It is like El Dorado, the golden city from human myth, or Shangri-la,' he paused, 'or whatever it was called.'

'It must be there, I came from there, I had to come from somewhere, it must be there . . .' There was an almost magical, solemn tone to Jacky's voice, as if he was reciting a religious litany, as if the existence of Jerramungup was the thread by which his sanity was hanging.

'I am Johnny, who came from the stars, who wants to return there,' Johnny mused, appearing momentarily even more thoughtful than normal, 'who can never return. They call me Star, because that is where I belong.'

He laughed then. 'You must be Jacky Jerramungup.'

The whole group laughed. Jacky was surprised but he was not offended. After a moment of red-faced silence his laugh rang out with the others.

'If we cannot get me home, and I assure you we cannot, maybe we can get you home.'

'How? Nobody seems to know where Jerramungup is.'

'Simple,' Johnny said, in a tone that said things would be anything but simple, 'we need a map.'

The news arrived when they were just leaving a small shabby inn in the tiny town – barely a dot on a map – of Bloodwood. Jacky had been seen raiding a homestead with Johnny Star's gang – news that could almost have been calculated to annoy the hell out of Sergeant Rohan. However, the Native who had brought the information, who was still breathless from the run, was still surprised when Rohan pulled a gun on her. Backing away carefully, as one does from a dangerous snake, she got far enough away to feel safe enough to turn and flee.

It would have given Rohan some small satisfaction to pull the trigger, and there was no clue on his face why he did not. He simply shrugged and slipped his gun away. Jumping onto his mount he didn't even bother to look if his deputies had joined him. They followed him as he rode off too fast in the direction the Native messenger had come from.

That damned Native was becoming a thorn in Rohan's side, was already a thorn in his side, a thorn being pushed deeper. He could only imagine what the Settler Administration thought of it, thought of him because of it. It had become a matter of pride, his pride and that of his race. Native servants cannot be allowed to run away. Any who succeeded would tell others it was possible. He had to catch that annoying little turd before more damage was done both to the Settlers' peace and Rohan's career.

Johnny Star, what a bastard. Adding him to the equation had just made Rohan's job a hell of a lot harder, while also making it more urgent. That traitor was even worse than a Native; he had Settler skills, Settler knowledge, Settler intelligence and a deplorable tendency to teach those skills to the Natives in his gang. Jacky was already cunning and hard to find. Now with the addition of Star he would be hard to find and also hard to catch. Rohan would now have to be extra cautious. He was in no position, with only four useless deputies, to take on the Star gang.

His mount looked so much like a long-legged crocodile, a Native animal, that many less educated Settlers saw the Native reptiles as proof Settlers had been to this stupid planet before, that they somehow belonged here. If they had visited here before, there was no other evidence of it. Crocodiles were fast, but the Settler mount was faster – its long legs giving it a half-sinuous, half-loping run. It also had better stamina than a crocodile, able to move at speed for hours.

Unlike a crocodile it was a herbivore, luckily, for finding meat for such a large animal would be crippling – pretty much impossible – on a mission like this. He had seen horses on this planet, even ridden one just to prove he could. His mount was faster and stronger, yet a horse felt like riding a table, it was so easy to ride.

There was no reason to look behind, so he didn't. Either his deputies were following or they were not, he had long ago ceased to care about that. Then again, there was little chance they would not follow – they needed direction or they would be lost, literally, since he had the only map. It had been hard enough to replace the stolen one. They had better follow. Even with them he was now outnumbered by the Star gang.

The trail wound wildly, ripping a jagged path through the trees. Nobody could really steer at speed through that place. If not for the intelligence of his mount he would have fallen, would have crashed off the path; he let his mount find its own path. That was why the animals were used rather than a mechanical conveyance.

Mounts were also better on dry land than anything other than a flier. Being a species that had evolved in a swamp from a swamp creature, there had been no need to develop the wheel. All their transportation at home had been aquatic before the invention of the flier. They were an intelligent race, so they had quickly absorbed the human technology of wheels and wheeled vehicles, improving on them soon after the Invasion. However, they were still not of any use on bad or non-existent roads. The mounts were perfect for this sort of terrain.

There was a strangled yelp behind him, a rustling, a thud, as one of his deputies, less experienced a rider, fell or was thrown from his mount. Rohan was too enraged, too engaged in his own world to care, to even notice. The young men were fending for themselves, helping each other. He was entranced, unaware of how long the ride was when he reached the farmhouse, when he was greeted by the farmer's wife.

She was tall, even for a Settler; her waxy grey-green skin stretched over a frail, probably malnourished, frame. Her clothes were even wetter than normal – she was sweating mucus as their kind did when distressed. Rohan had no time for that, no time for compassion.

'I am Sergeant Rohan,' he spat in her direction, 'what happened here?'

She started crying. This was not the sympathetic help she had been hoping for. 'One of them,' she cried, almost screamed, 'was one of us.'

'Yes,' Rohan's tone warned against wasting his time, 'that would be Johnny Star, the criminal, the traitor. I was told he was here so I presume you or someone else here identified him. We will apprehend the entire gang, but only if you help. What happened?'

'They came in the night, we were asleep, my husband and I, then they came. The traitor, the one you call Star, had a plasma rifle.' The Settler's voice was breathless with fear. 'We don't have guns here, except what we need for farming. They didn't even bother to tie us up. They knew we couldn't stop them taking what they wanted. One of the Natives had a plasma rifle too, a plasma rifle. I was so scared.'

'What did you do, what did your husband do about it?' Rohan fought hard, but failed to keep the contempt from his voice. He knew there was probably something they could have done to stop Star; they could have tried.

'We did nothing, we are just farmers,' the snap of her teeth audible as she bit off the words, 'he had a plasma rifle.' Anger had made her stupid, or she had found a clearing full of courage in the middle of her fear. 'I already told you that, can't you pay attention?'

Rohan was an overheating boiler, close to explosion, or at least that is what he sounded like, even to himself. 'And where is your husband?'

'He has gone to raise a posse. We cannot let the filthy Natives, or that outlaw you call Star, get away with it. They were armed!'

She sounded smug, where before she had sounded scared. 'The posse will come back with guns, and they will do the job you should have been doing. They will kill every Native they see until they find the right ones.'

Rohan agreed it was a good plan but he would get in significant trouble if he allowed vigilante action to go unchecked and unreported. 'You are aware that I would have to report any illegal posse to the authorities? As far as I am concerned any posse is illegal. Your husband could be up on charges. I will report him myself if you continue to annoy me.

'So could you, you could be charged, actually, as accessory to his crime.

'You could, of course, request permission for a posse to cut down Native numbers on your property, but you cannot and will not get permission to hunt down Johnny Star. If you hunt Natives without a permit – a permit I cannot tender, I might add – you will be breaking the law.'

He wanted to tell her that the important thing was not to refrain from hunting the Natives, the important thing was to not get caught hunting the Natives, but he couldn't tell her that in case it got back to the department. Not for the first time he wished that he had no notion of what was going on. Now he had to report it, and he didn't want to.

@

Grark was not even remotely happy to be in the colonies, not anymore. At first it had been an adventure, an experience, but that soon paled as he discovered more and more abuse and immorality he would have to report. There was cruelty and slavery everywhere, in every corner of the colony; almost every Settler was involved from the lowest worker who had a slave he called an apprentice right up to the highest level of government where they turned a blind eye to these abuses.

The entire system would collapse, the colony would cease to operate, they would all have to go home if slavery ceased tomorrow. Not if it was outlawed – it was already illegal. The disaster would occur if somebody enforced the law. Not only were his people, on the planet the Natives called 'Earth', becoming increasingly arrogant, decadent and lazy, but were, from the moment they landed there, biologically unsuited to the planet. There was not a task they could perform without slaves. Actually, that was untrue – they could do anything but it would require more work, technology and money than simply using the Natives.

They tortured and enslaved, they seemed to have no limit to the cruelty they would use to keep their slaves under control. They stole children – that to him was the worst crime. Everybody was guilty, even those not directly involved, for they allowed it to happen, they absorbed the wealth that the system brought. The entire colony was culpable.

He had written report after report to send home, and sent none of them. He doubted now anything would be done about the criminal abuse and slavery of the Natives. The Church was powerful but he doubted they were powerful enough to make the necessary changes, such as enforcing the ban on slavery, that would destroy a colony completely. For all his reputation for temper he was a kind man, so he would rather give them the benefit of his doubts.

What he discovered, what was in his latest report was so inflammatory, so condemning, he was sending it that very day. His tolerance for the people of this planet had finally expired. The people in the colony seemed to believe the Natives to be completely unintelligent, nothing more than animals. Therefore, they were proud when they took Grark on a tour of a certain facility.

It took him some time to understand it. It looked from the outside like a factory, an industrial meat farm maybe, but there was nothing particularly impressive about the place. It was when he got inside that he had difficulty controlling his disgust and subsequent anger. Only years of experience enabled him to keep his face, his voice, expressionless.

There, where he expected to find a factory farm, or something similar, he saw lines and lines of beds with pregnant humans strapped to them. 'We breed them here,' the proud Director said, 'using the latest animal husbandry, the latest genetic engineering techniques.'

'Interesting,' Grark replied, just enough to let the woman know he was listening.

'Unlike us, who sensibly deposit eggs in pools to grow, these Natives grow their eggs on the inside. Therefore we must remove them surgically.

'You can see there,' she pointed, 'the zippered aperture . . . well, it's not really a zipper, it's more complicated than that. It took a lot of research to create a suture we can easily open and close, but we all call them "zippers". We have added the zippers through which we remove the eggs from the ovaries. This is a new feature; we perfected it only a couple of months ago. Before that we had to remove the ovaries completely and keep them in culture.

'It is surprising to the uninitiated when they learn how hard it is to keep organs alive in culture; it is easier to keep the ovaries in and let the Native grow the eggs for us.'

Grark nodded, hoping this would be enough to satisfy her. He could not speak. If he opened his mouth he might say what he really thought. If he opened his mouth he might vomit.

Meanwhile he walked around the Native on the bed, one of hundreds in that room alone, strapped down, connected to wires and tubes. Feigning interest in the medical modifications that had been done he instead took the chance of looking the human in the eye. There it was – almost hidden behind the haze of tranquillizers – the same spark of intelligence he had found in the eyes of every human he had seen.

There, also, was madness. Her mind had been broken by the immobility, the being treated as an object. If she had not been dazed by drugs she would be screaming. This confirmed his suspicion: the Natives have minds, intelligence, you can't break a mind that isn't there. He had to somehow end this breeding program even if he could not end slavery here altogether.

'You might have noticed the Natives are immobile. We had a couple of escapes in the recent past,' the Director continued, 'so we have increased the tranquillizers and developed a paralytic. They can no longer move while we feed them the drugs through the veins. There have been no escapes since the new drug regime.'

Grark nodded again, feigning agreement in action because he still could not trust his mouth. He composed himself. He was an Investigator of the First Church, he should have more control than this. He had seen horrors before, he had felt sick from them before. Steeling himself he managed to speak.

'This one,' he pointed to the human woman tied down before him, 'is it . . . pregnant? Is that the right word?'

'No, this one gave birth only four local months ago. We have had less than satisfactory results when they are not allowed to rest for at least six local months. In the wild they go longer – they do after all suckle their babies from glands that produce a substance they call "milk".

'We, of course, modify the fertilised egg,' the Director continued, 'taking out a code here and there, adding a couple we devised, all very technical. We have almost completely domesticated the species. When we breed them and then train them right they are obedient enough. We try to keep most of the characteristics we find useful – the ability to survive with less water than us, and the animal intelligence that makes them such useful servants. That has been the hardest work – removing the tendency to rebellion while leaving enough intelligence to make them useful.'

The Director led Grark through the rooms where the embryos were implanted, which looked like a cross between a hospital and a computer factory. The storage bank where the modified embryos were stored was nothing more than a long line of freezers.

'Do you fertilise, is that the right word, and modify the eggs here?' Grark was curious how large this operation was, how many people were involved.

'No, sadly, the equipment needed for that is too expensive for every farm to have so it has been centralised. It adds the inconvenience of transporting the live eggs to the technicians, and transporting the completed embryos back, but unless more money is found we cannot change the way things are.'

Grark knew the Director was continuing but he was too deep in thought for the words to penetrate. Training and experience kept his mouth flapping and his head nodding just enough to make the woman think he was still listening. Instead his mind was racing: this was larger, more immoral, more pervasive, than he could have imagined.

How many of these places must there be to require a centralised genetic modification facility? He could no longer delay reporting to the Church, to Colonial Administration. This was worse than any of them could imagine.

It was only when he prepared to send his report, and with it a request for more orders, that he was reminded of the worst inconvenience of working in the colonies. Electronic communication works perfectly well within the colony – at least in the cities it does. However, nobody had yet devised a way to send messages faster than light, so all mail between planets was carried on ships.

Out here, the furthest colony from home, mail took many weeks to arrive. He would send his report and it would be weeks before anyone at home saw it, if it arrived at all – ships sometimes got lost on the way home. Once it arrived it would be more weeks while the contents were debated, then weeks again until he received further orders also by mail.

He would be lucky to hear a response, receive extra orders in less than six local months.

There was nothing for it, he had to send it anyway. Printing out several copies of his report and carefully signing each one, he sealed them in Church business diplomatic envelopes that explode – destroying the contents and normally the hand holding them – if they are not opened by the correctly authorised hands. Three were addressed to his superiors in the Church, the other three to his contact in Colonial Administration.

Following standard procedure for one in his position they were dispatched on three different ships home: one from where he was, the other two went by speedy courier to other star ports to be sent. It seemed unlikely they would lose three ships at once when all three were on different routes.

There was nothing to do but wait. Nothing that is except investigate the school in the outback that was his official, but really a cover, mission on this planet.

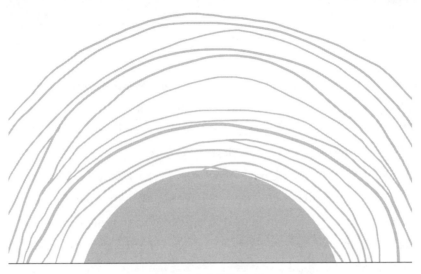

CHAPTER 16

For too long we have seen the Native as either a hindrance or a cheap, if somewhat unreliable, source of untrained labour. Their technology was primitive, they lack our education, they are provincial and naive, having never seen someone from elsewhere, having barely left their planet. They had never even sent anything more advanced than an unmanned drone out past the moon of their own tiny planet.

Being technologically more advanced than them, we have always assumed they must be stupid; after all, we build FTL drives, we invented the plasma cannon, we use fusion generators. It has taken us too long to realise they are not stupid, they are not primitive animals.

Until we came here we had never heard of the thing that humans call 'Art' – forms of creative decoration, forms of expression that our culture has never produced. Humans have made Art, it seems, for as long as they have been humans, if not for longer. Humans have been producing Art since before we started talking. Using Art they can say things we have not ever learnt how to say.

Now, having consolidated our control of this planet, having enslaved its people completely, we have time to better examine this place, this planet, this culture we have taken over. It has taken us too long to understand this Art thing that humans create; we are only now, decades after the colonisation, learning to appreciate it.

We are searching for Art and discovering, too late, that the works of Art we destroyed when we destroyed museums and galleries were the greatest treasure we have ever found in the galaxy. We want more Art, yet we have discovered that we have mostly destroyed the vibrant human culture that created it, that nurtured it, that made it possible. Years on and we are desperate to salvage what fragments of human Art are left. The 'junk' we destroyed, that humans guarded with their very lives, was an irreplaceable treasure. From what we discovered, from the scraps we can find, we destroyed a lot.

What Art we have collected has been taken by ship back home, there to be kept safe in universities and museums. What Art we have salvaged has amazed and astounded, delighted and enlivened the people back home. What's more, our collection is the envy of all the other planets in the Home Sector of space.

Now we want more, Art is potentially the most valuable commodity this planet can produce, and we can get more. Although the cultures that created the most profound of the Art we lost are also gone, the human tendency to produce Art still exists. Children when left alone, when they have a moment without something important to do, will 'doodle' to use a human word, will scribble small fragments of Art on whatever surface they have with whatever medium they have available. If there is nothing else, not even a rock and a piece of blackened wood, they will draw on the sand with their fingers. Seemingly the human tendency to produce Art is innate and cannot be eliminated, even if we now wanted to.

I call upon the Colonial Administration for help. Humans who know about Art, humans who remember any culture at all, must be found. Native children who draw, who 'doodle' must be collected. We must bring these humans together and give them nothing to do, no task other than to produce the Art that is, as far as we know, the unique talent of the humans.

– JULAS SALIS, CHIEF EXECUTIVE OFFICER, LOUVRE ART CENTRE AND GALLERY, PARIS

JOHNNY STAR SET a punishing pace as they raced south-east towards Jerramungup, and away from the inevitable pursuit. As they had hoped, the homestead they had raided had a map, something they had not bothered to look for before Jacky came. What use was a map when it didn't matter where you were going? Johnny had used one many times so he controlled it, he consulted it regularly – an electronic device smaller than his palm that projected a hologram of the terrain around them.

He knew that humans once had paper maps – strange 2D representations of the land. He had seen them, had confiscated them from human rebels in his old life. He had once even seen in a museum a device humans called a GPS. It was small and plastic, and he had heard that when it was working it was a lot like a map, although surely the small 2D screen it displayed on would not compare favourably to a Holo.

Rising as the sun peeked over the horizon they walked towards it, keeping away from the Settler roads, deep calm canals cut through the forest, through hills, caring not what damage they did. Settler roads, crossroads, beacons, were used as navigation aids, and the map made navigation easy. Whenever they could do it while invisible in the scrub they watched the road; how better to see if Settlers suddenly entered the area, suddenly got too close.

With caution again bordering on the paranoid, they even avoided what was left of the ancient Native roads – ribbons of hard black stones held together with solidified petroleum. Johnny marvelled at the effective, efficient use of low-technology materials – a perfect road for wheeled vehicles. The petroleum base, a bi-product of fuel production, gave the roads a flexibility and durability that was frankly astounding. If he needed more proof that the humans were more intelligent than other Toads believed them to be, here it was.

Now the roads were cracked and potholed by the ages, cut through in places by the Settler canals that disregarded the Native roads when they did not follow them. The Settlers often utilised the already cleared ground, using the cuttings through hills the humans had made long ago.

Surely they were still pursued; Jacky was wanted for absconding, at least, and the Settlers must have identified Star's gang when they stole the map. The Troopers would be coming. Their best hope was that the Troopers didn't know where they were going, if they did then they would take fliers and get there first. Nobody complained, although you could tell from their laboured breathing by the middle of the day that they were suffering. How could they talk about the heat and the dry, about their discomfort, when Johnny, less adapted than them, suffering more than they were, did not whine?

The landscape dried out as they walked east, the trees first getting taller, more impressive. Breaking eventually out of the tall-tree country they found a more open area, drier, grasslands with scatterings of trees. The trees were young, they might have not been there when the Settlers took the planet.

'There were over six billion, maybe even seven billion Natives, humans,' Johnny quickly corrected himself, 'when we arrived here, and all this land looked empty then,' he mused. They walked a bit longer in silence. 'I think these fields were used to grow grain, for humans to eat, or maybe it was grassland for those animals you called sheep.

'I saw a sheep in the zoo back home. There are still some out here in the wild I have heard. Not the woolly ones – they can't live unless someone trims their wool and the humans are not caring for them anymore, we won't let them; but there were other sheep – they shed their wool, they might have survived. Them and things called "goats", which are like them but tougher. If there are any human farm animals still running wild it would be goats, I think. There are other human animals that survive out okay on their own; they are apparently still out there. I wonder if we will see one.'

'Why did you even come here?' Jacky sounded like he was struggling to articulate his thoughts. 'You don't belong here, you have another world, one that is yours.' Johnny turned to look at Jacky and stopped, the young human's face was writhing with thoughts and emotions he could not begin to articulate.

'Other worlds actually, although this one was the least well-suited we have colonised. It's too dry, the whole planet is too dry, this continent is even drier, this continent is as dry as bone.'

'Then leave,' Jacky snarled, 'leave and let us have our planet, leave and take your animals with you, take it all with you. Go home and let us have our home.'

'I would love to go home.' Johnny's tone was strange, he tried to show Jacky with his eyes how he felt and saw nothing but anger and confusion on the human's face. 'They will not let me go home, they will kill me if they catch me, that is one way of being rid of me I guess. Besides, if I go home it won't help, I can't make them all come with me.'

A silence descended that everyone was scared to break, the tension threatening to tear them apart. Johnny felt like the whole gang was made of tissue, of spider's web. What was it that was keeping them together? They knew from the map that Jerramungup was not far. Jacky started to walk like the drive to move was all he had left, like he was walking a race where the prize was survival, forcing the others to almost run to keep up, unable to contain his excitement, unaware he was almost running. Tucker admonished him for running several times and then gave it up as pointless. After that the gang just matched his punishing speed.

Entering a cool dark thicket of trees, tall and straight, narrow trunked, the undergrowth wild and dangerous, they slowed. Johnny Star stood for a moment, relaxed in the cool shade as he could never do in the hot, dry grasslands. His stance, his walk, felt subtly yet recognisably hopeful, he even felt hopeful. Maybe he would finally be able to do something useful, something right, in the pathetic, selfish, pointless shadow of a life he had been living. Maybe he could do something other than just survive.

'I can't go home,' Johnny mused to his friends, 'and I don't even have to, if I could get passage on a ship. There are other worlds. I could try and find a way onto a ship, go to one of our other planets, or even to another empire. There are other people nothing like us, they have planets too.' A cool breeze flowed over Johnny's skin bringing memories of home. 'We would never let them come here, the other species, even the ones we have conquered, even the ones in our Empire, even when we lie to them and tell them they are equal citizens. This planet is for us, for the Toads.' He did not see the filthy look Crow Joe threw in his direction.

'Ah, what's the point, I don't want to go to another world, another empire. I want to go home and I can't. I may as well die here where I have friends, looking after my friends is all I have left.'

Returning Jacky to his home, to his family, might not quite make up for all the evil Johnny had done, all the evil his people had done and were doing, but it would be better than nothing. He hoped it would be better than nothing.

@

Reaching the daylight at the edge of the trees they stopped, cautious, curious, staring out onto an old human road, a distant town. It did not look promising; weedy trees, clumping grasses, strangling vines grew among damaged buildings. The gang just stood there and stared, a bleak hopeless look on Jacky's face. Johnny recognised the look, he'd seen other faces wear it; what the face wears when the soul behind it has lost everything, even hope.

Nothing like a family could live there, in that emptiness. It was as bleak as Jacky's experience, as his life. Surely this was a home for rats, for rats and ghosts – even dogs would desert this place. They could not even see a sign of a Native camp; if anyone lived there they were well hidden. There was no noise from the tiny knot of men, no noise from the ruin before them as Jacky fell to his knees.

He only stirred when the wind changed, blowing the faintest whiff of old smoke into his nostrils. Jacky followed the scent like a questing dog. All the others, all but Johnny, reacted like they could smell it too. They slowed, holding back so Jacky, frantic as a moth batting itself to death against a light, could find whatever, whoever it was first. He dashed this way and that, down cracked roads and weedy paths, through dead buildings and around rusted hulks of cars. Pebbles and ground glass crunched underfoot as he ran, then small stones scattered like a scared school of tiny fish when he suddenly came to a halt.

The man was wiry and old, dressed in rags, seated with his back to Jacky, hunched almost into a ball. Before him were the embers of a fire, smouldering, dying, merely glowing, a thin wisp of smoke fleeing to the sky. Maybe he lacked the strength or the emotional capacity to get more wood, maybe he was lazy. His hacking cough – surely his lung was trying to escape – was the only sound in a world holding its breath. His grey hair was as long as a woman's, greasy enough to cook with.

'Excuse me, sir.' Jacky's voice was shy, shamed, tentative, yet still it broke the silence like a gunshot. The old man showed no signs of hearing.

'Excuse me,' Jacky said again, louder, as the group with him held their collective breath.

The old man turned, casually, as someone who had heard a noise but was clueless as to its source. It took his eyes a moment to focus, to see that he was not alone. The scream he released then almost ended his life as every armed man drew at once. It was not a human-sounding scream, nor was it Settler; Johnny was reminded of the screech of a terrified rat.

Backing away on his arse he continued to scream, the painful noise only getting shriller as his watery eyes lay on Johnny's Settler face.

'Whu? Wha? Whoareyou?' When he found the words they poured out in a rush, 'whayoudoing here?'

'Please, friend,' began Johnny in his most amicable voice. The rest – 'we mean you no harm' – was buried under the weight of the screaming that rose in tone and lost the rest of its intelligibility.

Shrugging away the futility, Johnny stepped back, behind his friends.

'Please, sir,' Jacky tried, pushing the nearest drawn gun down with his hand, 'we will not harm you, we need your help.' The old man stopped screaming, then stopped his desperate back-pedalling when his hand, leading the way where he could not see, contacted the hot edge of his fire. The fire was almost dead but was still hot, the burned hand must have hurt a lot, he screamed again. Jacky walked a pace closer then turned to Johnny and the gang.

'Please, gentlemen, this poor old man must be cold without his fire.' Although the air was not cold, they nodded. 'Could you help him with some wood, so we can sit around his fire and warm ourselves?'

When finally alone with the old man Jacky sat on his haunches reducing his unintended threat. 'Please, sir,' again, 'is this Jerramungup?'

'It was called that,' came the belated, surprised reply, '"the place of the tall trees" in the language of the blackfellas who lived here, who lived here through two colonisations. There aren't any left now. Now this is nowhere, and I must be nobody to still be here.' The old man chuckled at that, clearly accustomed to laughing at his own jokes. 'Who are you and why do you care?'

'My name is Jacky, I think I was born here. I was taken from my family from here.'

The old man stared hard at Jacky's face, as if it was a book to read and he was missing his reading glasses. 'I think I know your face,' he said finally. 'Your parents were here – you look a bit like old Fred anyhow, so you must be his kid they took. Your name wasn't Jacky then; you were Fred Junior, or little Freddie.'

Jacky leaned in closer, ready to jump into the old man's eyes to steal the memory of his parents he did not have. 'Where are they now?' The hope in Jacky's voice was louder than the words. From nebulous connections, from nothing but a name and a direction he had something, someone who knew them. He felt almost home.

'They aren't here,' the old man said in a tone that dropped 'you idiot' at the end of the sentence. 'The Settlers cleaned this place out years ago. They took everyone to the missions – everyone they didn't kill that is. They came in the morning, first thing, took us all by surprise. We thought they wouldn't bother, we kept to ourselves, never even stole anything.

'No matter, they came talking about stealing, about someone stealing their livestock, they took everyone who couldn't or wouldn't fight.'

'What about my parents?' Jacky seemed trapped halfway between eager and terrified – here was the answer to the whereabouts of his long-lost family. 'What about my parents?'

The old man nodded, beaming, proud to deliver good news. 'Your daddy, Fred, he fought hard, he had been a soldier before the Toads came, but, well, their guns were too strong. He's rotting out there,' he waved his hand vaguely, 'near the old war memorial. Your mum, old Hattie, she gutted a Toad with a kitchen knife, bless her soul, she died just about right where you are standing.'

Jacky's heart followed his body to the ground, the ground where his mother had died, embraced him, nursed him, held him up.

©

'We must be prepared,' Esperance was firm, adamant, 'they will come for us and we will be enslaved or worse, the women could end up in a baby factory . . . The lucky ones might be those who get killed.'

The council sat in a circle in the middle of the biggest open space in camp, their grey hair the main reason, it seemed, for their status. Esperance paced the open space like a caged tiger, her agitated movements the main indicator of her mood. One of the elders, Old Bob, spoke, his scraggly white beard dancing with the rhythm of his whiny voice. 'If they come, if they come, we will run as we always have.'

The other grey-hairs in the circle nodded, their nods varying in tone from wise to sleepy, sometimes both. Exasperated, failing in her attempt not to show it, Esperance turned to look at her grandfather. The bemused smile on his face broke into a wild grin of affection; he looked almost ready to laugh. He seemed to be enjoying himself when the safety of the entire camp, their entire mob, was at stake.

'We have moved and moved, every time we are worse off, every time we lose ground, lose possessions. Each camp is worse than the one before; we arrive weaker to a worse place and have less material to set up. One day a time will come when we don't have the strength, the resources to move.' Esperance was sick of repeating herself, surely they were sick of hearing it too.

'There is no way we can stand and fight, we will all die.' Another elder had spoken this time, and again they all nodded sagely, except Grandfather whose manic smile just got wider.

'Of course we cannot fight them,' Esperance said in a tone and with volume that was almost a shout, 'that has been tried, I never said to fight them.' She let that soak in their heads before going on. 'What we need to do is move before they find us, when we choose to move. Make it our decision – start acting, stop just reacting. We need to move further than we ever have before, further into the desert, then move again even further. When we have moved somewhere safe we need to train, to prepare, so we can be prepared for defence when they come.'

'And what would that achieve, young lady?' This elder had a voice like a child asking for Toad candies after being refused once already.

Grandfather stood suddenly. 'It would achieve, I believe,' he said, his tone as frustrated as his granddaughter's, 'the chance to choose our ground rather than it being chosen as the place we have fallen down after being chased. It might achieve, if we are in the deeper desert, if we are deep enough into the desert, having a place to live for a while, for the children to live for a while, in relative safety.

If we train some fighters they might last long enough in defence to give others, like you, a chance to run.'

'Maybe,' Esperance added, 'if we go far enough they might not find us at all.'

Esperance had hoped to sway them on her own, hoped she had earned that much respect, hoped they could have listened to her logic, the wisdom of her thoughts. On the other hand, she was glad for Grandfather's help – maybe they could convince the council between them. At least Grandfather believed in her wisdom; she thought it unlikely that he would agree with her just because they were family.

'Even that is not enough,' she said, pacing again, 'we need to send out patrols, scouts, we need communications so we know when they are coming.'

'They aren't coming,' said one of the elders, a laugh in his face, 'why would they bother looking for us?'

'They are always coming,' she said as she turned her back on the group. There was no use trying to convince the elders. Her grandfather's face had said, do it anyway.

Her face showed nothing but submission as she walked away from the meeting. Grandfather made an excuse and followed her, catching her before she left the circle of shacks that marked the unofficial edge of the camp.

'Esperance,' he said in a quiet but firm voice, 'don't run too far, you have our defences to organise.'

'Grandfather,' she snapped, 'nobody wants me to organise the defences. Either they genuinely believe we don't need to be defended or they want defences but don't want me to do it.'

'Who cares what the elders want?' He laughed. 'I am one of them and I don't really care. Their lack of desire for planning the defence of the camp shows they are out of touch, you are not the only one of your generation, or even your parents' generation, to believe that more defensive planning is needed.' He laughed again, 'Though I think I must be the only one of my generation.'

'I know they would run from any trouble, like we have always run.' Esperance sounded frustrated as she spoke. 'What would they do if an enemy came before they knew they were coming, what if there was no time to run, what then?'

'They will die,' he replied, 'just like you, I, everybody will die. We will all die.' They stopped. Esperance was staring at nothing, Grandfather was watching the children playing.

'You would know what to do if you just relaxed and thought about it,' Grandfather said. 'Your generation, your parents' generation, they know the danger, or will if you explain it to them. They trust you, though they might not be ready to actively disobey the council. Nor should they, but if you work with them to plan how to protect the camp if sudden attack comes it would not be a bad thing.

'It is important to respect the council, respect the elders, but as you and your generation will be the ones who would die defending them, you should make the decision about defence. There is nothing wrong with the fighters deciding when and how to fight. That was the mistake we all made too many times before the Toads came – always old men decided when and how to fight, and young men died fighting. We never let the young men decide how and when to fight and die, old men decided for them.'

He smiled at her. 'One of the council believes in you. I do.' He stared at nothing, his thoughts elsewhere, his mind in the past, or in another world. 'Have I ever told you what your name means? It was an old word even before the Toads came, a word that nobody used even then. Your father, he learnt much from books in the early days out here, before he and your mother went scouting and never came back. I found their bodies some time later, plasma burned.'

Tears ran down his face leaving runnels in the dust. 'Your father named you, he told me what it meant. I didn't understand then but I do now. You were named after a town, a human town that doesn't exist anymore, but the name means more than that. In an ancient language of Earth, one I had never learnt to speak.

'Your name means "hope".'

Devil arrived at his office, and looked out the window, as always, at the streetscape outside. The road was empty at that time of the morning; there were not yet any Natives arriving at the office with forms, requests or petitions for him to deny. Something was wrong; it took a while to register, as his eyes saw yet his mind refused to. Across the street scrawled on the walls in fluorescent paint were the words 'JACKY LIVES'.

He buzzed his secretary, irritated that nobody had taken care of it yet. They should have called the Troopers straight away, they should have had someone from the city council clean it before anyone saw it, before he saw it. He wanted to scream; instead he steeled his face, became a statue, making sure his secretary would see the quality of his self-control.

All around the colony, Natives were dying. Always afraid – that would never change – they had, regardless of the fear, lost some of their habitual inertia. If Jacky, barely a man, could run free, stay at large for so long, why not they?

So they rebelled, taking his initiative, learning from his lesson. All made mistakes: they fought when they should have run, ran when they should have hidden. These mistakes, these deaths, the recaptures leading to torture, the men, women and children in jail – they did not seem to dampen the drive to rebellion.

Every violent death that had before bred fear, now made the humans who witnessed it more angry.

It was as if the humans, enslaved for so long, had been looking for a role model, for someone who would fight and not give up. Devil and his department could not understand why this time they could not restore order, why this rebellion was not easily crushed. There was nothing special about Jacky. Others had escaped, others had been at large longer, yet his freedom had become a rallying cry.

Devil blamed the media. They would not shut up about Jacky Jerramungup, as he was becoming known. How the hell had they learnt that name anyway? Someone must have talked, must have been one of his victims. The damned media got everywhere – he would not be surprised to discover some of them were even talking to Johnny Star.

Opinions were divided, some seeing Jacky as a scourge, seeking endorsement to exterminate the entire Native race, using him as an excuse. 'Jacky Jerramungup is the Proof that the Native cannot be Pacified' said one headline on the news net. 'Bring Me the Head of Jacky Jerramungup' cried another. Jacky was the proof, the excuse, the incentive – 'the Native must be Destroyed'.

The other opinion was what worried the department most, some commentators calling for emancipation of all the Natives. If Jacky Jerramungup showed such initiative, such a desire to be free maybe they were people after all. It was bringing too much attention to the Natives, to the department, to Devil himself. The headlines espousing that opinion were less flowery, less attention grabbing, yet far more dangerous for all their subtlety.

However, in the end it mattered not which opinion was leading, which opinion was going to win. What mattered was the mistake they had made in teaching the Natives to read. So long as the debate continued in all the media, online, printed and otherwise, the Natives would know that Jacky Jerramungup was free.

It was too late to suppress the information now – the news, the debate had gained its own momentum, and Devil knew nothing could shut up either side. All he could do was expedite the fugitive's capture without seeming either to spend too much or too little resources on the problem. It was a balancing act the department was familiar with: both sides of the debate must be appeased.

Moneys and staff were diverted from other projects, in subtle and complicated webs of paperwork. A special contact circuit for information on the fugitives was set up, the extra staff minimal, while staff were diverted to actually spying.

The hardest job was getting information out of the Natives. The subtlest form of rebellion they could perform was silence, refusing to supply the needed answers. It was a rebellion they relished, one that was unlikely to lead to punishment. It would not do to remind them of Jacky by asking them if they knew where he was. Sadly, most of the spies for the department were not subtle enough for that task. More disastrously, the department sometimes did not know that.

So Natives continued to rebel, and continued to die. Natives continued to rebel and continued to be imprisoned, to be tortured, to be executed. Natives continued to rebel.

It was an old road, an ancient road, a human road – a river of cracked and potholed tarmac, dead straight, stretching, before them and behind them, to the western and eastern horizon. The air above the black tar shimmered and crackled with heat. The scattered desert trees, stunted and twisted growing out of the reddish earth, were the only things not drooping from the dry. Johnny Star, Jacky, and their small band stood in the middle of the road, the silence broken only by the morning cries of small birds.

Eagles circled lazily over the road, riding the thermals that the black ground produced, searching for the tiny animals that would fill their bellies and keep them flying. Even first thing in the morning the heat was noticeable, and when the sun made it overhead it would become unbearable, driving everybody but the eagles into the dappled shade under the trees.

'I don't understand why he didn't come with us. He must have been lonely there, in Jerramungup all alone.' Jacky wouldn't let it go.

Johnny Star decided it was time for the truth, they were far enough from the town. 'He couldn't come,' he said.

Jacky stopped dead, the others walked only a few steps on before stopping too. 'What do you mean he couldn't come? He was old but we could have given him the chance. He might have kept up, we can't just leave him there alone.'

Johnny turned to stare Jacky in the face, watched Tucker step behind the young man, silently applauded his caution. 'When the Settlers destroyed Jerramungup they captured everyone they could – better to take slaves than kill them all I guess. He tried to run, that man; a few of them got out of their chains and tried to run; he was the one who got them loose. He was the only one they caught, the others got away.'

Johnny broke out in mucus all over his skin, displaying how nervous, and emotional he was. 'They cut his hamstrings, in front of the slaves who had not escaped, who had not even tried to escape. Made sure they would know what could happen to them if they tried to escape. They made sure he could never walk again, then left him to die.

'A couple of the people he had helped escape came back days later, they found him there. They looked after him for years, fed him and gave him water when they could have left him to die.'

'Where are they now?' Jacky hissed, looking like he wanted to vomit.

'The food ran out,' Tucker drawled behind Jacky, 'they had to leave and find more. They left him enough to eat and drink, enough firewood for a few days, then left him to look for food. That was two weeks ago.'

'We have to do something,' Jacky was frantic, 'he is going to die.' Tucker caught him as he made to run.

'We did do something,' snarled Crow Joe, 'we did everything we could. We left him food – more than we could spare – we collected water, filled his bottle, we collected wood. We are going to hurt the next Settlers we see.'

'Why didn't you tell me? We can help him, we can take him, we can't leave him.' Jacky was screaming.

'You were unconscious when we found out,' Tucker said slowly, as if talking to a madman. He released the painful grip he had on Jacky's arm.

'And we knew how you would react,' growled Crow Joe.

Nobody spoke more, nobody moved; the gang stood waiting. Dip and Dap were so tense they were vibrating. A quiet so deep it was almost silence descended onto the desert.

A faint cough in the distance broke the stillness, resolving rapidly into a stuttering, throbbing whirr. Dazed by the early hour, lulled into complacency by the purely earthling scene, by the heat, by the painful discussion, nobody immediately reacted to the sound. Even that quiet, even so far away, it was already filled with menace, a menace they should have reacted to.

'Flier,' the word slipped out of Tucker's mouth, in his characteristic slow drawl, almost swallowed by the surrounding emptiness.
'Flier,' he drawled again, turning to stare with dark eyes towards
the sound.

Johnny did not respond, failed to react as if for a moment he
had thrown away the paranoia that had kept him alive for years,
forgotten who he was and where he was. Tucker reacted first, broke
from the group heading into the meagre cover, the darkness of the
scraggly trees on the side of the road. The other Natives, all but
Jacky, followed, disappearing with practised efficiency.

The noise got closer and louder, its creator not yet visible,
thunderous in the quiet, powerful, threatening. There could be
no doubt left that a flier was headed their way, following the road,
maybe using it as a navigation aid, maybe thinking refugees or
outlaws would be unable to resist using it. Still the two men, one
tanned bronze, the other mottled grey-green, stood seemingly
oblivious.

Maybe they had not even heard the flier, had not heard Tucker.
More likely they were both tied up in memories, in reverie, in
deep thought, in the flights of the eagles, in the dark green of the
desert oaks. So deep in thought they were oblivious to the hissing
cries, the loud whispers of the men hiding in the trees. The flier
was almost roaring in the emptiness before Johnny finally reacted,
grabbing Jacky and diving with him into long grass under the scant
cover of the grey-green canopy of a bloodwood.

When it passed overhead the flier was definitely searching for
something or someone; it drifted slowly down the road, too slow
to be simply travelling. If the Settlers in the flier were uncertain
that what they were searching for was using the road, they gave no
clue of that. Johnny Star thought rapidly as the flier passed; there

was no way of knowing how many Settlers were in the vehicle, but he desperately needed supplies and ammunition.

As the flier whirred its way past, Johnny barely moved, the small movements he made invisible even at the low height they were flying. They were less than fifty metres past when Johnny stepped out of the trees, his slippery-looking Settler rifle in his arms. Taking careful aim he fired one shot, the superheated plasma hitting the underside of the flier. With a bang even louder than the flier's roar one of the lift motors exploded – metal, ceramic and plastic spraying out from under the vehicle.

The pilot was good – he almost kept his flier in the air, the remaining motors roaring and shuddering. There was simply not enough power left for any pilot to use, no matter how skilled, and the vehicle landed on the road with a deafening *crump*. It had not taken Johnny's men long to realise what was happening; they were running at his side almost immediately, carrying what weapons they had at the ready.

A Settler climbed half out of the wreck, he must have been more worried about potential danger within the flier than he was about the danger outside. He stopped suddenly when he saw the barrel of Johnny's rifle pointing at the centre of his face. Around the flier in a ragged half circle stood the little gang – Jacky the only one not armed with some sort of firearm.

'My name, is Johnny Star. No doubt you are looking for me.' He circled around them with an almost human swagger, keeping the barrel of his gun pointed at the terrified Settler. 'They call me a thief,' he said, 'they call me a murderer.

'I guess I am a thief, I have stolen quite a few things.' He laughed, 'I have stolen guns, ammo, food. I have stolen money, for that money helps me and my friends here,' he waved in an arc, 'survive.

'I steal little things, and people get hurt when I do it but I don't set out to hurt people. Our whole race are a bunch of thieves. You came here, I came here and helped, we came here and took their planet, took their children for slaves, took their future.' There was a distinct snarl in his voice, his face expressionless in anger. 'Stealing something to eat, that is a crime that would get me flung into jail. Stealing everything, that is just good government.

'I have killed people, that is true, I have killed my own people. All those people have been trying to kill me. I killed people before that too, when I was one of you, a trooper. Most of those people you don't even think are people. Those deaths will haunt me forever.'

There was no doubt the flier had communicated its position, informed home base it had been attacked and had crashed. Taking no chances Johnny's gang ran off into the trees; they were short, twiggy and scarce but they were cover. They were better than nothing. It would take some time for another flier to be dispatched but it would be coming. Before it got there they would have to be well gone.

Their bags were heavy, filled with ammo and rations. It might have meant death for the troopers they had left behind, tied hand and foot, but they took all the water, bottles sloshed in their packs, a comforting sound for the still thirsty, always thirsty, Johnny.

Every member of the gang now carried cream plastic Settler rifles, carried them nervously as if mistrusting that they were really dangerous, would really work for them. Every member that is except for Jacky who was so afraid of the alien equipment they could not convince him to touch them, or even carry a spare for someone else.

'I am taking too many risks,' thought Johnny, almost letting the words escape into the world through his mouth. The water, the ammo was worth it, but only just. Maybe he should have hidden from the flier, kept running from the Troopers as he had always done.

It did not presage well. His habitual caution was wearing thin.

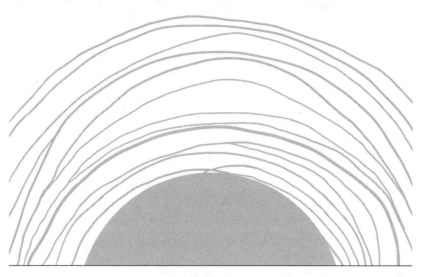

CHAPTER 17

Jacky Jerramungup will go down in history with the other outlaws, real or legendary, who have fought a more powerful enemy, one they could not really defeat. Robin Hood, Jandamarra, Yagan, Haasheh Gaarnch, all fought with whatever small resources they had, all became thorns in the sides of the administration they were fighting. All became legends in defeat. It does not matter if we capture Jacky Jerramungup. In allowing him to become famous, in allowing him to become a role model, we have already lost.

– J. R. KAASHAKK, HISTORIAN

SERGEANT ROHAN FINALLY gave in to his frustration – something he had wanted to avoid, something that would be supremely unhelpful. The thin veneer of stuffy civilisation, that too-tight coat that kept the savage inside, where it belonged, had been scraped and dragged off, torn to shreds by the rough land, by the heat, by too many days in the wild. He lashed out – his grey-green, wide-mouthed face in a contorted, uncontrolled grimace – the ceramic blade in his hand sharper, stronger than steel. The headless body of his informant collapsed, the tumbling head kicking up puffs of dust from the bone-dry ground.

'They took down a flier, that flier we heard about that went down. Somehow that Star, that traitor took down a flier,' Rohan said to his deputies as he strode past them in a fury. Turning he bared his teeth to his terrified, horrified deputies. 'Somehow they shot it down and stole their guns, the water, the food, all the ammo, and left the men in the flier to die.' He did not tell them that the men from the flier had been recovered, alive. He wanted the boys good and angry.

The Natives were laughing at the Settlers. So many of them and so strong, yet Jacky and Johnny remained impossible to find. That was the thought occupying Rohan's mind as he leapt onto his mount and turned again to yell at his posse.

'We are going to need a few more men – we cannot take Jacky and Johnny Star, and their whole gang without some serious help. They are armed, they outnumber us and are not as pathetic as you.' He ignored the gasps of disgust, the looks on their faces.

His inability to catch Jacky, even to find him, had led him to unconsciously imbue the Native with almost supernatural abilities. The thought of him with Johnny Star, who had escaped the Troopers for years, who killed Settlers and troopers in an almost mocking way, was chilling. They were almost his equals in his grudging esteem. They were almost certainly dangerous. Rohan respected dangerous.

It was not far to the nearest Settler military base – at least not as the crow flies, as humans said – yet in that wilderness, in that desert, it took days. Too many days, as Rohan knew the fugitives were getting further away, though he hoped not too far away.

He was merely a trooper, hunting a mere Native, despite the addition of a Settler rebel and a few more Natives in the mix. Therefore, he did not warrant a heavy flier, well armed and thickly armoured; he did not warrant a platoon of troopers or soldiers. Thirty more men and a utility flier, barely armed, not much more than a truck, was all they would spare him.

Uncontrollably savage now, Rohan snapped and bit at the supply clerks who did not pack his flier fast enough for his liking. His new men were volunteers, from the ranks of the Troopers, not that he had asked for such but before men could be chosen they put up their hands. The traitor Johnny Star was a target many a trooper wanted to pin their name on. Oh how they would boast if they returned from the mission having captured both Jacky, who some now named Jerramungup, and the notorious Johnny Star.

The eagerness of his small army made Sergeant Rohan slightly nervous, even a little nauseated. He had to wonder, again and again, whether any of the men throwing themselves into the fray had ever been in the desert, ever risked their lives against anything more dangerous than women and children.

Johnny Star, Jacky and the gang strolled up a ribbon of red sand that looked like it had once been a river. Here and there were boulders, deposited by what must have been a torrent, on the rare occasion that it rained. The sand even looked a little like water, although the wrong colour; the flow of the last rains, who knew how long ago, had made swirls, streaks, ripples that had stayed carved in the sand when the water retreated.

It was hot as hell out there. Johnny hated the heat, hated the dry but there had seemed little choice but to travel north, north and east deeper into the dry lands, deeper into the desert. Here even the tough native trees, with their dry waxy leaves, the tougher native shrubs, all spikes and scratchiness, seemed confined to the edge of the river. Beyond the riverbanks there was nothing but spinifex, a grass that tore at the ankles.

What sort of a planet, what kind of a continent, can produce a grass that can tear at your skin until it bleeds?

Six days after shooting down the flier the gang were desperate, they were hungry, they were almost constantly thirsty. It had taken all of Tucker's skill, all of Dip and Dap's luck and tenacity, all Jacky's will to live to keep the group alive, to keep finding barely enough water to survive. Johnny was tired of the taste of mud and sand, the flavour of the puddles they drank from, of the holes in riverbeds where they dug for water.

Johnny walked in a silent daze, dreaming of cool water, of lying in a pool, soaking water in through his soft, thin, porous skin. He could not of course do this, when there was little water to be had, and that hard to get, he could not pollute it with his flesh, he could not even spare the water to wash. The nearest he got to lying in water was rolling in the damp sand the more energetic humans dug out when looking for water. They nearly left him there, threatened to leave him when he lay in the damp sand and refused to move. As always Johnny wondered how his people had managed to overwhelm this planet so quickly. The Natives here were stronger and more resilient, better survivors than his own people. He was enough proof of this. Despite his training as a soldier, as a trooper, despite his years surviving in the swamps back home, he was now completely reliant on his human companions. He hoped desperately that they did not resent him.

With threatening suddenness, Tucker, again leading the way, stopped, his dusty face frozen. The rest of the gang were slower to react: Dip and Dap freezing a moment later; Deadeye lifting his rifle stock to his shoulder with breathtaking, frightening, reflexes; Crow stopping like a ball that had just been caught, too much restless energy to stop softly.

Even Jacky was faster than Johnny, startled by his companions' reactions. He scanned the trees with lightning eyes although he knew there was nowhere to hide. Johnny was too tired, too dehydrated to react. He stumbled, almost fell when he blindly staggered into Tucker's shoulder.

Here the water must have held on longer – the trees were healthier, taller. The hot breeze had suddenly ceased, the thicker woodland an efficient windbreak. Cooler, without the drying wind, darker in the shade of the trees, they breathed, the air so much cooler than before it felt almost damp.

'There have been people here, many people,' Tucker said after he had stared at the riverbed for some time. 'A great mob of people, all human – men, women and children – carrying weight, travelling slowly, some barefoot, some in boots, some in shoes like I have not seen since my family was killed, and some look like they have just tied skins over their feet.'

'People would be nice, people other than you lot. I am getting a bit sick of your company,' quipped Crow Joe. His voice was its usual deadpan – only long association let the others know he was joking. Dip and Dap laughed at once, in disturbing unison; Johnny was too tired to laugh; Jacky was still silent, as he had been for too long.

'We follow them, and stay alert. They might help us, they might at least be company for a time.' Johnny was glad to have a decision to make finally, something proactive. 'Unfortunately they might not be as glad to see us as we would be to find them.

They have not had the benefit of all the shit we have been going through. Surely nobody can be as tragic, lost and lonely as us.'

'We'd best get moving then,' Tucker replied, 'they were here many days ago, maybe a week. They would be far ahead unless they have stopped. There are less of us – we should be faster.'

Johnny stared where Tucker was looking, marvelling as always at the Native's tracking ability. Where the Toad saw nothing but scratches and the slightest indentations in the sand Tucker was reading the signs like a book.

There was a spring in their steps when they moved on – they had a destination of sorts, some sort of target ahead, better than just running away. It was hard to maintain caution – they wanted to skip and run, to get to the humans ahead of them as soon as possible. They walked fast, vibrating with the excess energy.

Why would such a group be ahead of them? Were they free humans, somehow staying away from the Settlers, keeping free, keeping alive? Were they a group of slaves on a forced march, would they get somewhere ahead and find a work camp, a death camp, a mass grave, a rotting pile of corpses?

When they broke out of the trees, back into the heat and light, into the scouring wind, they lost the tracks. The tracks of more humans than they had seen in a group in years had been swept away by the weather. No matter, the gang would follow the river, there to find more tracks, to find the people before them, or not. There was nothing to do about it.

Another clue was not long coming, and again Johnny Star, to his embarrassment, was not the one to see it. In his hot, dry, almost delirious state, he didn't at first understand the significance of the find. At a bend in the dry river, sheltered by a bloodwood tree, there was a slight depression in the sand.

There the ground was slightly damp; they could smell it, especially Johnny in his dehydrated state. It was just the sort of place they would have dug for water. Johnny dropped to his knees, grateful they had, at last, found a soak. There would be a little water there.

Nobody was digging, nobody was searching for the precious water, nobody was breaking branches off the trees to use as digging sticks. They were merely staring at the place where the water would be as if they had all lost their minds.

'Someone has already dug for water here.' It took some time for Crow Joe's words to penetrate. Belatedly Johnny realised that all his companions had alert expressions, hands on weapons. He stumbled to his feet, so unsteady, so uncertain he almost fell again.

'Are you sure?' The Settler was not sure of the significance in his depleted state but knew it was somehow important.

'Yes,' Crow Joe was sardonic, 'I'm sure.'

Johnny examined the slight depression, heat and dehydration chasing his thoughts down a blind alley. Again he felt it was important, yet he could not say how. 'Why do I feel that matters, why can't I think why?'

It was Tucker who answered. The words came out in a rush, more excited than Johnny had ever heard him be. 'It matters because Settlers would carry water, they don't dig for it, and a group who are being marched somewhere wouldn't dig either, they wouldn't be allowed the time, and if they did dig for water they'd probably not fill in the hole, or make the least effort to hide their hole, to hide their presence here.

'What's ahead of us, Johnny, is a group of free humans, a group like us but much bigger. They might be refugees, they might be escapees, freed slaves. They might have never even been controlled by your people. I've never seen evidence of such a large group in my life.'

'Then what is ahead of us,' said Johnny Star, his mouth half open in a Settler smile – on a human it would look like they were panting – 'is hope.'

@

The children were so filled with excitement and energy when the flier arrived that it was almost impossible to control them. Sister Bagra stopped trying. There was no way to keep them in class. They were rebelliously heading for the doors, they were standing at the windows – she let them go, it would do no harm. She could hear the banging of doors, the hammering of feet as the other teachers released their charges. Like a flock of gulls they squawked and flapped out the doors and into the open space between the buildings.

Some had never seen a flier, they landed so seldom there, yet even they responded with joy, aping the other Natives. She would have expected them to fear the sound, the noisy machine coming from the sky. Such enthusiasm, such vivacity was not really acceptable, yet if this was the inspector arriving it could not hurt to have him see the children happy.

What would hurt was for the inspector to see her disciplining the children for nothing more than being too happy, too noisy. She let them run and scream although the noise hurt her head.

When the inspector alighted from his still-whining craft the children rushed, consumed with curiosity, and the pointless energy they often had, to examine the new arrival. To someone unaware of the excitement that something, someone, new can bring, someone unaware that excitement does not necessarily equate with happiness, the children would appear to be filled with joy. Bagra hoped the inspector had not learnt enough about Natives to learn to be cynical about their fleeting and unpredictable moods.

Apparently not. He stepped out of the flier, a soft-coloured almost ivory-white man, going to flab like all their people do as they age, yet somewhat larger. Despite his vow of poverty he was overweight. He reached out to muss the hair of one of the children crowding around. Bagra noticed that, the touching of the hair; likely a gesture learnt from humans, possibly calculated to inform her subtly that Natives are to become citizens, equals.

She avoided touching the hair of the Natives, except when they were shaved as punishment for almost every minor infraction. Hair, which only mammals have, that someone had told her was actually dead tissue, was disgusting. Even if not inherently disgusting, it was definitely dirty. They shaved the children when it got too dirty; it was almost impossible to clean otherwise.

There were no shaved heads among the children. Discipline had been lax lately, few punishments had been handed out. She was relying on the short unreliable memory of the children to ensure there was no 'cruelty' to report.

Bagra was certain she was not supposed to see the look of distaste that flickered almost invisibly across the inspector's face. Behind her mask she laughed. Big words, big gestures, yet he too felt the revulsion that all their people feel when touching a human. Hopefully he felt crowded, infested, dirty and claustrophobic having the Natives pressing against him like that. If so it would certainly not hurt her cause to make sure he had as many opportunities to feel that way, as many chances of being crowded by the children as she could manage.

'Children,' she flustered towards them, 'you can all talk to the inspector later. I am sure he would love to spend time with you all.' Was that a look of alarm that showed briefly on his face?

'Oh, it's okay,' Grark boomed over the cacophony, 'they are just excited.' He did not sound particularly convinced. Bagra smiled triumphantly behind her mask.

The flier took off with a scream as she herded the children towards the other nuns who were fluttering like crows. She spoke firmly. 'They need to return to class, we cannot neglect their education, there will be time for a more formal introduction to the children later.' With the flier gone she knew now that it was not to be a short visit; he would be staying.

Grark nodded, relief again? 'Of course,' he said, 'we must continue to improve their lot in life. Nothing, nothing at all, is more important than education, except faith.'

Gesturing for the gardener to take Grark's ostentatiously minimal luggage – so like an inspector to demonstrate their self-declared piety by packing so little – Bagra led the way to the guesthouse. 'It would be best to not interrupt the children at class – learning order and discipline is an important part of their education. When the children first come here they have no concept of sitting down quietly, they are unused to keeping to a timetable. If we interrupt class now it will teach them the wrong lesson about discipline and self-control.'

Bagra did not look to Grark to see his reaction to this, so she did not see the expression on his face. 'Yes, self-discipline is important, discipline is important,' he said. His voice was curiously flat in the manner of someone keeping strong emotion from their voice. They walked on in silence.

'We will have a meal outside tonight. The children can show you some of their work, show some of their Native dances. We have been teaching them some spiritual songs, they would love to sing you some.' If not for her own flat tone, sounding like she couldn't choose an emotion to place in the words, Bagra made sure she sounded enthusiastic, even proud of the children. She dared not look at him but hoped he was convinced.

@

There had been a mass grave here once, from one perspective it was a mass grave still. Johnny stood right where the mound had collapsed, where the bones poked through the dry red sand. Nothing grew on the mound but some weeds. The desert plants grew slowly on thin soil, and the disturbance when the bodies had been dumped had interrupted them. Erosion from the last rain, years ago, had been enough to open the grave. There was no sign of life in that place, as if the birds and small animals shunned it, as if life itself was holding its breath.

Johnny was envious of humans, for they had the capacity to cry. All around him his gang, his friends wept, tears streaming down their faces. Only his face was dry; he lacked the moisture to even ooze with emotion. He knew they were receiving catharsis – that after they had cried they would feel better for a time. He had no such luxury.

An eagle cried overhead, a message he knew he was incapable of reading. He didn't know if even Tucker knew the language. He wished the eagle would talk to him, tell him everything would be okay, that one day there would be peace, that one day he and his people could earn the right to belong there.

'I was not at this one,' Johnny said eventually. 'These bones are old, twenty years at least, back then I was still in the swamps back home.'

'They are older than that,' Tucker said, 'might have been from the beginning, from when your people first came from the sky, when so many of us died.'

'I was probably at school then, if I was even born,' Johnny said. 'I hated school, the teachers were even worse than parents, worse than the parents I only saw at holidays. As soon as we were hatched they took us there to that school, taught us to obey, to follow their damned rules, no matter how stupid the rules were. I have never known for sure how they kept track of whose parents were whose – just tagged eggs, hatched at the school, surely they get mixed up.

'I hated them and they hated me, those things I called my parents. They didn't care what happened to me, they didn't help when I was arrested and sent here.'

'I love my parents,' Jacky said in an almost whisper, 'I don't remember them, at all really, but still I love them.' The other humans nodded their understanding.

'You people,' Deadeye hissed at Johnny, 'your people, they think we don't love our children, that they can just take the children away and we won't give a shit. You monsters are the ones who don't even know what love is.'

'While I regret you have placed me in the same category as the other Toads I have to agree with the sentiment.' Johnny had slipped back into his mask of the suave outlaw; the conversation had helped him regain his composure. 'My people don't have the same family life as yours. We put society first and family second, you are the opposite. Yes, that makes us monsters compared to you.'

That first night Father Grark was at the school they picnicked under the alien stars – the adults, the Settlers, seated at a long table, constructed from boards laid across trestles. They sat along one side, Grark in the middle with Bagra at his right side. The table was covered with an abundant, if simple, feast. The children sat on blankets, on stained sheets of canvas, on unrolled sheets of scuffed and scratched plastic, on the ground, getting up when brave enough to raid the food on the table. All of the Native children were too nervous, it seemed, to talk to the Settlers.

There was nothing notable about the feast, except the quantity, but the children, though subdued, nevertheless reacted as if they had never seen so much food. Maybe they hadn't, but that did not prove they were abused; maybe there had not been a feast for a long time. Certainly he would not expect to see a feast like this every day — it would be lacking in piety. Maybe they were just children — those of his own people would eat too much with a feast before them.

'The children cooked the food in home-economics class — we take great care to teach them to cook well,' Bagra said. 'They don't get to cook so much party food often. They are very excited to see what you think of the food.'

Grark nodded and smiled, turned to the children and shone his smile over them. 'It is certainly delicious and abundant, and they have got the spicing exactly right. Everything is pretty much perfect. Well done, little ones.'

'We have found that young ones who can cook fare better when they leave here and look for work.' Bagra looked pleased with herself as she spoke. 'Most houses look for cooks, they will hire a cook even if they cannot afford any other servants, so we concentrate on teaching domestic chores, particularly cooking. Even if they do not find work as cooks it serves the girls well to learn how to do it. They might have families one day and will need to cook good food for them. The food they ate before they came here was not always the best, sometimes not even edible at all.'

'How did they eat before, before we came?'

'Their parents were neglectful – they seem incapable of feeding their children to a standard we would think even adequate, even edible. The children in the camps live short, empty, pointless lives, those we cannot get to a mission to teach. We do our best to educate, to care for the Natives, but their parents don't seem to want us to bring them in, they resist, but they seem to forget their children after a while. At least they stop looking for them.'

Grark nodded slowly, politely, although he was unsure what he believed. The Natives he had seen seemed to care for their children as much as his own people did, maybe more. What free children he had seen outside the mission seemed to be as well looked after as the conditions the parents lived in allowed. Schooling his expression well, he simply kept nodding, not trusting his mouth should it fall open.

That night, as the moon rose, the Natives demonstrated their Native dance and song. Grark noted to himself, not yet trusting his mouth, that all their culture was considered worthless, except those parts that his people found beautiful. After the dance they sang a haunting lullaby from his own people. They performed it perfectly, with a soulful quality he could not pin down, a quality missing when the song was performed back home.

There was something unfathomable about the Native voices; no two sang exactly the same note, yet the different tones combined to make the whole unfathomably much larger.

He was surprised to be so moved – if he had been human he would have been moved to tears.

'It's called "harmony", something primitive the Natives do,' said the nun who had taken an interest in teaching the children to sing, 'we don't teach it to them. We cannot even get them to stop it when we try.' Grark didn't think it primitive at all. It was the most beautiful thing he had ever heard: massed voices singing in 'harmony', turning a song from his language – admittedly relatively tuneless compared to Native songs – into something that filled the ears and heart.

When he went to bed, after being introduced to the children, that sound, that singing was still playing in his ears.

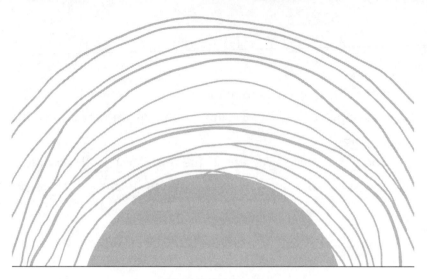

CHAPTER 18

We have overwhelmed them completely, we have taken them down, we control everything, everywhere and every one of them. They were defeated almost as soon as we landed, we rule this planet. There is nothing the Native, the human, can do to stop us or to kick us off the planet. Why, therefore, are you so damned scared of them?

– CAPTAIN BAALAAS, COLONIAL TROOPERS

ESPERANCE DIDN'T OFTEN go hunting, although she wanted to. She had other jobs, other draws on her time, things that were much more important and far more boring. There were always arguments to break up and people to placate, water to cart and children to mind, shacks to repair and first aid to administer. When there was nothing else, Grandfather's failing health was a constant presence, though she did not begrudge that work.

It had been a surprise to her, as much as it was to anyone else, that she had shown real talent for hunting in the desert. When

Paddy took the women out into the sand, showing them what he knew of the traditional 'women's work' of his people, none had shown much ability except for her. Now whenever she went out she could find a lizard if not more, preferably one of the frightening large ones that haunted the spinifex, to bring back to the communal cooking fire.

Lizards and desert rats, rabbits and feral cats. These were the foods they lived on out there in the drylands, where they were safer.

Since their last move they no longer cooked and ate as families, as individuals, well mostly not anyway. Food was in such short supply that a kind of emergency socialism had ensued – everyone who could manage it gathered food, everyone who was hungry ate. Nobody was really getting enough, no matter how long the group spent hunting, yet nobody took more than their share even though the food was cooked then left for whomever wanted it.

Esperance suspected that many, especially the older women and her grandfather, were consistently taking less than their share, to the detriment of their health. As the food got short there were even suicides – people who believed they had nothing to contribute, who believed they were a waste of good food, who felt too powerful a weight of despair, took their lives or, in some cases, wandered out into the desert, staying hidden until they died.

The discovery of her natural talent for tracking and catching small game such as lizards and rabbits came as a relief to everybody in the camp. Everyone was hungry, so volunteers had taken on Esperance's other tasks to free her for hunting. Nobody was particularly keen on lizards, yet in their desperation they would eat pretty much anything; unfortunately the desperation would not stop any of them whining about the food.

The men went hunting with spears and bows; they could not use guns, they were too noisy and ammunition too precious. The large game they could find would feed many, but too often they hunted all day and found nothing. So Esperance led a small group of the younger women in the search for forage. Armed with sticks and crowbars, shovels and empty tins, they had wandered off on a meandering trail through the spinifex following the slightest of tracks.

They found a rabbit warren in the bank of the dry river, some way downstream of the camp. This was a boon – rabbit was the most popular small game at camp. There were smiles all around, snatches of song, as they dug out the small hole wider. It was hard work in the baking sun – it was unfortunate that the hole was not under an overhanging tree, or on the side of the river shaded by the high banks.

A rabbit bolted out through the legs of the girl whose turn it was with the shovel. Another girl, laughing, chased it down, thwacking it on the head with her stick. The digger went back to digging, other girls watching for more escapes as a couple went to look for lizard tracks. She loved being out there looking for food to feed their people, far from the questions and complaints of the old and infirm.

Esperance was the oldest of this group. It was a delight for her to not have the old people question her every move, every decision, even every word. Out there with those girls she was the elder.

They were tired from the digging. All singing, laughing and chatting had stopped, and there was no noise but the sound of the shovel hitting the sand, the swoosh of girls emptying cans of sand outside their circle, the breathing of those waiting to see another rabbit.

Therefore the hunters were as surprised as the Toad looked when he almost tripped over them while walking down the river. A yelp burst out of his mouth before he could stop himself. Surprised as they were, the women reacted faster. The girl with the shovel threw the shovelful of sand in the Settler's direction as the others stepped towards him armed with their sticks and crowbars. He backed away, making no move towards any weapon. If he drew a gun, or even attempted to there were two most likely ways it would go. Either these women would kill him, or he would be forced to kill one or more of them.

He backed away slowly down the riverbed. 'Please,' he said, 'I mean you no harm. My name is Johnny Star, the outlaw.'

To his visible surprise, his name caused no reaction at all. He shrugged while still backing away. 'I thought I was famous, damn I wish my face didn't cause such a reaction,' he laughed a hysterical facsimile of human laughter. 'Please,' he almost sounded like he was pleading, a very human tone, 'I'm a friend, I mean you no harm. I like humans, my only friends are humans. I . . . my people want to kill me . . . I like humans so much. My friends will explain. I don't want to hurt anyone, you want to hurt me – I don't blame you for that but I am a friend, truly.'

It was Esperance, crowding him to make sure he had no time to draw, who spoke. 'You are alone,' then continued to advance.

'I hate Toads,' Johnny's voice was frantic, panicked, 'no, that's not true, I don't hate all Toads. I had friends back home, I don't hate them, and there are, I am sure, some Toads who are okay people but I hate what the Toads have done on this planet. I want them to go home, I want them to leave you alone.'

'But you are a Toad,' Esperance half laughed, half screamed, he was so infuriating.

'I know that,' Johnny's laugh was manic, terrified, 'I want me to go home too.'

Johnny backed away from the girls as fast as he could as he spoke. They were, however malnourished they appeared, fitter than him and he, unlike them, was walking backwards. He tripped and staggered, just managing not to fall. Esperance wondered what he was doing out there, further out than a Toad should be, alone. He should be dead.

'Excuse me,' the drawling voice came from the trees and a brown-skinned human followed the sound out, an axe in each hand. 'They call me Crow Joe, and you are scaring my Toad.' Crow Joe was bouncing on the balls of his feet with manic energy. He looked ready for a fight, dangerous, violent, unhealthily energetic. Esperance froze.

'Gentlemen,' Johnny Star said more calmly than should have been possible, 'let us not hurt anyone, there has been enough killing. These ladies and I have merely had a misunderstanding, they would not really hurt me, I am sure they don't want to hurt me, and I know you won't want to hurt them. They might feel better if you came out and said hello, surely we can talk all this over.' A young scared human appeared, like a ghost, from the trees behind the women, unarmed, harmless. Two more, so alike they had to be twins, stepped onto the riverbank, one on each side of Johnny and stopped there, lowering their guns. A man, made of wire and leather, slipped out of the trees and was standing erect between the women and Johnny before anyone really noticed him moving.

'Deadeye, don't shoot anyone, I am in no danger now, we are all going to be friends.' Johnny Star sounded as nervous as Esperance felt.

For a time those standing in the riverbed would never be able to measure, the tension was almost unbearable. Nobody moved, nobody felt there was time to move, there was no space to move, it was not safe to move. Nobody breathed, there was no time to breathe. There was a nearly imperceptible noise, like a rat running over sand, and Deadeye appeared, at Johnny's shoulder, just behind. Esperance could tell the sudden arrival was as startling to the Toad as it was to her. Automatically, almost as a twitch, she raised her crowbar slightly.

'Please, let us not fight,' Johnny said amicably, 'we can be friends, my friends were out of sight, they could have hurt you, but they did not. I am armed, I could have drawn on you, I did not.'

'What are you doing here?' Esperance's voice was toneless with enforced calm, fear and anger kept barely under control. She would not let it show. 'If you had reached for a gun I would have gutted you, if you reach for a gun now I will dash out your brains, armed friends or not.'

'We are on the run. I am Johnny Star, outlaw, fugitive, deserter – they will call me all those things. What I really am is someone sick of watching your people, any humans die. They made me join the Troopers, brought me here, then one day I had only two choices: keep assisting in the murder of humans, or desert and go outlaw.'

'I bet you killed people – you are a Toad, you were a trooper, you must have killed people, my people,' Esperance said, continuing to talk for all the women with her, for they all seemed too scared to talk.

'Yes, I have killed people, it was my job to control humans and often that control was done through violence. Then one night during a raid on a human camp I . . .' he paused, panting as his people do when upset, 'I realised we were killing people, not the animals I was taught you were. I sickened, I couldn't fight anymore, I killed nobody that night although death was all around me.

'The very next day I ran. I would have died from heat exposure, from the dry, if Tucker here hadn't done a humane thing, a very human thing, and saved my life. Your people are better than mine – mine are monsters. If it is in my power, no human will die in my presence. If I could send my people back home, I would.'

Esperance turned slightly to stare Tucker in the face, then back to Johnny, finding his large watery eyes. There was something in his face she did not expect to see. She believed she could see he was a good man. Things like that turn up in the eyes of humans, yet rarely in the slimy eyes of the Toads. It was as if somehow his eyes, his face, his expression had been humanised. 'Is what he said true?' she asked. 'I can't trust a member of the people, the things, who killed my family, killed countless people, yet I can't kill him outright in cold blood while he just stands there.

'This must be why the Toads won.' Esperance sighed, 'They have no mercy, we have too much.'

'Hand her your weapons,' Tucker said, 'I am sure she will be calmer if you are unarmed.'

Johnny looked nervous, but he appeared to have no choice. He could either hand his guns over or he could fight the humans he said he didn't want to harm. Esperance stared. Would he take the risk, the gamble? It was not a risk really – if his 'friends' were really friends he was not truly defenceless, surely he knew that as much as she did.

'I doubt she wants to see them in my hands, Tucker,' Johnny said finally, nodding with what was again a very human gesture, 'please disarm me, hand the humans all my guns, then we can all relax.'

Tucker walked behind Johnny, pulling his cream plastic pistol from his hip and the Settler rifle from the holster on his back. Walking back to the front he handed the two guns to Esperance. 'Now you are armed and he is not,' said Tucker, as she took them.

'Please remember, my new friends,' Johnny said, 'you did not capture us. We surrendered. We had you out-gunned.'

Esperance nodded, then stepped behind Johnny. 'You surrendered but I would feel better if I could see you. Walk along the river, and don't do anything to make me regret accepting your surrender.'

Johnny laughed – a nervous giggle that came out like the hissing of a snake, the croaking of a bullfrog. At the end it was an almost human snigger. 'Don't do anything to make me regret surrendering.'

The small band of outlaws were silent as they were led up the riverbed through the evidence of human occupation. There were the remains of a hole, dug for water, another hole that looked like it was dug to find small game, the kind of hole the human women were digging. The tracks up and down the ribbon of sand were now so tangled and overlapped that they were impossible to read.

The other girls had been alert, Esperance was glad of that; they had run ahead and made sure everyone was ready. Before the Toad in her custody was a line of eight men, all holding the biggest, most threatening, weapons they could get their hands on. They held axes and clubs, spears and even a sword. She was glad to notice that not one of them held a gun. If all had gone to plan – and for now it looked like it had – all the guns were held in reserve, the people armed with firearms in the trees outside camp, or in the shadowy doorways of huts.

Esperance was glad they had not shown all their strength – that part of the plan was working although she was not sure this gang would be tricked. Johnny Star appeared to be unusually attentive and astute, and his friend Tucker was almost frighteningly alert. She knew the newcomers would see her signalling but did it anyway. Surely they used a different hand sign than she and the other refugees had worked out. There was another slight noise in the painful silence and another group appeared behind the Toad and his friends. 'Hello, friends, I am Johnny Star.' He pulled away from Esperance as he spoke, projecting as well as he could while sounding polite, calm and conciliatory. 'I know it might be hard to believe looking at me,' he gestured at his face, 'but I am truly a friend. Please believe I hate the Settler government, the bastard Toads, as much as they hate me, and they hate me more than they hate you.'

Esperance spoke behind him. 'We will not harm you, but you will not be allowed to harm the camp, you will be searched for more weapons, for communicators, for anything that can endanger us and you will be bound. The same goes for your friends.'

Tucker shrugged, then stepping forward handed his Settler rifle to the nearest human. 'We mean you no harm, this Toad is our friend, he too has no intention to harm anyone here. If he is to be disarmed, searched and imprisoned, I will share his fate.' Esperance's eyes went wide as Tucker removed weapon after weapon – a Toad rifle, an old hunting rifle, an ancient police revolver, a knife as long as his forearm, an ancient butter knife sharpened as keen as a razor, and handed them over.

One by one the gang handed over their weapons and stood with Johnny. 'It's a shame,' he said, 'that we would have to be captured before I understood that my friends love me.'

The youngest man was last. Esperance noticed he was less connected to the others, more reluctant to be bound.

'I am Jacky, they call me Jacky Jerramungup. I am a fugitive, sought for running from a homestead – I was a servant, a slave there. Since I escaped things have got worse and worse. I have been forced to run, forced to fight, forced to hurt people I don't know because almost anyone I have met, Native,' he paused and gulped for breath, 'human that is, or Settler, has tried to stop me. When I met this Settler he was close to death, I needed his help so I saved his life. I felt pity for him so I saved his life.

'In all my life I can remember nobody who has stood by my side as much as Johnny and his friends, nobody has ever risked their life for me since my parents died and I was just a little baby then.' Shaking he handed his knife over, walked over and stood by Johnny. 'I will stand by this Toad's . . . this man's side, stand with his friends. They risked death, risked their freedom for me.'

Esperance was speechless. The men guarding the camp entrance tied Johnny's hands behind his back. To their surprise the humans with him refused to move until they were bound as well. The camp had never taken prisoners, never had any need or opportunity to do so. They led the small band to the centre of the camp near the fire and sat them in a group, guns trained on them.

All around them the camp seemed to come alive – children and the elderly came from the tents and shacks, armed men and women appeared, spilled out of every shack, every tent, from the shadows, having hidden even where there seemed to be nowhere to hide. Some appeared as if by magic, just suddenly there with no intervening movement. Everyone fit enough to fight seemed prepared to do so.

There were ancient rifles, bows both handmade and the pinnacle of old-human technology, axes and spears. One man, seemingly unable to find anything better, was armed with a club, a heavy stick. Everybody carried a knife – they were on most belts, in most hands – even down to the smallest child.

'Damn it's hot here,' Johnny hissed from his seat on the dusty ground, 'it's gonna kill me.'

'Probably,' smirked Tucker, then he laughed. 'If you die from the heat they will probably untie us and give us something to drink.' Every human in the gang laughed, including Jacky.

'Not funny,' Johnny said with a laugh in his voice. Turning to Esperance who was watching still, he spoke: 'I will die here rather than kill another innocent human.'

@

Devil was furious, although you would never know it. Not for him the blanching white that other Settlers couldn't control, a physiological response to anger. Not for him the thin mouth, straight and expressionless. Not for him the slight bulging of his large liquid eyes, the open panting mouth. He had too much control for that.

Instead, the only clue – and one that his staff had learnt to look out for – was a slight, almost invisible quivering of the muscles of his back and neck, a sign of energy suppressed, of fury controlled by pure will. His stillness was terrifying; all who passed his open door looked away quickly, frantically, walked away with studied calm, making no noise. None of them wanted to be noticed, to be the one to be hit by the splash over from whatever it was on his mind. They would have reported sick to go home if only the request could escape his attention.

How dare that festering pile of dirt, that pathetic, useless nothingness, that ungrateful animal, that moronic creature, that Native, be so hard to find? Already the affair was eating into his inadequate budget, forcing him to write to the slippery bureaucrats to ask for more money for the hunt. If they did not give him what he needed, he knew other Natives would try it, try to run, try to go back to whatever it was they called their lives.

If anyone was watching they would have taken some hope from his faint, slightly smug, smile – hope that the impending thunderstorm had passed over, leaving them safe. It was not just his problem, not anymore. The Native – unfortunately his responsibility – had been seen with a fugitive, criminal Settler. That was a job for law enforcement, the Troopers, to finally take care of this so-called Mister Star. So far the mission had been paid for using Devil's budget even when Enforcement staff did the work. That had to change.

Quickly, perhaps too quickly, Devil drafted a letter, his hands a blur. Enforcement should, he believed, split the cost of the mission with his department. The mission was already underway to hunt down the fugitives; this would decrease the costs for them. Just as quickly, he screwed the paper into a ball and threw it in the bin. It was not his problem anymore. Johnny Star was someone else's problem, the fact that he had been seen with one of the Native fugitives just proved that Enforcement should have taken care of him long ago.

The next letter was written with more care, more diligence, and with a faint almost-smile. Information, that was what he offered, all he offered: he knew where to find Star, had men already on the way to apprehend him. Above all he had a pretty good idea where they must be headed; Sergeant Rohan would find him. When they found him Enforcement could pay for the retrieval, alive or dead, of Johnny Star and all with him.

Sergeant Rohan had already done all the hard work, Devil had already paid for the search for the fugitives with his department budget. All Enforcement would need to do was pay for the actual apprehension of the gang. All Devil and his department required in return for this information was Jacky the Native or proof he was dead.

There was a spring in Devil's fingers if not in his step, a dangerous little smile on his face, when he pushed the button that would summon his secretary. Her relief at seeing the grin on his face was palpable, he almost giggled at it. It is better to be feared than loved. She rushed out with the draft letter, it would be typed up, someone would check it and then it would be transmitted.

Someone would pay, and it would not be Devil.

@

Johnny, again, indulged the curiosity of the young. He had spent days tied up, questioned by the elders of the camp, none of them believing he was a friend and had no desire to harm them. He had responded to their distrust in the only way he knew – by being as polite and friendly as possible. The children in the camp had never, for the most part, met a Settler – they being, until Johnny came, legendary demons, creatures of terror. All their lives they had run from the Settlers before they had even seen them.

What a dilemma. He wanted them to trust him, yet he could not teach them to trust Settlers, Toads in general. The children could not afford to lose their fear of the Settlers. Careful to ensure they knew he was different to others of his species, he told them all he could about Settler society. Fortunately, what they were most interested in was the stories of his life as an outlaw, a highwayman. He had to admit, to anyone looking at that life from the outside it must have seemed romantic. From the inside it was terrible, dangerous, tiring, painful and, most of all, thirsty work.

He told them the stories – of narrow escapes, of prison breaks, stealing food and fleeing from towns. So that they would understand the danger they were in, he told them of the gunfights, the injuries, of the cruelty and arrogance of his people. He did not tell them of the times the gang had nearly died from starvation and dehydration, the times they had been wounded or sick and had no access to medical assistance. The children already knew what it meant to be starving and sick.

Most importantly he did not tell them of the time before he went outlaw, when as a trooper he had captured, imprisoned and killed people like them and their parents. He told the stories of those raids, but was careful to write himself out of the action. It was strangers who killed the Natives, strangers who arrested them and took them to jail, never Johnny.

His friends, despite their protestations, had been released already. Whenever they could, they spent their time by the fire in the middle of the camp, with him. They did not get much free time. They were survivors, they were skilled effective hunters and there were many hungry people in camp to feed. They had wanted to stay with Johnny, show their support, their solidarity, their love, yet they could not watch these people starve. Johnny supported their decision to abandon him.

Although careful not to show it, Johnny was desperate to end his captivity. The humans needed him. Around the camp could be seen barely working remains of human technology that could, if working more efficiently, make their lives more comfortable, make them all safer. He was not human, but part of every trooper's training was simple engineering and mechanics so they could repair any human tech they found and make use of it in the field. He was better than most; when he was alone in the swamp he had needed to fix everything himself.

At the end of the camp was a mound of camouflage netting covering what must have been a shabby collection of human vehicles before the Invasion. In the many years since they must have been turned by rough use and rougher repairs into wrecks barely able to move. Glass glinted around the cars – solar panels, he thought, a rough human technology for producing electricity that worked well enough out here on this planet, in this sun. They were something his people would never have invented; their planet had not enough unfiltered sunlight to encourage the development.

There were other signs of old human technology too. Hunting parties and sentries carried small, hand-held communicators – radio most likely. They would need charging for sure. Occasionally from the direction of the cars would be heard a burst of white noise, not for long, but there. Maybe they had a radio tuned to human bandwidths hoping to hear someone, anyone else, talking.

Johnny was saddened, more than he expected to be, by the prospect that this might be the largest group of truly wild, truly free humans left in the world. Unless the group that once was home to Paddy, the enigma, was still out there, still free. He could hope they were; it would be a terrible sadness if they had gone the way of the rest of the humans.

Days into his captivity, only freed from his bonds long enough to eat, he felt he had made some friends. The woman he had surrendered to, Esperance, approached. That young human had impressed him, though she was not in charge of the camp. Leadership was clearly in the hands of a council of elders, mostly men, her grandfather the oldest of them. However, all the younger, more active residents of the camp – the hunters and fighters, the builders and scouts – automatically turned to the girl, Esperance, for leadership.

In a more civilised setting the elders would be the parliament but she would be the general. If she had been his commander in the Troopers he might not have taken off and gone outlaw.

'Good morning, Esperance,' he said with saccharine, false cheerfulness, desperate to make her laugh, 'it was a lovely cool night last night, I hope you slept well.'

Esperance sounded unusually conciliatory, she almost laughed. 'Your friends have been so useful, helping find food, taking a turn at guard duty, scouting for resources. My people have come to trust and even rely on them.' She paused for a moment, seeming uncertain. Johnny nodded, and she went on. 'Trust in you has come slower. My people have learnt to never trust your people, because you have done everybody here some harm. If your people have not directly hurt someone they have indirectly. Almost everybody here has lost family to the Toads, and everybody has a story of pain at your people's hands.

'You personally have done nothing to us, have been nothing but polite, nothing but an apparent friend. Your friends speak highly of you, saying that you have repeatedly saved their lives, that you would endanger yourself before you would allow one of them to enter danger.'

'Yes,' said Johnny, 'I have come to love my friends, and through them your people, all your people, all your race, your species. There is no doubt in my mind that we – I mean the Settlers – are nothing but a plague on this planet. I do not hate the people back home. They might have sent people here to colonise, but that could have been a stupid mistake, it could have been mere short-sightedness, but I do hate the Settlers here.'

Clouds scudded overhead, bringing with them a momentary shadow, a waft of cool air, a relief for Johnny's dry, hot skin. For a time the light was less painful to his large, open, liquid eyes. The constant watering, constant weeping, that protected them from the heat momentarily abated. It seemed for just a second that he had been crying and had stopped.

'The council have voted to unbind you, allow you to help at camp if you desire,' Esperance said, 'though so far they do not trust you enough to give you back your guns.' She raised up her hand as Johnny started to speak, 'I know you would be a great help if we were suddenly attacked, but at the moment most of the elders and most of the hunters are not certain enough that you are not a greater danger than an attack by the Troopers.'

She glared at him as if daring him to argue. 'I like you Toad, Johnny,' she said, 'but I cannot yet trust you enough to let you walk around here armed. Your friends say I can trust you, the council have agreed with them for now, we need your word.' Esperance stared at him, and he felt she was trying to cut through his skin to the flesh beneath. 'Do you give your word to do nothing to harm anyone in this camp, and to not contact your people?'

Johnny nodded. 'I swear to harm nobody in this camp even if they harm me first –' he held up his hand as Esperance opened her mouth to speak. 'Even if they harm me first,' he repeated, 'and I swear not to contact any Settlers. I cannot swear to not contact my people because if my friends here, and your people here, are not my people,' he paused and sighed, 'then I have no people.'

Esperance leaned over with a nervous stiffness that made a lie of the confidence she was professing. She was still scared, Johnny could see that, so he made no move, trying to not even breathe in a threatening way. Visibly steeling herself, she cut the bonds around Johnny's hands then stepped back.

Stretching his arms Johnny sighed then smiled. Looking at his feet pointedly, he said 'I would stand better if you cut the bonds around my ankles too,' and laughed. Esperance surprised him then, turning the knife in her hand and holding it out to him hilt-first.

'It's your knife anyway,' she said, 'I could count it as a weapon but around here a knife is almost part of somebody's clothing, you can't even eat properly without one.'

'Thank you,' he said, the words somehow managing to carry most of the weight of the planet.

'You're welcome,' Esperance replied before turning on her heel and walking swiftly away.

Days into his stay in the mission, living in the guest quarters on the men's side of the compound, Inspector Grark from the First Church realised that he and at least some of the missionaries were working at cross-purposes. The Mother Superior certainly had something to hide, yet so skilful was she at such subterfuge that he had not noticed for days. It would be many weeks before he could have any evidence to hand to someone else, if he found it at all. The children seemed happy, there was no overt cruelty that he could see, they took to the education and mild discipline of the mission like ducks to water.

However, something made him uneasy. Maybe the children were too obedient, too quiet, too much not like children. Wherever he had gone on his visit to Earth, to this continent the humans used to call Australia, he had seen slavery. Yet, wherever he went he also saw children being children whenever they could get away with it – they were noisy, rambunctious, they almost reminded him of the young back home.

Here the human children were quiet and passive, perfect little angels, far more disciplined than the children of his own people. He had received no answer to his questions: Why were the children so quiet, when human children are so hard to control? Why was obedience and religion given more time in class than all other subjects when the school was instituted to prepare the Natives for life in the Empire?

Most importantly, what were those small buildings for, the ones that looked like lockable kennels for animals? The buildings the children were so scared of, so scared they wouldn't even look at them. They looked for all the world like punishment cells. There was no doubt in his mind, none at all, that punishment cells is exactly what they were, yet he could find no member of the mission staff, even the Native tracker, who would confirm this. He could not even find the missionary who had sent the letter to his superiors that led him to this baking hot place.

He could not find the evidence he wanted in the security cameras. He had clearance to access them, should have been able to find all he needed, yet a reported computer failure had destroyed random chunks of data. What was left was full of holes – either the computer was intermittently failing or it was being systematically hacked. Either someone was more skilled than he would expect or they were getting help; the hacking was so good he couldn't even prove it was happening.

Trying to put an end to it, he called for help from the Mission Authority technical division. Unfortunately, they were too far out and the staff too busy – it would be months before anyone could be spared to send out to the mission. If anyone was going to arrive at all . . . He hadn't been on the planet more than a few weeks, but he thought it unlikely technical would come.

Waking early, he again walked over to the dormitory hoping to see the children waking, hoping he would catch someone at some sort of abuse before they were alert enough to hide it, before they could guess he was watching. Again he was foiled. The children were already up and eating a nutritious breakfast. They did not seem to skimp on food here, yet there was another mystery. Even with little experience of the species he could see that every child showed evidence of longstanding malnutrition.

Soon the sun rose high enough to notice the heat; it was as hot as hell again. Returning to his room Grark slipped into his wet-suit – the waterproof fabric keeping in a thin coating of water, kept cool by a tiny battery power cooler unit. He had no idea how it worked, had no interest in finding out – that was a job for engineers, technicians. It was heavier than he would have liked it to be, adding what felt like thirty kilograms to the weight being carried by aching knees. At least his skin was cool and wet again and he was thankful for the suit more than he was horrified at its unnecessary weight. Surely some sort of antigrav would be possible, they had been talking about it for years.

The nuns, obedient to their tradition of simplicity and poverty, were pointedly wearing their heavy, plain habits; shunning, scorning climate control. They must have adapted to the climate a little but he wondered how they survived living like that; it would kill him in a heartbeat. It was obvious they did not approve of his wet-suit, the looks they gave him made that abundantly clear.

Wandering the mission he tried to discover anything he could, anything at all.

Another day went past, the yellow-blue sky cloudless, the too-yellow sun too bright, the heat and the dry air oppressive, without him discovering any more. He could not wait for a crisis, for something to go wrong, for someone to make a mistake. Either something had to happen soon or he would have to admit defeat and go back to the city. If he hung around it would be too obvious that he was waiting for something to happen.

There was never enough water in the mission, yet there was always cool water to bathe. Likely it was not considered an indulgence by the Order because cleanliness was one of the virtues they espoused. Bathing was essential for his species – without it they died after first going mad from the pain. However there was bathing and there was bathing – surely twice, three times a day, as he had seen from some of the nuns, was more bathing than one needed for simple cleanliness, or for health.

There would be more water for drinking, more for growing crops if there was a little less bathing. Not that he would consider complaining to home about it. Bathing was an inalienable right for his people and he could not complain when he was as guilty as anyone.

Bathing went some of the way towards returning his sense of goodwill towards men, and women come to think of it, even towards humans. The tub was small but he'd got the water temperature perfect before climbing in. If he had been anywhere else, he might have burst into song but here, among the austere nuns, it was ill-advised. Actually, a hymn might be acceptable, a hymn was almost always acceptable. He had not much of a singing voice but nevertheless he croaked out one of the more popular but now less acceptable hymns as he climbed out of the tub.

'Father.' The voice at the bathing-room window stopped him dead in the middle of a rousing line with plenty of oompah and pomp. Still singing, to reduce suspicion from anyone who was watching him, he paced over to the window. When the song naturally ended he spoke quietly.

'Who is that?' He had his hopes but was careful not to let any emotion other than bland curiosity into his voice.

'Father, I cannot speak long, she is always watching.' He tried to identify the voice of whoever was talking but had not heard any of the sisters talk enough.

'Who is watching?' He thought he knew, though there was no harm in seeking confirmation.

'Sister Bagra, the Mother Superior,' the voice hissed, 'she thinks whoever wrote the letter was a traitor, she is seeking them, she is always watching.' The voice went silent for twenty of Grark's excited, ragged breaths. 'This place is not normally like this. The children are just children but she has threatened to kill them all if they do not behave while you are here. Those little sheds, they are punishment cells . . . the children call them the "boob".'

There, the proof he needed – if only this nun, this terrified nun, would testify.

The voice when it went on was almost unintelligible, overcome with an emotion he could not identify. 'There was an epidemic reported here – children died, were reported dead. The doctor in town who looks after the children here, he writes whatever

Mother wants on the reports. He hates the Natives. It was not an epidemic, there was no disease. Those children died from lack of water. She locked them up in the "boob", the punishment cells, and left them there. She said their screaming was a lesson to the other children, she forbade us to help them. She told the other children they would be next.'

'You have to testify,' Grark hissed out the window, realising too late that he was talking to nobody – the voice outside had disappeared. He had to find her, this mystery informant, right now.

Not yet dressed, he pulled his blackest robes over his nakedness. They would cover him enough and in the night he would be hard to see. Running from the bathing room he saw the nun sprinting off into the darkness.

His bulk belied his speed, he had trained to be fast, kept the bulk as camouflage. Catching up with her just before she reached the door of the convent proper, he lay his hand gently on her arm. It was the youngest nun, he realised, the one called Mel. Soft-hearted, she seemed to be the one most convinced that humans were sentient, yet she was as soft and wet as a used tissue. Surely she could not have had the gumption to have sent that letter home.

'Was it you who sent the letter and informed us of the abuse here?'

She shook her head, even in the twilight he could tell she was perplexed. 'I know of the letter,' she said, 'but I didn't send it.

'I would be too scared, I wished I had said something but I was too scared.'

Camp was at the edge of a small, forgotten waterhole. Grandfather had told Esperance that it must have been a farm dam once, a dam built by humans when they ruled, when they owned this place, when they lived free. Now it was not much more than a muddy puddle. All the water that was left after the low mud and clay wall had collapsed; a victim of time and lack of maintenance. The tiny water supply was welcome, an oasis in the desert, one that hopefully the Toads would never find.

Birds lived there, the remnants of Earth species. Out in the desert the Settler animals had not yet displaced them, or hunted them extinct. Waterbirds, living closer to the waterways that the Settlers frequented, had suffered the worst. The animals brought in by the Settlers, farm animals and pets that went feral, had taken care of the few waterbirds that the Settlers hadn't eaten. It was nice to see waterbirds, to see wading birds, even ducks. She had seen ducks in books, in a bombed but not burned library, yet before they had arrived in that camp she had thought them a myth, or extinct at least. She never grew tired of looking at the ducks.

The refugees were well fed – the hunting and scavenging had been good so nobody had killed any of the birds. It felt wrong, killing them, when they were clearly almost extinct. By unspoken agreement they were being left alone. How could anyone contemplate eating a rare bird that had been so common before the Invasion, that was such a strong thread through human history, culture and myth?

Esperance was alone, as she so often was these days. The despair in the camp had been too deep, she could no longer swim it. The trees there were thick, good cover for the camp, she hoped it would be enough, though she thought nothing would be enough ever again. The new arrivals were settling in well, even though she had not expected them to. Again she was pleasantly surprised by her people.

Not that it was easy having new people there, people who had been through the fire, who were still being hunted. Hiding was even more important than it had ever been before – there were more fliers, no doubt looking for the new ones, the fugitives. Despite the risk, despite the fact that they were new, despite even the fact that one of the new arrivals was a Toad, nobody considered turning them out. There were almost silent mumbles but none were prepared to go out on a limb to reject them.

Again there was surprise – Johnny Star had become an important part of the camp, of the community, the family. His knowledge of the Troopers from his time with them, although none wanted to think of how he had learnt it, was invaluable in planning their defence. His charm and easy, though dark and sardonic, humour lit up the camp wherever he went.

Grandfather, although normally slow to warm to anyone, got on with the Toad easier than anyone. Esperance supposed it had to be because both were once soldiers, albeit on opposite sides. Maybe there was more similarity between soldiers on different sides than between soldiers and civilians. Soldiers are soldiers no matter who they fight for. It was strange to see Grandfather and Johnny deep in conversation, heads close together as if keeping secrets, laughing in unison, their very different laughs clashing.

She was glad, though, that her poor lonely grandfather had a friend to talk to.

An early riser she went bush earlier than everyone else, almost every morning. She liked the peace, she liked to hunt before the sun hit the sky – it was cooler and more comfortable on her skin that humans had called 'white' before the Toads came, before skin colour became irrelevant. The lizards she hunted most for food out there; they were cold-blooded, they would still be asleep in their holes if she was early enough.

In the near silence of the forest there was a strangled cry, a magpie singing a half note, a timid sound, a frightened sound. Magpies are like that; they sing to warn off intruders, they sing to warn each other. Esperance had been even more careful than normal so it was unlikely to have been her who alerted the birds. Besides it was somewhere away to her right, the wrong direction. Presumably it was only birds in her path who would cry out. Neither could it have been someone from the camp, carelessly scaring the neighbours; camp was far away and nobody else had left when she walked away.

The cry of that magpie, her favourite song cut short, was like ice-water pouring into her veins. Frozen for a moment by that influx of ice she stood, as the trees, as the rocks. There was no thought, no volition, nothing but that fear that reinforces, from the deep unconscious, the need for utter silence.

When she could breathe again she stood, loose, relaxed, and listened, trying to turn her whole body, her entire being into a device for hearing. There, off to the right, the sound of people, several of them trying to move silently, people not familiar with these woods, people from the city perhaps. It was unlikely they would be human.

Sliding the walkie-talkie from her pocket, praying she had set the controls for silence, she pressed three times on the 'press to talk' button. She could not risk a word, but if someone at camp was listening they would hear the three bursts of static, the new camp code for 'beware, someone is coming'. Hoping that someone had heard the signal, hoping someone was getting ready to defend the camp, having no choice but to act on the assumption the others were doing what they should, she moved towards the noise with the silent grace of someone for whom silence has long been a matter of survival.

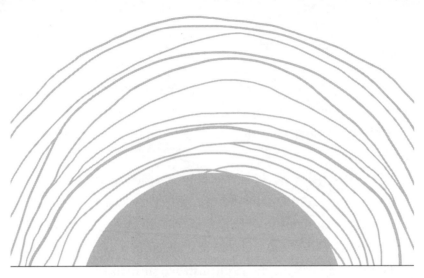

CHAPTER 19

There have been calls by some citizens, some subjects of the Empire to allow full freedom of movement within the Empire, to allow subjects from one planet to move to another freely regardless of species. We should think carefully before allowing such a privilege to anyone who is not of our race, the race that created this Empire. Think on this: would you tolerate humans from Earth migrating to Shalis or Shalisians migrating to Earth? Shalis and Earth are our Colonies, and only we should be allowed to move between them.

Even less tolerable would be allowing citizens of our allies to move to planets in our Empire. Only our people deserve the right to free movement in our Empire. That is the way it has always been, that is the way it will always be.

– TISSHAK GALISS, HEAD DEPARTMENT OF IMMIGRATION, COLONIAL ADMINISTRATION

THE SURVEILLANCE SATELLITE over this part of Earth was shiny and new, recently launched and barely operational. There was no astronautics factory on this ridiculous, primitive planet so it had been sent all the way from home. They couldn't even co-opt the Native technicians to unpack, assemble and launch the satellite; they did not understand the technology and besides, they could not be trusted.

That was not why it was barely operational, it was barely operational because Colonial Administration back home had for some reason not sent the right technical staff, again. Techs in other fields had been co-opted and told to do their best using the manual.

Home had not sent the right instruction manual either.

It was a hard thing to admit but there was essentially nobody in the colony who knew how to repair the satellites, or even unpack and launch them properly.

Sergeant Rohan had been firm. Then he had been aggressive. Finally, he had been vicious, almost screaming over the communicator. None of that had freed up the satellite to search where he thought Jacky had gone. Much to his despair and disgust he eventually had to call his superior officer, who tried a different tack, calling in favours. All attempts were unsuccessful. Even the notorious Devil, who wanted to find Jacky as much as Rohan did, could not mobilise the satellites to the effort. It was when Rohan resorted to threats, threats he was notorious for carrying out, that with a startling suddenness the satellite was both in operation and not tied up in routine searches for water.

Therefore, finally, Rohan had somewhere to go – a target less nebulous than tracking some footprints across the desert. In the fugitives' last known direction of travel there was a ragged feral Native camp, a number of tin and canvas roofs scattered among the trees where nobody should have been living. If they had not arrived at that camp yet, surely they would soon; there was nowhere else to go.

He smiled as he handed the coordinates to the flier pilot.

@

Johnny Star and Jacky were drinking tea, something neither was particularly familiar with but a tradition that was rapidly growing on both of them. Not that there was any actual tea in their tea; instead they were drinking what the refugees had been calling tea, a constantly varying mix of herbs and leaves that is sometimes, but not always, quite pleasant. Tea was not a drink, not in that camp. Tea was really just a chance to socialise, a reason to sit down.

They both heard the three staccato, almost percussive, blasts of static on the radio in the communications tent.

Both men leapt up reflexively, though their reactions immediately after standing could not have been more different. Johnny drew his handgun from the pocket in his belt in a single fluid movement. Reaching out, almost without looking, he placed his hand on Jacky's shoulder, arresting him in the process of fleeing.

'Stay, kid,' Johnny said, his voice filled with barely controlled tension. 'If someone has come for us the least we can do is help these poor people fight the enemy we brought down on them. I understand the desire to flee, I feel it too but we cannot give in to that desire, not this time.' Jacky relaxed; Johnny could feel the muscle tension leaving the young man as he was enveloped by inevitability. He was not relaxed, not really, but he was doing a damned fine impersonation. 'I've run, and run, and run, how can I stop running?'

'There are too many people here, too many children, too many old, sick, injured. They cannot all run. We have to at least give them a chance. Besides, we don't even know for sure who is coming, it might be refugees.'

Around them the camp was exploding into activity. Anyone who could fight, men and women, older children, all who carried arms, scrambled to prepare to defend the camp. All those who were unable to fight grabbed their most precious belongings and as much food as they could carry and scattered into the trees in small groups.

If they could defend the camp, they would, and then those who had run would return. They were no longer safe there; they would pack and move again if they fought off this attack. If they could not defend the camp, if the enemy were too many, or too well armed, they would delay the foe with their deaths. Maybe someone they loved would get away, maybe somebody would get away.

@

Sister Bagra carefully concealed her rage. Such anger was not becoming for a nun of her rank, that was reason enough. However, the real reason was that the excremental inspector, Father Grark from home, was still at her mission, still watching. If she was seen to lose her temper he would surely believe what was said in the letter.

She had only a few days to go, he was being recalled home. She had discovered this fact only that morning.

'Well, Mother Superior,' he had said when they met outside just after breakfast, 'it seems that the accusations in the letter must be untrue. I have seen no evidence of cruelty and abuse against these Natives.'

'Of course not,' she replied, 'I would not allow anything in my mission that would cast the Order or the First Church into disrepute.'

Grark nodded. She could see nothing on his face that gave any clue to what he was thinking.

'Of course. The only concern we have,' he continued, 'and by "we" I mean the Church as a whole, is that you, and the other sisters, need to follow the official line on the status of the Natives.'

'Which is?' Bagra's voice was so carefully emotionless it froze the air.

'The Natives are sentient,' he said with utter certainty. 'They might not be as intelligent as you and me but they are sentient beings. Thus they are people, they are our equals in the eyes of the Church if not yet in the eyes of the government, and are to be treated as such. We have concerns about reports, about evidence of slavery in the colony. Slavery cannot be tolerated.'

'Of course not.' Bagra's voice was too adamant. She almost flinched away from her own tone.

'Once you treat them as our equals I have no doubt that the slavery will end. I don't know if you are aware of this, but the servants you send from here are generally paid nothing but rations, nothing but room and board. They are arrested for running away if they ever find the courage to do so.

'If you are working without pay, and arrested for leaving, you are, by definition, a slave. Slavery is illegal in the Empire and against the strictures of the Church.'

Bagra fumed inside. Surely this imbecile didn't actually believe the children, the Natives, were people? He had been there with them, he had seen what she was working with, what the children were, how could he have concluded they were people? She had one path of appeal left against this madness and she fully intended to use it.

'God created the universe, he placed life on home, it says nothing in the Holy Book about other planets, about this place. Therefore, he could not have created life on this planet, therefore they are monsters, or demons, or animals. In fact, by the scriptures they cannot even be alive, they should not even exist.'

'Then the Book is wrong. It makes no mention of the other planets in our Empire or of the other empires we have fought in the wars either.'

Bagra choked back a scream, turned and walked away. He followed, faster than she would have expected from someone of his age. 'Sister Bagra,' he said when he finally caught up, 'I have to leave in a few days. I received communication stating that I have to return to report my findings back home. It must be important – they sent a fast courier with the letter.'

Bagra carefully controlled her features, letting not even the slightest sign of triumph escape, walked away fast, yet calmly. She would be disciplined, she would be strong.

The sun was setting, it was time to go inside to finally eat, when Bagra caught Mel walking towards the visitors' quarters. 'Where are you going? It is almost time to eat,' Bagra said, all sweetness, no sign of her anger at all.

'Ah, I had a question, a spiritual question to ask Father Grark,' the girl said, sounding nervous.

'Surely,' said Bagra, frost forming on her words, 'you can ask such questions of me, your Mother Superior. If you cannot find me, there are other nuns in the mission with about as much knowledge, as much authority. You can speak to them.' Her voice became somehow even colder, 'Surely you have nothing to speak to an outsider about.'

The girl hissed and sighed, her breath heavy, her eyes were darting as if she was trying to see everything in the world at once and was therefore seeing nothing.

'It was you, wasn't it?' Bagra had reached the end of her tether, she had no ability left to hide her displeasure. Anger turned her voice into the hiss of a venomous snake; she had to speak or she knew she would explode or do something worse, something unforgivable. 'You sent that vile letter, such horrible accusations against your own people, so vile. You are one of us yet you would betray us.'

Mel shook her head from side to side, a bad habit she had learnt from the disgusting humans, and then lowered it in firm submission. 'I . . .' her voice was tiny, almost inaudible. Bagra leaned closer to hear better. 'I . . . I did nothing, I didn't.'

'Nonsense,' Bagra hissed, 'who else could it have been?'

Turning suddenly and wailing, Mel ran out into the descending night. Bagra was not sure it had been a good idea to provoke the girl but nevertheless she quietly went back to her cell. Grabbing her plaque, she slipped her tap into the security cameras, watching the guestroom.

@

Father Grark was triumphant though he was careful not to let it show.

He had gone to bed early after a simple repast. Nothing was likely to happen that night so it was no good getting tired waiting for it.

When morning came he checked his plaque as normal, expecting to see nothing, yet this time something was there. A flashing code on the screen told him that someone, and he would know who in a moment, had hacked into the security camera system. Highly illegal, and all the proof he needed. Success! His own hack had detected and identified the hacker, or the hacker's plaque at least.

Sister Bagra. He might not be able to prove abuse of the children but he could at least have her removed.

Dressing quickly he stepped with false calm out the door of the guestroom. Striding across the compound he noticed an unusual turmoil. Nuns paced around the compound, children ran, searching for something. One of the nuns, a younger one, walked over so fast, with so little grace she might as well have run.

'Father,' she puffed, 'have you seen Mel?'

'Pardon, who?'

'Mel. She was the newest, the youngest here, she is missing. Her bed was not slept in last night, she isn't anywhere.'

'We will search, we will find her.'

Some hours later, when she was not found, a runner was sent to find the tracker. He was glum when they returned with him, though completely professional. Grark understood he stayed in the nearby camp because, just like everyone else there, he had a child in the school. At least being the tracker gave him access to the school. He could, unlike the other parents, at least see his daughter even though he could never get permission to speak to her. Grark was not even certain she knew he was her father.

Later that night, Grark held off confronting the Mother Superior for to do so would throw the already tense mission into deeper turmoil. The tracker returned. He had followed tracks; they staggered like those made by someone insensible, he said; he had marked where to begin tomorrow morning.

The next morning broke clear, the sky yellow-blue, terrifying to those born under the grey, damp, skies of home. The tracker was gone before light, starting at dawn in the place where he had left off when it got dark. Grark strolled around the mission, waiting for news, waiting for the opportune moment to confront Sister Bagra.

Not waiting for the tracker to succeed or fail, all the nuns led groups of the children on a search. Seeming to not understand the gravity of the situation they were screaming and giggling, delighted to be outside. The noise was piercing, threatening to give him a headache, though it was good to see the children acting like children.

That night, again, the tracker returned without the missing nun. The other searchers staggered in with nothing to show for a day in the heat. Grark then finally thought of checking the video stored from the mission's cameras. Making sure to lock the door to the guestroom he entered his access codes to the system. There she was, on the night she disappeared, walking through the convent rooms. He programmed the system to track her movements; when she left the view of a camera the screen automatically flitted to another.

She left the building, with all its cameras, and for a moment the system lost her, then it picked her up again on an outside scan. It was too far away to see clearly but she appeared to be heading to the guest quarters. She must have been on the way to see him but didn't get that far.

Suddenly another nun appeared out of the darkness into view of the camera. He could not see who she was, it was too far away, but maybe the computer could. Typing a command he let the artificial intelligence analyse shape and movement while watching for what happened next. It appeared to be a confrontation. Mel was taking a submissive stance, the other nun was aggressive, dangerously so.

Mel walked away from the confrontation, breaking into a run just before she left the range of the camera. A line of text appeared at the bottom of the screen, 'Subject lost', as if he did not know that. He had at least discovered why she had run, even if he knew no more about where. The tracker was searching in the right direction.

He kept staring at his screen, watching the 'processing' icon whirl. Finally it stopped and he saw what he had suspected: 'Second Subject – Mother Superior, Sister Bagra.' He had found some proof of wrongdoing, enough to get her removed. Fearing another 'incident' with the servers he backed up the relevant video and went to sleep. Tomorrow would bring conclusion, or it would bring more crisis, there was nothing more he could do that night.

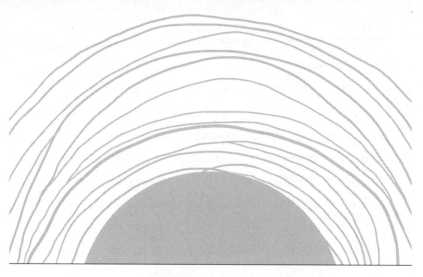

CHAPTER 20

You think you are smarter than us, you think your brains are bigger, you think we can't learn. We know more than you, we have stories and songs, we have art and culture. What do you have? You have guns and fury and hate. The war has so far been about guns and death. When you think we are defeated the war will change.

The next war will be about resilience and survival, culture and art. When that war begins you will discover you are not well armed. You have no art, your stories have no power.

– GIGI GREYHAIR

ESPERANCE WAS FOLLOWING when the Troopers and Rohan picked their careful, meticulous way towards the camp. She had turned the radio off as soon as she sent the warning. The noise of a radio would not help, she knew where the enemy were and unless her radio made a noise they would not know where she was. There was no way for her to get to camp before the interlopers. There was no choice but to hope, to trust that someone, everyone, had responded to her alarm.

It was the first time she had drawn her gun in preparation for using it, first time that was not just dry-firing practice. As always there was the fear: what if she was unable to pull the trigger, what if she failed to shoot and somebody died? What if the gun, not fired for who knew how many years, didn't even work? She and Grandfather had maintained it well, but the fear was still there, it was always there. Again she wished there had been enough ammo in the camp for her, and everyone else in the camp, to learn to shoot by actually shooting.

They thought they were being quiet and sneaky, these Toads, dressed in camouflage as if their mottled grey-green skin was not already the same colour as the few trees scattered around the landscape. Esperance had spent most her life in the bush, her senses were tuned to survival. The small rhythmic noises of someone trying to sneak, like the rustle of a giant goanna scurrying through the undergrowth, were to her like sirens. She did not even have to use eyes to follow the interlopers, she could just follow her ears.

She was still behind them, carefully not being seen or heard, when they halted, confused. The camp was empty, seemingly abandoned. Esperance smiled. Someone had listened, someone had made the right decisions; that meant that some of her people had run for it. They would not necessarily survive this attack, coming as it had from nowhere, but as she had warned them, some of them might get away.

Despite herself, she choked back a squeak when she felt a hand on her shoulder. Turning with studied calm she saw the face of one of the camp's best hunters, Art. He too was armed, with a short bow, silent, deadly, a far more sensible weapon than the pistol, as noisy as it was, that Esperance was holding in shaking hands. Then again, he would have to stand to fire.

In rapid hand signs, glad they had developed and practised that language, they discussed the situation. As Esperance had hoped, what non-combatants there were, the elderly and infirm, little kids, the one pregnant woman, had hidden when she had alerted them. The hunters, the fighters, the stronger and larger children, they were all hiding as best they could in the surrounds, waiting to turn the easy victory the Toads had expected into a deadly ambush.

Unfortunately there were just too many, Esperance knew that, and they were simply too well armed. There was a good chance that none of the defenders, none of her people waiting in ambush would walk away from there alive. She hoped they did not know that, or if they did, she hoped they would not fear it, hoped it would not stay their hands. If they fought hard enough those who had run, who had hidden, might get away.

Jacky was torn. When the desperate plans were made he could have run, could have joined those running, they at least had a chance. He doubted any of the fighters, those preparing to die to give the others that chance, would hold it against him if he ran. Yet he did not. Always he had run, when injustice, when torture, when pain threatened, he had fled, yet he did not. He was not a man of action, he was not even really a man, not much more than a boy; he was no fighter, no soldier, yet he did not run.

His whole life was behind him, a road travelled mindlessly, his barely remembered childhood, his incarceration in that place they called a school. He winced internally to remember his slavery at the Settler farm, the casual cruelty, the conviction in the minds of the Settlers that he was just an animal. Nothing in his life had prepared him for these unaccustomed thoughts, the pride in his humanity that rose unbidden.

Not for the first time he wished he could remember his parents; he searched for them yet could not remember their faces. Anyone there, in those trees, running for their lives, or preparing to die, could have been his family. Maybe they were.

'We are here for the fugitive Jacky Barna, also known as Jacky Jerramungup, and the known outlaw Johnny Star,' a trooper's voice rang out. 'My name is Sergeant Rohan, of the Colonial Troopers. If you have heard of me you will know I am not known for my ability to control my temper. I know somebody is out there, I know you can hear me. Hand them over and I will let the rest of you run away like the cowardly animals you are.'

He turned to his men and spoke again. 'Boys,' he said, 'they are not going to cooperate, so I guess we get to go hunting.' He laughed. 'This is not war, this is not murder,' he growled theatrically, 'this is pest control.' The troopers around him grinned like skulls. Jacky did not expect it, and was unprepared for it when he paced calmly into the centre of the camp. Therefore, nobody else could have possibly known what he was going to do, he did not know what Johnny would have done had he been prepared. A part of him watched himself from the sidelines as he stopped still in the centre of that open space, facing down so many guns without visible fear.

'I am Jacky, some call me Jacky Jerramungup,' his calm voice said. 'I think you are looking for me.'

Carefully keeping his face as expressionless as he could, a facsimile of the impassive face of the hunters, of Paddy, the man from the desert who showed no fear, Jacky watched as Rohan, smiling, walked towards him with cuffs in his hand. He thought he would die with fear when Rohan reached out and put the cuff on his right hand. Rohan bodily turned him to cuff the left hand, and Jacky, using the momentum the trooper had given him, added speed to the turn. He pirouetted on his heels faster than Rohan was ready for, and spinning, dug his stolen kitchen knife into his captor's ribs.

If his life taught him one thing, he would never be captured again.

The stifling hot air was filled with the tension of everybody, Natives and Settlers alike, holding their breaths. Even the air was silent, dead, unwilling to breathe on the land. Heat and the weight of history caught in a hundred throats, oppressive, as thick as treacle. Rohan folded over the knife, his wide-mouthed face stuck in an expression between shock, awe and horror, mingled with a touch of surprise. He did not speak, maybe his lungs had been punctured on the way to the organ the Toads use for a heart.

With a soggy, weak thud he hit the ground.

There were over thirty Settlers out there, surrounding the camp. When they fired it was like a song, a slippery discordant tune, magpies amplified and distorted, requesting a dance from Jacky. They must have hit him twenty times at least, each hit adding a step to his dance. He fell, a look of total contentment, utter peace on his face. Again the breathless silence descended. Jacky made not a sound, everybody watched as he lay on his back with his head turned to one side. Everybody watched his chest rise and fall, the breaths getting more laboured. Everybody, human and Settler alike, was watching when Jacky Jerramungup, faintly smiling, breathed his last.

@

For an immeasurable length of time – it felt like forever, yet might have been only a few breaths – nobody knew what to do. The fugitive and the hunter, both were dead, there was no purpose left to the already pointless-seeming search. None of the troopers wanted to be there, facing an enemy, unknown, who knew how many Natives were out there? For the Natives, the refugees, Jacky was a stranger, he had brought this attack upon them, they owed nothing to his memory.

Nothing but that he had died bravely, died on his feet, died standing strong, died to stay free.

There was a moment of indecision, a moment when both sides could have ended it there, when the troopers, already uncertain, could have retreated, when the Natives could have stayed hidden. Only Johnny had impetus and energy. Esperance heard a noise and looked over, as he writhed against a strong arm around his shoulders, a hand over his mouth. It was Tucker, the only man who could stop him charging into the circle alone to avenge the human, to die. The tension broke suddenly, the blood-chilling wail of a Settler dying, gutted by a well-sharpened blade, followed almost without pause by the *whaaarp* of a Settler gun.

In the melee that followed Esperance seemed only intermittently present, never still long enough to be a target. She had never fought like this before, her only experience of actual combat was breaking up fights in the camp, stopping friends and family from killing each other. She was no soldier, to stand and fight, untrained, afraid. Her fear seemed to have given her the right instincts to survive, for this was not a good place and time to stand and fight.

Running from cover to cover, she had no idea what to do, how to fight this battle against an overpowering, better-armed enemy. Screams chased her everywhere, screams of her friends and family, screams of pain and anger from the Toads. She barely had time to look where she was going.

In the chaos that had fallen into the camp it didn't matter how good a shot she was. She was slightly less surprised than the Toad she bumped into, and pulled her trigger first. It was the first time she had killed but there was no time to think about it, though her stomach churned for a second. Count your shots, that was what Grandfather had told her. Two was a shot at a distant amphibian as it attacked, drawing a plastic-looking gun on a refugee armed only with an aluminium spear. Three was a shot at the same Toad when she missed and he turned on her. That shot did not miss, she was far enough away to see it properly – the spray of blood, the surprised look on the Toad's face as he fell.

Four and five were fired as reflex when a flailing Toad knocked her down. The fight was by then completely impossible to see, nobody could see the fight for the fighters. In the chaos that followed she fired shots six and seven – one a miss and the other splattering through a Toad's shoulder. Shot eight took that Toad out of his misery.

There were only two shots left, and before her was a trooper in armour, a difficult target and an impossible target for her small handgun. Around her, people died or were dying, the screams of her people forcing blinding tears from her eyes. She blinked to clear her vision and in that instant the Toad raised his gun to fire. She did not run, did not jump or dive, she merely ceased standing, fell boneless to the ground. The surprised trooper fired where she had been and missed; she fired wild, the shot ricocheted off the impenetrable armour.

The noise should have been deafening yet she could not hear – her ears, her brain had shut down from over-stimulation. There was too much death; it painted the ground beneath her feet, it filled the air with a red mist. We all bleed the same colour, Toads and us, we all bleed the same colour – it looped through her brain.

She had one bullet left, a bullet that had always been meant for her, reserved for her from the day Grandfather had given her his gun. From the ground she was vulnerable, down to her last shot, afraid, despairing. There were too many dead of her people in the trees, on the ground near her. Blood pooled on the ground, a rivulet inching towards where she lay. Raising her gun to under her chin, as Grandfather had taught her, she tightened her finger on the trigger, praying to the god that her people had believed in before the Settlers had arrived.

The shot went wide as a Settler grabbed her hand and pulled it aside, her last shot disappearing with a flutter through the leaves. The air was now filled with the screams of the dying, her vision filled with the smirking grey-green face of the Toad. In silence she waited for death, praying for death, in fear that death would not come; there were worse things than dying.

So suddenly she almost didn't notice it, the Toad above her died even as he leaned over her with cuffs in his hand; his large, liquid eyes opening with surprise, his head thrown back, mouth open, silent. The face of Johnny Star appeared over his shoulder, his feral smile almost a mirror of that her attacker had been wearing. Johnny helped Esperance stand, the smile on his face turning grim.

He fired past her ear, and she heard a Settler yelp; she did not know how many Johnny had killed but surely he had killed more than anyone else. His clothes were wet with mucus, a sign of his exertion, of his emotion. Looking her in the eye, taking his eye off the fight, it was then he finally earned her respect.

'There are too many of them, too well armed.' His breath was laboured, his expression pained, surprising Esperance in that moment with its humanity. He gave her a shove, 'Run, damn you,' slipping into a human expression, 'run!'

'I can't.'

'Run, we are all dead, I would run if I had somewhere to go, something to live for, RUN!'

Giving her a last shove, one hard enough to hurt, hard enough to almost knock her down, he turned to fire. She heard a chirping noise from his pistol, the warning tone, warning that the charge was low. She hoped he had more ammo, and then she heard the flier.

It was flying low, its engine emitting a throbbing whirr – a utility flier, it was not well armed, but what weapons it had it was firing fast and indiscriminately. A sound like a tin roof in a hurricane erupted and again the air was filled with screams and wails as her people, already close to utter defeat, were decimated, massacred. This time there was definitely nowhere to run, the flier would kill them all, she was dead.

She had assumed that Grandfather had run, that someone had packed him away, led him into the woods and safety. That was until he stepped out of his hut, walking more erect than she had ever seen him before, more confident than he had been in her entire life. He stopped in the middle of the camp, standing among the dead, and lifted a sky-blue plastic tube to his shoulder. Again the world seemed to hold its breath, time seemed to slow; if anyone was moving, if anyone was fighting still, Esperance could not see it. Then her world stopped.

She wanted to scream 'no' but no words came out.

Grandfather fired his Settler rifle, with the fire-power of a howitzer, at the same moment that the flier fired its rapid-fire pulse cannon. The plasma splattered into Grandfather's skeletal chest; there was no blood, not right away, maybe with the heat of the plasma there would never be. The only family Esperance had, the only hope she truly felt, her entire world, died at the same moment that the flier stalled and accelerated to earth at the speed of gravity.

@

As Grark had hoped the morning did bring conclusion but, to his despair, not the conclusion he had hoped for. The tracker rode slowly into the mission, bringing the feel of dust, of heat with him, drooping on his saddle with exhaustion, even the mount, that tireless beast, hanging its reptilian head with fatigue. Dismounting slowly, he dragged a bundle off his pommel. It was thin, but the length of a body.

Grark feared what it was, knew what it was, and that was quickly confirmed. The tracker stood back in utter breathless silence as one of the arriving nuns unwrapped the bundle. Mouth open yet silenced forever, skin impossibly papery, lay the remains of Sister Mel. As Grark had feared she had not found water in the two days – at most two days – their people can survive without it.

Striding over to the wailing nuns he grabbed Bagra by the shoulder. She turned, mouth open, eyes seething. 'Sister Bagra,' he snarled, 'what did you say to the girl the night she ran off?'

'I did not see her,' she hissed, looking not at him but rather at the other nuns.

'You and I both know you are lying,' Grark stated with confidence, 'you because you are lying and you are not that delusional, me because, unlike you, I have security clearance and saw you argue with her on camera. I am angry with myself about that. If I had thought of it before last night we might have known more to let us find her.'

'She betrayed us,' she said surprisingly haughtily, almost arrogantly. Did she not know the trouble she was in, did she not care? 'She sent that letter that brought the Inspectors down on us, that brought you here. She had to know I knew, she had to feel sorry, she couldn't live with the consequences of that. She must have killed herself when she knew I was on to her.'

One of the older nuns — one so old, so nondescript she was almost furniture, stepped forward. 'She did not betray you, Mother Superior,' her voice thin and tired, old, quavering with the need to stay calm, 'you betrayed the Order, betrayed our duty, our mission, with your cruelty. She did not even send the letter,' she paused, sobbing, 'I did.'

'Why?' Bagra gasped, knowing with the death of Mel and the old woman's words the investigation would send her home, knowing it was all over.

'You are too cruel to be a Mother Superior,' she stated matter-of-factly, 'and I have been a member of Save the Humans for the last ten years.'

'Spy, traitor, bitch,' screamed Sister Bagra before collapsing to her knees. Hands on the ground, she wailed.

@

Johnny Star had always known he would die alone, that his own people would end his life. The only decision he had the power to make was how, fighting to the death, fighting to stay free or public ritual execution. A blaze of gunfire or the mocking, laughing, faces of the smugly 'civilised'.

This death was neither. All around him were the bodies of the dead and dying, some he had brought with him, some he had just met. All of them were his friends, his family. The death he had brought with him, the Settlers chasing him and his little gang, had killed this place, for a camp, a village, is not the ground it is on, it is the people who live there. On hands and knees he crawled, too pained even to scream from the plasma burn in his gut, the section of intestine scraping in the hot dust. The firearms of his people kill his people even more efficiently than they kill the Natives.

He was already dead, he knew that; there was no hope of survival. Even with the best of medical care he would most likely die of that wound, and that medical care was too far away even if he was not denied it. He did not know why he was still alive; his heart beat with nothing left to beat it, his blood surely could not be flowing. Yet alive he at least appeared to be to himself, and nobody else's opinion mattered.

Why was he still alive, what was driving his clear, ridiculous, desire to stay conscious, keep moving? Covered in blood, the blood from the ground where so many had died, the blood from corpses, Settler and Native, Toad and human, that were nothing more than obstacles on his path to who knows where, who knew why, he kept moving. There was so much blood it had flooded the dirt under him turning it into dark red mud.

Finally, after an age of crawling, no longer on hands and knees, an age of sliding on his torn-open, burned crispy, belly, he found a corpse that did matter, that he recognised even in his depleted, agonised state. It was a destination of sorts, one his unconscious had chosen for him once his conscious mind switched off. Through blurring eyes he could see the contented human face of Jacky, dead from the moment the fight had started, from before the fight had started. His body lay untouched, lying on his back, with his head to the left.

Johnny had not known Jacky for long, yet the human's death had been something for him to die for. Staring into that beautiful face Johnny from the stars breathed his last. He did not know if there was a heaven, or if he deserved to go there – he had killed so many of Jacky's kind – yet in that final view of that peaceful human face he felt he was as close to heaven as he would ever deserve to get.

@

Grark examined the room with a look of disgust he no longer even wished to disguise. Those walls, how could anyone stand to work in a room with those walls? He had never seen something so busy, so densely layered with bullshit. The contrast between the empty, obsessively plain desk and the walls was painful, nauseating, distressing.

It had taken too long to organise this meeting with the Head of the Department for the Protection of Natives, the legendary Devil. Strange that no matter how hard Grark tried, he couldn't find Devil's real name; the name that should surely be on government records was apparently not known to anyone in the colony. His real name if it existed at all was either hidden or excised from the records. That was madness. That was impossible.

Finally they were to have a meeting and yet the famous – infamous – Devil was not there, and not currently available. It was only Grark's supposed status as an important representative of the Church as well as having some power in government back home that prevented his banishment to some dreary waiting room. Instead he rated the right to wait in the Head's actual office, although having now seen it he could not imagine how any waiting room could be worse.

This was pure and simple power play – making him wait when a meeting was scheduled. If Devil was trying to annoy him it was going to work, yet Grark knew he was too disciplined to lose control. Losing control here, in the office of a senior bureaucrat, would lose him everything.

When Devil finally opened his door and walked into the office like he owned the place, which for all intents and purposes he did, Grark was ready and calm. 'Inspector Grark,' he said in an artificially cheerful voice, 'how good it is to finally meet you. I have heard so much about you.' 'Nothing good' was implied in the tone.

'Mr Devil,' replied Grark just as falsely, 'I must admit to being impressed with the efficiency with which you run your department. Everything seems to be operating extraordinarily well. If only all departments were as well run as yours.'

Devil beamed, delighted at the compliment, seemingly unaware of the sarcasm dripping from Grark's voice. They could both play at that game.

'We do our best. It is our job to manage the safety and quality of life for the Native. They are like children, they don't seem to be able to look after themselves, and it is our duty to ensure that they are protected from the suffering their position and lack of civilisation might cause.'

Grark nodded. He had heard all this before, and a nod was at least safe while saying nothing. 'And what would you say to the accusations that your idea of protection, taking children, taking complete control over their lives, forcing them to work without payment,' his voice was ice, 'is not helping them at all, is in fact far worse than leaving them alone?'

'I would say it's unfounded, ludicrous rubbish,' Devil snapped. 'The Native Rights Association, or Save the Humans –' he said the name as if he was vomiting '– if that is who you have been listening to, don't know what they are talking about.'

Grark stood, took a few paces. It was obvious all his considerable mental strength was focused on containing his anger. 'What do you say then, to the further accusation that paying the Natives nothing but rations is actually slavery? You know of course that slavery has been outlawed in our Empire.'

'Of course I know slavery is outlawed, I read the news, I read the endless memos I get sent from home. It is illegal to enslave a citizen, and all members of intelligent species have the same right to citizenship, that is the law.' Devil was so angry he was shaking, yet the quivering of his muscles was the only real clue. 'You can't enslave an animal. It is not slavery when we ride a mount, when we keep pets. It is not slavery because the Native is an animal.'

'The Church has been studying the Native,' Grark continued in a conversational tone. 'We have concluded they are intelligent – whether or not they are our equals is still being debated, but the debate regarding their intelligence is over. So is the debate about slavery of intelligent species, that has been over a long time now.'

'You people from home, you know nothing,' Devil was almost screaming, drops of saliva spraying from his mouth. Grark backed off, more to keep himself clean than for fear of that vapid little man.

Grark turned to leave. Trying for a passing shot Devil would have no chance to reply to, he turned as he reached the door. 'Of course, I will have to report to the government and the people back home about the slavery here.' He could no longer keep the scorn he felt for Devil from his voice. 'It cannot be tolerated. Pray the administration is merciful and you get to keep your job.' With that said he stepped out the door before Devil could respond, walking away from the furious squalling behind him.

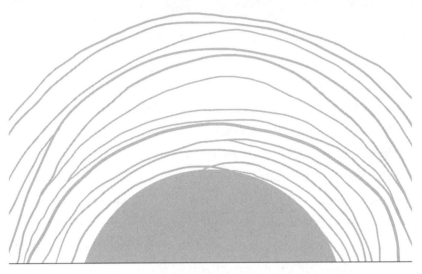

CHAPTER 21

Many recently have called for the ultimate end to the so-called 'Native Problem'. The Natives are intransigent, rebellious, uncontrollable and ultimately destructive. Whilst some have been trained to be useful in some small roles in our society, others have refused to learn our ways, follow our laws, and become useful servants. These rebellious uncivilised Natives collect in camps in and around towns, they drink and consume drugs. Having no means of support they survive by begging and by theft.

This problem is far more obvious in the frontier cities on the edges of the deserts, near the land where we cannot live. For so long we have been reliant as a society on using Native workers to manage our concerns in those areas, and the Natives who work are also harassed by those who will not – begging from working relatives is almost an institution for those Natives who do not work. Increased policing will, of course, take control of the problem, allowing the punishment and imprisonment of the Native, but would be costly – a cost we would not wish to bear as increased taxes.

The recent rebellion by the Native Jacky Jerramungup was relatively short-lived, but far too public; it drew attention back home to the

'Native Problem' while seeding rebellion in the minds of the other Natives. In the months since then the Native population has been even harder to control, harder to tolerate than usual.

In the aftermath of that short rebellion some have even called for the complete extermination of the Native, the arming of hunting parties or the use of a controlled virus to eliminate the problem. It would be neither desirable nor ethical to exterminate an endangered species. We cannot allow a situation to arise where the few Natives we have in zoos are the only survivors of the once numerous animal.

It is with those thoughts in mind that I make a suggestion that would be unpopular with some. In the old days on Earth before we settled it, a small country called Britain historically transported their undesirables to the island they called Australia. The country of America handled their Native problem by forcing their Natives into reservations. Note, the 'Natives' the Americans dealt with were a different coloured and culturally distinct race of their own species.

I propose that the 'Native Problem' in this colony can be solved in a similar manner. The island Australia is large but almost entirely useless to us, the Settler community. The rainfall is almost non-existent and the soil is almost completely infertile by our standards. Desalination of seawater and irrigation of the land would resolve some of the problems there but the natural environment we would be forced to work with there and the sheer size of the island would make conversion to a healthier environment prohibitive.

In addition, Australia, being about ninety per cent uninhabitable by our people, has a Native population more difficult to control. Not only do they possibly outnumber us there – although with the difficulties involved in recording a census we may never know – but the desert, ninety per cent of the vast island, gives fugitives the opportunity to disappear. Evidence has arisen that the Native has never been under complete control on that island. Native workers do not so much run away, it is more like they can come and go at will. They have learnt we lack the resources to run them down when they escape.

The island of Australia must be abandoned: it is too costly to manage, the Natives there continue to have the upper hand. This would produce a dividend that few have identified. We can take a lesson from the Natives and their activities in the past and transport any rebellious and difficult Natives to Australia to live out their worthless lives. This would have a twofold advantage: it would remove those rebellious Natives and would act as a deterrent for others.

I say let us turn inevitable defeat in Australia into a resounding victory and give Australia back to the excremental Natives. Let us abandon the island of Australia. Then we can take other rebellious Natives in a flier and abandon them there too.

– DR DES ASPER

IT HAD BEEN many years since Sister Bagra had been on a ship and things had changed more than she had expected. She would have thought that such mature technology, in use since before she was born, would have no room for improvement but clearly she was wrong. Gone was the shudder of the ship when it entered hyperspace, instead it slipped in like a hot knife through warm butter. Gone was the constant vibration of the ship that put everybody travelling in it on edge, made people angry long after they became unconscious of it. The ship was silent – you might as well have been sitting in a room at home.

She was as always travelling light; it would not do for a nun to be seen carrying too many bags, it would bring the Order into disrepute. All she had was two habits, her underthings and a copy of the Holy Book. Even if she wanted to carry more she couldn't; they would not have allowed her to take anything else from the mission. Even her plaque, a constant companion, had been confiscated.

'Evidence,' Grark had said.

Sitting in the third-class lounge – the only seat she had access to, her room being no more than a tube with a bed in it, not even really enough room to sit up – she carefully avoided making eye contact with anyone. She did not want to talk to anyone; if she was foolish to make eye contact someone surely would have a spiritual question to ask her or need help with an emotional matter or some other such foolishness. Being a sister of the Order she would be obliged to talk to them.

She could stay in bed for the entire trip but that would surely drive her mad with boredom. She had not been still with nothing to do since last she was on a ship, leaving home to her new posting in the colony, decades ago now. The only other way to keep from talking to anyone would be to take off her habit, but she had worn it all her adult life and didn't know how otherwise to dress.

Besides that, she was in disgrace, returning home to be questioned, to be re-educated, to no doubt spend the rest of her long life in contemplation in a convent at home.

Heading home she had only one thing to be thankful for: she was being trusted to return on her own, not being returned home under guard, as shameful as that would have been. She was, for the time being at least, still a Mother of the Order and she would conduct herself in a manner befitting. One other thing kept her from crying, not that she would let anyone hear her cry, after all these years. She was finally going home.

There had not been enough troopers left alive to clean up all the mess, so they collected their own dead and carried them away from the carnage. A flier was dispatched at their urgent call – the rescue was as immediate as could be managed. The Settler dead were taken home for a decent military burial. The bodies of the Natives were left where they fell to rot. There were not many buildings left – those still standing were put to the torch or destroyed by plasma fire. The weather and time could be relied upon to do the rest.

If there were any survivors from the camp, they did not return, not even to wail over the dead. Crows and magpies, eagles and small furry things came and feasted, scattering some bones, cleaning up what meat they could as the rest rotted. Weeks later there was little more than bones, still brown with dried blood and flesh. No bones still lay where they had fallen, all were churned up by the actions of the feeding animals.

Months later the bones were white and wildflowers and tangling vines were overrunning the remains, blurring the edges between the dead and the living. Among them, so scattered with the bones of Jacky Jerramungup it would have been impossible to separate them completely, lay the bones of Johnny Star.

@

Grark had reported all he had discovered to the Bishop, and to the Governor of the colony, a pompous arrogant man who seemed more interested in the latest fashions back home. Handing letters to both the government and the Church to a courier, he packed for the journey home. Finally it was all over and he could return to his cool monastery. Sending his bags ahead to the shuttle he decided on one last meal – not that he could get a good meal anywhere on that damned colony.

Leaving sated in quantity if not even slightly satisfied with the quality of his repast, he took perhaps a little too long to notice the footfalls behind him. Stupid, thinking it was all over; couriers could be stopped, letters could be lost. He had never unearthed completely how high the corruption went. His complacency had led him down a dark back alley.

A silhouette broke the faint light at the end of the alley before him. When he stopped the footsteps behind him also did. It was far too late to regret that his masters had sent him to the frontier unarmed.

'Let me guess,' he said, 'the government or the Church don't want me reporting. Which is it?'

'I don't ask.' The voice was cultured, gentlemanly, sardonic. Grark gasped, did not scream when the knife was stabbed through his lung from the back. Collapsing to his knees he said nothing to his murderer, keeping his last breath for a prayer to his god. Whatever happened to his body, his soul would surely be safe.

A hundred million years of weathering had carved the top of the hill, once solid rock, into tombstones. The branches, the dark hanging needles, of the desert oak embraced the desert flowers, a loving embrace but strong enough to strangle. The rock and sand here, the dust, were a deep red, almost carmine. The blowtorch-yellow sky, the grey-green, the gold of spinifex and the red earth paradoxically gave the world a violet tinge.

Esperance picked her way carefully through the rocks, through the spinifex and the thorns. Her clothes were ragged, torn short by the rough ground and a desperate need to cool down. A wide hat protected her eyes and a thin scarf kept the dust from her face; only her eyes were visible, watering from the heat and dust.

On her belt, worn openly now, was her grandfather's handgun, out of ammo, but she could never part with it. She carried no pack, no food, no extra clothes; all she had was a stick, and a billy can held in her left hand. Strapped across her back, seeming to repel the dust that blanketed her, somehow managing to stay mysteriously shiny, was a Settler rifle.

They had lost another battle. For the rest of her camp it was their final battle, for her grandfather who had raised her it had been such an end. She had nobody; her parents were long gone, the aunties and uncle she had never met were long gone. Necessity had led her to create a new family from whoever she could find. Friends, comrades became family – new aunties and uncles, brothers, sisters, cousins. Now they too were gone.

At least some of her people had run, though she would never know how many, if any, had made it to safety. Some would be rounded up, would become servants or breeding stock. Those she could not save. Many would not be taken – would die first – old men, women and children would die, or were already dead. Some, hopefully, had made it to other camps, if there were any other camps left.

They were no longer her problem. She could not, would not risk herself to look for them. It would be suicide; she had to live to save everybody.

Somewhere in the gorges and caves of this desert land, almost too hot for humans, there would be survivors – free humans. The desert tribes were never oppressed even by the white men when they invaded hundreds of years before the Settlers, and the white men could live in the desert far better than the Toads could.

Somewhere out there were a people supremely adapted to this environment who had been there for tens of thousands of years. The opposite of foreigner, the opposite of alien, they were the people who belonged, who could survive here naked and unarmed.

Esperance's people had just lost their final battle, so she would find more people. The battle that ended her life, killed her family, was over, the war for Earth had not yet begun.

We think of the Settlers, who we call Toads, as inhuman. They are not – what they are is nonhuman. In all other ways they are more like us than we would like to admit. There is nothing in their behaviour that humans are incapable of: we have invaded cultures more peaceful than us, we have murdered and enslaved. There is nothing in their hearts and minds that does not also exist in the hearts and minds of the human species.

– TRANSLATOR'S NOTES, *THE TALE OF JACKY JERRAMUNGUP*

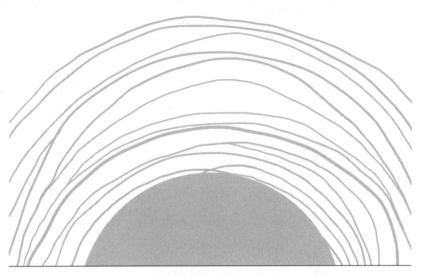

AUTHOR'S NOTE

THIS IS A work of fiction yet was influenced both shallowly and deeply by Indigenous Australian survival narratives and works of post-colonial historical fiction. Some, but by no means all, of the works of fiction that influenced this novel are *My Place* by Sally Morgan, *Benang* by Kim Scott, *Follow the Rabbit Proof Fence* by Doris Pilkington Garimara and the film based on that book (name shortened to *Rabbit Proof Fence*), *Jandamarra and the Bunuba Resistance* by Howard Pedersen and Banjo Woorunmurra and *The Chant of Jimmie Blacksmith* by Thomas Keneally (and the film of the same name). *Jandamarra* was co-authored by a white man and *The Chant of Jimmie Blacksmith* was written by a white man based on the true story of Jimmy Governor but they are powerful nevertheless.

The historical context was provided by more books than I could possibly name and the anthropological context to the understanding of technological imbalance was provided by Jared Diamond's excellent *Guns, Germs, and Steel*. There are many other works that have had an influence on my life and work.

All these influences were important to the development of *Terra Nullius* and their authors deserve and receive my deepest gratitude.

The content and feel of this novel is not alien to an Australian audience and certain themes are almost certainly universal. However there are some cultural contexts that might benefit from explaining. When Australia was invaded by the British in 1788 (they would say "colonised") the land was taken by defining the continent as "Terra Nullius", meaning empty land. This doctrine, that formed the entire basis for Australian land law, was overturned in law by the Mabo decision in 1992. However, nothing has really changed. Many white Australians still act as if First Nations people did not exist. People, my nation included, are still fighting for Land Rights, the legal system still privileges settler land title, built on stolen land, over Native Title.

Despite the Australian idea of what the country is; slavery existed in this country up until the late 1960s. Indigenous workers were not paid and for a long time were not allowed to possess money. People were forced onto stations where they had to work for rations. In the late 60s laws were passed forcing station owners to pay their Indigenous workers and those workers were immediately fired and expelled from the stations.

The "Stolen Generations", a concept well known in Australia, refers to Government policies that allowed police and welfare to take mixed-race, First Nations, children from their parents for no other reason than for being mixed-race First Nations Children. The cultural after-effects of these policies have not yet ended and maybe never will.

The quote from 'Solid Rock' by Goanna at the start of the book is the only quote taken from a genuine source. All other quotes to introduce chapters were created to reproduce the feel and content of the assorted historical texts and documents written about and pertaining to my people and other First Nations Australian people in the past.

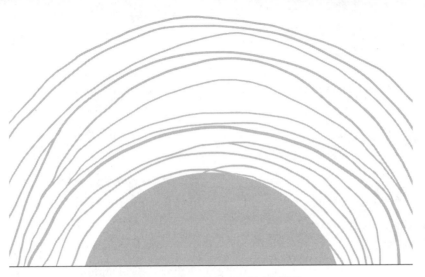

ACKNOWLEDGEMENTS

FIRST I WOULD like to acknowledge my Noongar ancestors without whose resistance and resilience I would not be alive today. Most of this novel was written travelling around the continent now called Australia; I would like to acknowledge the traditional owners of all the lands that so inspired this work. Thanks also to Kim, you showed me what is possible.

This manuscript won the State Library of Queensland's 2016 black&write! Indigenous Writing Fellowship, a partnership between the black&write! Indigenous Writing and Editing Project and Hachette Australia.

I would like to thank the team at black&write! and at State Library or Queensland for their support and my editors at black&write! Project Ellen van Neervan and Grace Lucas-Pennington. Your assistance was invaluable.

Thanks also to Hachette Australia for publishing the Australian edition of novel and for supporting the black&write! Project. My publisher at Hachette, Robert Watkins, sometimes believes in me more than I do and provided an essential lifeline when I needed it. Thanks also to project editor Kate Stevens and the rest of the team at Hachette Australia.

Copyeditor Alex Craig smoothed off the rough edges I had left on the manuscript and Grace West designed a stunning cover; thank you both.

Thanks to Gavin and Kelly at Small Beer Press for this North American edition. I am so delighted that they decided to take my book out to another part of the world.

Last but far from least, thanks Lily, you helped me get up in the morning, you always believed, you were my first editor and critic. Volim te.

CLAIRE G. COLEMAN is a Wirlomin Noongar (Indigenous Australian) woman whose people have occupied the south coast of Western Australia since time immemorial. Claire wrote her debut novel, *Terra Nullius,* while travelling around the continent now called Australia in an old, tumble-down caravan.

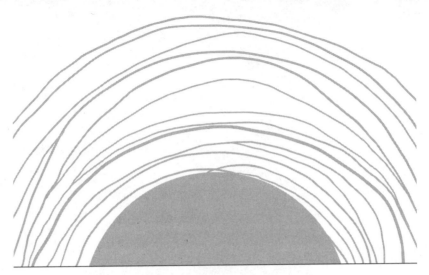

TERRA NULLIUS READING GROUP GUIDE

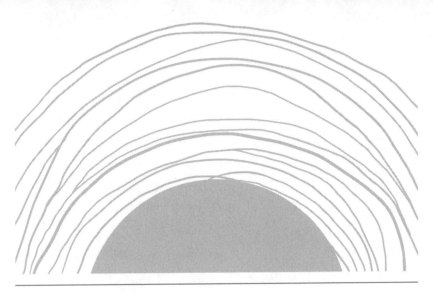

CLAIRE G. COLEMAN INTERVIEW

by Jenny Terpsichore Abeles

Q.   I AM very interested in how different writers talk about their "process." Yours stands out to me, as described on your website and other places, as writing this novel while driving around the country in a caravan. Can you describe a bit more about how the experience of traveling through the landscape of your novel affected its creation? Do any particular moments or anecdotes stand out to you where the landscape you were in became imprinted on your novel?

A.   I have been asked many times what it was like to write a novel while traveling around the continent. It was hard to answer because at the time I had not written under any other conditions. I do know one thing though, I would not have written the same novel had I not been traveling, the conditions under which a novel is written is often deeply embedded in the book's DNA.

Landscape is all through *Terra Nullius*, the places I travelled were in the feel of the landscapes in the book. I described few places accurately and many places were unsettled in space because I used them metaphorically not literally, but they were there nevertheless. Someone pointed out to me that most the characters in *Terra Nullius* are moving for most the narrative and I was moving too, so movement is important in many ways.

There is one example I can remember well. We were traveling through the Pilbra, in Western Australia. I stopped so my partner could photograph the colours, they were so vivid, the purple-red stone, the wildflowers, the grey dry-adapted foliage all conspired to cast a purple tinge over everything as far as the eye could see. I leaned against my car and looked at the other side of the valley. There was a rocky hill, it's top cracked and jagged, like crooked teeth or gravestones, where a massive rock had weathered and cracked. That very hill, that scene, that place, is in *Terra Nullius*.

Q. You've spoken about the "hidden history" of native peoples in Australia, one that is more brutal than historiography typically wishes to account for. How do you think that history, and the hidden histories of colonized/indigenous people across the globe, could be revised more honestly? How could colonized and colonizer alike work to face and accept more truthful versions of history in order to proceed together into a more just future? What steps do you see (museums, monuments, legislation) being taken in that direction?

A. It is vitally important the truth of colonisation is acknowledged; lies are one of the weapons used to continue the oppression of colonised people. It seems unlikely to me that the truths of colonisation will be understood if only the victims are telling the truth, if only the victims are fighting for truth and justice. It is also important for settler individuals and institutions to do their bit.

I have friends and acquaintances working in the institutional environment who are working to change the way those institutions manage the interface between coloniser and colonised. Museums and art galleries are part of a movement to change the dialogue, they pay a pivotal role.

Legislation, on the other hand, seems far off in Australia. Despite the work being done by many to change the laws; successive governments in Australia have worked to broaden the divides that are so damaging to our society. I hope one day to see a government determined to make things better or at least stop making things worse.

Q. Some of your Settler characters occupy a mindset that's difficult to relate to – Sister Bagra stands out to me, particularly. How did you get into the heads of such characters in order to tell the story from their perspectives? What historical or psychological clues did you use to imagine their thoughts and feelings?

A. It took a lot of imagination and a lot of soul searching. I imagined what sort of person I would have to be to do the sort of thing those people do. I believe there is no such thing as an evil person, only evil acts, so I had to imagine how someone could logically and emotionally decide to do evil. Their behavior needed an internal logic.

The character of Devil was based on a real person from history, A. O. Neville, the "Chief Protector of Aborigines" in the early 20th century. I did not have to imagine the things he did, they happened. What I had to do was try and understand his motivation. Once I had that the character was already there.

Q. How did you discover that you're a writer? Or, maybe, how did you become a writer?

A. I became a writer by writing *Terra Nullius*. I had tried before to be a writer but had never managed to actually do it, never managed to complete anything. When the story of *Terra Nullius* made itself known to me I felt compelled to write it. It was in the process of telling that story that I learned how to do it.

Q. You've mentioned in *The Gaurdian* that "The entire purpose of writing *Terra Nullius* was to provoke empathy in people who had none." At some point while reading the book, I began to feel that "Settler" and "Native" weren't valid boundaries between people, and the more meaningful distinction between people seemed to be empathetic and unempathetic. Apart from reading stories such as yours, how can we tip the human scales toward greater empathy between people who are not alike in immediately observable ways?

A. People tend to have empathy towards people they know. Getting to know people from other backgrounds tends to lead to greater empathy. It's important for people to approach people from outside their own backgrounds and communicate with them. People are generally nice, people generally get along and getting to know people from outside your own background is generally productive.

Q. As someone who appreciates seeing her favorite books made into movies, I'm wondering if it's possible with a book such as this? Have you given any thought to a movie or television adaptation?

A. I have given much thought to it, I love watching movies. However I cannot see how it could ever be done. I have been living with *Terra Nullius* for many years now and I still can't see how an adaptation would be possible. That bothers me a bit, I think if there was a way to dramatize the story it could change many lives.

Q. For American readers, some plot-details and historical cues in *Terra Nullius* might not feel as local and present as they do to Australian audiences. What do you hope American readers take away from this novel?

A. The historical cues are not as local for American readers but that does not mean there is nothing for American readers to gain. Many of the problems from colonisation are identical between our countries. Colonisation is colonisation, slavery is slavery, there is no way to separate them. I have heard many times of evils done there, in America, and many of them sound a lot like what happened here. I think there is a lot to gain.

Q. The end of the novel seems to suggest the arrival of a moment of change. Do you feel a similar zeitgeist in our current moment, in Australia or the world more generally? What catalyzes such moments and how can we best respond to them?

A. I think in the world at the moment there exists a potentiality. Things seem currently to be getting worse, the far right are on the rise, there are other bad things happening. On the other hand there are a generation of people coming up who are refusing to accept what is happening. Things will change for the better if we help those who are willing to fight for a better world.

Q. In a piece you wrote for *The Guardian,* you described how low self-esteem affected your ability to think of yourself as a writer, a feeling I imagine is familiar to many writers and would-be writers. What advice do you have for others who feel this way?

A. Just write. If you are scared then write anyway. The worst that can happen is that you don't get that thing published, submit it somewhere else, write something else. The best that can happen is beyond your wildest dreams.

I was scared right up to the moment when *Terra Nullius* was published. I am still scared now, with more books to come. Fear does not have to be crippling, fear can help us climb to new heights.

Q. Reading through your interviews, reviews, and articles, it's clear that you've become a voice for a particular justice movement. What has this metamorphosis – from private to public figure – been like for you? How do you handle criticism of your outspoken views on the rights of Indigenous peoples? What inspires, emboldens, fortifies, or motivates you to persist despite critics and haters?

A. I believe that the greatest good comes from people acting according to their abilities rather than doing only what will benefit them. I have a platform, a voice, I am capable of bringing society's attention to the plight of colonised people and asking for justice. I do it because I can and when I am attacked it just tells me I am having an effect.

The critics and haters, when they attack, are just telling me I am getting to them, that they are scared. If they left me alone I would not know whether or not my work is going to elicit change.

Q. Have you been to the United States? If so, what did you do or see here, and what were your impressions? If not, what would your ideal North American tour look like?

A. I have never been to the US. I would like to tour the US with a book one day, although admittedly sometimes your politics there scares me. I would particularly love the opportunity to speak with First Nations people in the US find our common ground in the effects of colonisation. I believe Australia and the US have both good and bad in common. I would take the opportunity to explore that.

Also fishing, lots of fishing, your fly waters look awesome.

Q. Who else do you think American readers should be reading, writers perhaps not already well-known here?

A. There are so many, many of them are my friends and family. I risk leaving someone off the list and upsetting them, therefore here is a partial list:

- Bruce Pascoe, particularly his amazing *Dark Emu*.
- Kim Scott, whose novels are stunningly beautiful, particularly the Miles Franklin award winning *Benang*.
- Ali Cobby Eckermann, a brilliant poet.
- Ellen van Neervan, whose poetry and short stories are ground breaking.
- Alexis Wright, the winner of the 2018 Stella prize and a past winner of the Miles Franklin award and one of Australia's greatest writers.
- Tony Birch, one of our most accomplished writers.

There are many many others. Our First Nation writers produce some of the best literature in Australia but are often unfairly ignored.

Q. Do you feel that people occupying opposite sides of an aggrieved history can learn to live together in mutual respect? If so, what are some crucial steps in that process?

A. I believe that it is possible. In Australia we are a long way from that even though some people think the discussion is unnecessary. There is a crucial step that is often if not always ignored, particularly in Australia. That step is "truth telling". Colonial propaganda has an uncomfortable relationship with the truth. For example, there are still people in Australia who believe that the "Colonisation" was peaceful and that there were few if any massacres. The truth is very different.

Although *Terra Nullius* is a novel it is built on a foundation of fact and I consider it part of the process of truth telling.

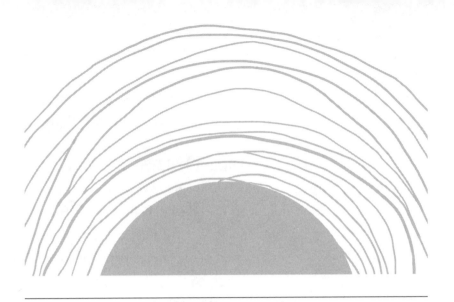

READING GROUP DISCUSSION QUESTIONS

1. WHAT DO you make of the title of the novel? How does Coleman elaborate in different ways on how the land belongs to no one? How does the idea work for or against the colonizers who used it to empower their colonization efforts?

2. For all its surprises, this novel remains a story about colonialism. What do you know historically about different colonialist efforts? How does this novel expand upon or surprise what you already know on the topic?

3. Where do you sense the earliest hints that this is not the colonization story you thought it was? How does the revelation of the true nature of this story proceed?

4. This novel is full of unhappy characters, Settler and Native alike. If Settlers are not happy in their new lands, what, in your opinion, motivates colonialist or expansionist endeavors?

Consider this from a variety of perspectives: psychological, sociological, political, economic, spiritual, and personal.

5. It becomes obvious almost immediately that many Settlers do not believe the Natives are human in the same way they themselves are. How many different kinds of evidence can you find of dehumanization in this novel? What kinds of moments lead certain characters to a realization of the humanity of "the other"?

6. In Johnny Star's first positive interaction with a Native, he thinks that ". . . he wanted to find the humanity in the Native" because ". . . he was looking for the humanity in himself" (63). How does dehumanization work against oppressors and oppressed alike? Weigh the benefits and drawbacks of domination for the Settlers.

7. What, in your opinion, constitutes a state of being that demands the same respect you believe yourself worthy of? What events or beliefs from history have caused dehumanization? What signs of dehumanization are evident in our current world? How can these be effectively countered or resisted by everyday people? Does the novel offer suggestions for this?

8. In the blurb at the beginning of Chapter 16, a Settler registers a completely positive reaction to an aspect of Native culture, "Art," lamenting that many galleries and museums were destroyed before they learned to appreciate the value of this strange, new phenomenon. How has the art of colonized peoples been denigrated, destroyed, stolen, redeemed, and appropriated? What examples of a particular culture's art stand out as particularly moving or appealing to you personally?

9. Who are the sympathetic and unsympathetic characters in this novel? What do the sympathetic characters have in common? The unsympathetic characters? What philosophies of human relationships can be drawn from each set of characters?

10. At the beginning of the novel, Jacky tells himself, "I belong somewhere, I had a family once. A family who misses me" (8), thus beginning a quest. Does he find what he set out to find? Does his quest come to a successful conclusion? Why or why not?

10. On page 37, Sergeant Rohan ruminates on how the Natives lived "pointless, aimless lives in the dirt" without "protection" from the Settlers. What seems to be the point or aim of the Settler's lives? The Natives? What in your opinion, should the point of human life be? How many different aims for human life can you think of? Which of these are consistent with one another and which in conflict with others?

11. Sister Bagra is a representative of the educational system the Settlers give to Natives. Since education by definition shapes the way we think, how can we ensure that true education differs from indoctrination or mind control? How does education in our culture work to enforce or resist oppressive tendencies? Try to give multiple examples for each category. How could education be reformed to create more equality amongst different kinds of people?

12. We are told toward the end of the novel that "Esperance" means "hope." In what ways does this character embody, aim toward, or fall short of the concept of hope? How is hope spoken of,

created, or destroyed throughout the novel? What kind of force is hope in people's lives – emotional, psychological, intellectual, spiritual, or material?

13. On page 219, Jacky is compared to Robin Hood and other outlaws who, as symbols of resistance, became larger than life both in their own time and throughout history. Who are the symbols of resistance – the outlaws, innovators, freedom fighters, justice seekers, heroes and heroines – you admire most and what thoughts, realizations, behaviors, and actions do they inspire in you? Think historically and currently when looking for examples.

14. Each chapter begins with a blurb from poetry, history, scientific studies, news reports, or other kinds of texts produced in a given culture. How do these kinds of texts affect the trajectories of individual human lives? Describe the reciprocal relationship between the stories we tell as a larger culture and the stories we live as individuals. How might this novel enter larger cultural conversations and affect the way we live?